HIS NEXT WIFE

BOOKS BY D.K. HOOD

DETECTIVES KANE AND ALTON PREQUELS

Lose Your Breath

Don't Look Back

DETECTIVES KANE AND ALTON SERIES

Don't Tell a Soul

Bring Me Flowers

Follow Me Home

The Crying Season

Where Angels Fear

Whisper in the Night

Break the Silence

Her Broken Wings

Her Shallow Grave

Promises in the Dark

Be Mine Forever

Cross My Heart

Fallen Angel

Pray for Mercy

Kiss Her Goodnight

Her Bleeding Heart

Chase Her Shadow

Now You See Me

Their Wicked Games

Where Hidden Souls Lie

A Song for the Dead

Eyes Tight Shut

Their Frozen Bones

Tears on Her Grave

Fear for Her Life

Good Girls Don't Cry

Their Haunted Hearts

Watch Over Me

DETECTIVE BETH KATZ SERIES

Wildflower Girls

Shadow Angels

Dark Hearts

Forgotten Girls

PSYCHOLOGICAL THRILLERS

The Liar I Married

HIS NEXT WIFE

D.K. HOOD

bookouture

Published by Bookouture in 2026

An imprint of Storyfire Ltd.
Carmelite House
50 Victoria Embankment
London EC4Y 0DZ

www.bookouture.com

The authorised representative in the EEA is Hachette Ireland
8 Castlecourt Centre
Dublin 15 D15 XTP3
Ireland
(email: info@hbgi.ie)

ISBN: 978-1-80550-395-8
eBook ISBN: 978-1-80550-394-1

To all the wonderful readers who have come along with me on this exciting journey.

PROLOGUE
PRESENT TIME

Willow

I married a man who has secrets.

In truth, I hardly know Jack. We've just arrived at the airport after a very romantic honeymoon and he guides me toward a new Porsche—yes, that's right—a glossy red Porsche—and I realize that his first secret is his wealth—but that's not all. The longer I'm with him the more secrets unfold. Why did I marry him? It's simple—I love him.

You may ask how I'm in this crazy situation. Well, many things in my life have come about by being in the right place at the right time. I just happened to be in LA at the auditions for a commercial for Jack Hunter's company and he'd taken one look at me and swept me off my feet. I went to lunch with him and we talked for hours, right up to dinner and then way into the night. We had what you might call a whirlwind romance, and I married him just three weeks later. Charismatic, handsome, with deep blue eyes to dive into, Jack is twelve years older than me but you'd never guess it; he's tanned and fit with only a couple of laugh lines on his face. I often wonder why he chose me; he could have just about anyone.

During our first date, he explained that he'd been married previously and has two children: Ava, nine, and Noah, eight. His wife died in an accident at sea seven years previously and, after going through the arduous task of pronouncing her dead through the courts, he'd decided that life must go on. Although he has this goal in life, I find it very strange that he speaks about Laura as if she's still alive. It's spooky—I mean it's been seven years. During our honeymoon, he made comments like "Laura would love this place", when we dined at a restaurant or whatever, and it made me feel like a third wheel. I guess as time goes by, he'll accept the fact she's gone.

I must admit, my life has changed dramatically. Wealth is intimidating and so are the people who surround my husband but Jack brushes my worries aside, assuring me when I get to the house I'll find my feet. I haven't met the children yet, which I figure is a little unusual. I can't imagine how they'll react to being told that I'm their stepmother. I've seen photos and Jack has told me stories about them but he doesn't seem to spend too much time with them at all. His life revolves around work and the Newport Yacht Club. I know nothing about sailing and googled the marina and discovered it's a historic and well-regarded yacht club located in the heart of Newport Harbor. We're heading into Newport now and the ocean comes into view. I adjust my sunglasses to avoid the glare of sunshine glistening on the waves and move my attention to the majestic houses of the rich and famous. "This place is amazing."

"I'll take Ocean Drive to the house. It's the scenic route." The engine of Jack's Porsche roars as we fly along the blacktop. "Beauford Manor is your home now. I hope you'll enjoy living here as much as I do. Laura loved it."

I look at him and sigh. *Laura again, as if she'll be there to meet us. Why does he do that?*

I shake off the feeling of being second best because every moment with him, I need to pinch myself to believe it's not a dream. I've never lived like this before, and being able to buy whatever I want is surreal. Money has a power that could easily get out of hand. I look at Jack. His company builds hotels, skyscrapers and upmarket housing. He gave me a brief idea of what he does in the company but insisted it's nothing for me to worry about. I lean back and enjoy the scenery but now we're heading along a driveway. Large wrought-iron gates slide open as we arrive and before me is a mansion. My mouth hangs open. It's old with windows everywhere and it has that sinister vibe you see in horror movies, or is my overactive imagination conjuring secret hallways and dark cellars with chains attached to the walls?

The surrounding land is impressive. I'm seeing manicured lawns and perfectly trimmed hedges. Vibrant garden beds fill the air with floral scents as we sweep along the winding driveway. For a few seconds the house is obscured by two massive oak trees, their puzzle-piece leaves spreading giraffe-pattern shapes across the driveway. My eyes widen at the sight of the grand entrance with marble steps and towering columns. It's intimidating, dominating the landscape like a medieval castle. I suck in a deep breath to steady my nerves. It didn't look so big from the front gate.

"This house is a testament to Newport's Gilded Age. That was a time long ago when wealthy New Yorkers built extravagant homes to live here." Jack grins at me. "Laura knew the family who owned it; she played here as a child and claimed to know all its secrets. I purchased it for our first wedding anniversary." He winks. "It makes a statement, doesn't it?"

I nod, though wonder why he believes he needs to prove himself worthy of his neighbors and bite my tongue. I've always been frugal, having to work hard for every cent means I appreciate the little things in life—but this? How much money does he need? This house is screaming overindulgence to me. Keeping it clean must be a nightmare. The gardens alone would take an army. Intimidated, I swallow hard. Suddenly wishing he'd brought me here before asking me to marry him. The huge house and the responsibility for two children I haven't even met weigh heavy on my shoulders.

We stop on a wide gravel driveway and the scent of roses drifts toward me. I can't resist and step from the car, turning to Jack. "Give me a few moments to explore the garden. It's so beautiful."

"Go right ahead." He indicates to a gray-haired man trimming a hedge. "That's Bill; he's been here forever. If you want to bring some of the roses inside, ask him to cut them for you."

I walk back along the driveway, turn and stare at the grand façade. Panes of glass stare back at me like the eyes of a giant fly and, in one of the windows, a pale face looks out at me. I wave and the face vanishes. I turn away and head toward Bill, who is watching me intently. "You must be Bill. I'm Willow Hunter. The gardens are spectacular."

"Thank you, but I can't take all the credit. I do have help these days." Bill's weather-beaten face wrinkles into a smile. "It's nice to meet you."

I indicate to the house. "It's not what I expected. It's very intimidating from the outside."

"Who were you waving at?" Bill rubs his chin, his eyes never leaving my face.

I look back at the house. "I assume it was one of the staff. I believe the children are away until tomorrow."

"No, it's not one of the staff; they'll be downstairs waiting to see Mr. Hunter. That window is only for show. It can't be seen from the inside of the house. The other Mrs. Hunter spent hours trying to find that window because she insisted she saw a face peering out." Bill rubs a handkerchief over the back of his neck. "It's probably a trick of the light is all. That window was bricked up on the inside during the renovations some years back. So, nobody can be up there."

The shivers sliding down my back stop as I turn to look at the windows, but this time I see nothing. "Does anyone else see a face at the window?"

"No, only you and the late Mrs. Hunter." He gives me a long considering look and lowers his voice. "Don't you go searching the house like she did. Strange things happen in the left wing. No one can explain them. It's not haunted, it's just weird. I figure the noises and suchlike drove the last Mrs. Hunter close to having a breakdown."

I stare at him, unease seeping into my bones. "How so?"

"It's not for me to say." His lips flatten into a thin line. "She just changed is all. The next thing I know, she died."

Footsteps come from behind me. I clear my throat. "I love the roses. I'll come and see you when I'm settled and I'll grab a bunch for inside."

"You have the rest of your life to tour the gardens, Willow." Jack comes up behind me and his arms circle my waist. "I'm anxious to show you the house."

Pushing the warning to the back of my mind, I smile. "It was nice to meet you, Bill." I turn in Jack's arms. "Okay, show me the way."

Before we climb the steps, a man comes dashing out of the front door. He's wearing a dark suit, with his gray thinning hair carefully combed. His face has a worried expression, and his pencil moustache twitches as he stares at me. His eyes are cold as if I'm an intruder he doesn't want to deal with. My heart sinks. Will all the staff have the same attitude toward me? The man stands to one side to allow us to pass and his attention moves to Jack.

"It's good to see you, sir. Your bags arrived yesterday and Amy has unpacked everything." He looks at me with a stiff smile but says nothing.

"Thank you, George." Jack waves absently in my direction. "This is Mrs. Hunter." He turns back to me. "George oversees the running of the staff. You can go to him if you need to know anything."

I blink as George hurries to collect our carry-on bags. "I'll be asking you first."

"Ah, but I won't be here all the time." Jack takes my hand. "You can ask George when I'm at the office."

He leads me through huge oak doors and into a mind-blowing entrance hall. The walls are decorated with glossy carved wood panels, depicting bowls of fruit with grapes tumbling carelessly over the edge. A polished marble floor reflects a huge chandelier in the high ceiling. Dumbstruck, my gaze moves up an ornate staircase and I stop mid-stride at the shock of seeing the portrait dominating the wall at the top of the stairs. The woman's eyes seem to look straight through me. It's unnerving. Why would anyone keep such an evil-looking picture? "Who is that?"

"That's Laura." Jack is watching my reaction. "She was a beautiful woman."

I meet the penetrating eyes of a woman dressed in red, her black hair tumbling over her shoulders. I swallow hard and shivers run down my back. There's something not quite right about her. It's as if she hates everyone. I can imagine how menacing she'd be in life. Her chin is lifted in an arrogant tilt as if daring me to take her place. "It's been seven years, why do you keep her portrait in such a prominent position?"

"She's the mother of my children." Jack shrugs and walks on.

I pause, staring into unforgiving eyes. It's as if all the happiness has been sucked out of the room—out of me.

ONE

SEVEN YEARS AGO

Laura

I'm angry—and who wouldn't be after what I've been through over the last three years? I figure I'm entitled because happy isn't in my vocabulary and never has been. I'm just existing day to day. Most people would advise me to walk away from my marriage—but I can't leave my kids. Trust me, I've tried to leave and take them with me but my handsome and very wealthy husband, Jack, just drags me back. If I don't stay, I'll never see them again. What would you do? My husband is a powerful and respected man, and now most people believe I'm unstable. I can almost hear them calling me "poor crazy Laura."

Tonight, Jack insists we celebrate our third wedding anniversary aboard the yacht. *Celebrate* is a joke—he barely tolerates me—but appearances are everything to him and I can play the part of a loving wife. The thing is, he doesn't trust me alone with my babies—*my babies*. No one will believe me about Jack's coldness toward me. His friends are loyal to him and tied to him by umbilical cords of money. He tells them I've been unwell since delivering our son, Noah, and they put on a good show of supporting him—not me. I hear them whispering behind my back and giving each other knowing looks as if evaluating my mental state. I ignore them and try to relax amid the smiling faces, bubbling conversation, loud laughter and the tinkling of champagne glasses.

Our guests lounge on the lush leather seats as staff move between them refilling their glasses or offering morsels of food on silver platters. The recessed lights almost blind me as they reflect on the wealth of diamonds worn by his friends. You'll notice I say *his* friends, as I haven't really had many of my own since we married. It's never been something my husband encourages, preferring me to move within his circle of acquaintances—it's safer that way.

Jack doesn't argue and it infuriates me. I need to give him important information about a member of his staff but he brushes me aside. When I insist, he hurries me into the galley. It seems I've embarrassed him in front of his friends. I need to get away and breathe some fresh air. I slip out on deck and sigh as the wind tousles my long black curls around my face. Out here, under the black sky, I'm free. An unexpected squall cools the mid-summer night, making the waves climb and break in white caps, and in the distance, lightning zigzags the sky. The boat pitches and rolls as I turn to see the captain illuminated at the wheel chatting with one of the other men. He doesn't notice me as I continue my way to the stern.

Beneath my feet the deck shifts and I slide toward the railing. I grab onto the cold metal, my knuckles white as I strain to regain my footing. Knees trembling, I call for help, but rolls of thunder cover my cries. Beside me, a shadow moves. Relieved someone has seen me, I reach out a hand for assistance but instead a violent shove sends me sprawling across the slick deck.

Rain lashes my face as the floor beneath me rises high and then dips. Waves crash over the stern, soaking me in salty brine and rolling me back and forth. I try to get to my knees but another wave flattens me. I'm in a desperate bid for survival as lightning flashes across the sky and thunder booms. Panic grips me as I slip toward the edge. I dig my nails into the deck but it pitches again and a wave washes me under the railing. I float in midair and seconds go by before I smack hard into dark, freezing water. Waves engulf me and I rise screaming. I must survive. I can't leave my kids without a mom.

A shadow looms on deck and I wave frantically, screaming for help. They've seen me! Something flies over the railing and strikes me hard in the face. Pain rocks through my brain and I sink. Icy coldness surrounds me and bubbles leak from my lips but instinct makes me kick to the surface. Waves crash all around me but the current is dragging me away in a slipstream of violence. Terror grips me as another massive wave of black water drags me under—there's no escape.

My lungs are bursting but I fight hard to catch just one more breath—I don't want to die. I have kids and I can't leave them alone—not in that house—with him. As I break the surface, pitch-black walls of water surround me. Salt stings my eyes as, for a few moments of respite, I bob up and down like a cork flowing to the will of the sea. I'm so cold and my head hurts. I gasp as another wave swamps me, rolling me over in the bubbling breakers. Cold seeps into my bones. I can't feel my fingers and my teeth chatter as I rise through the dark waves gasping and spitting.

There's no time to breathe before another wave crashes over my head, sucking me deep into the murky depths. Salt water fills my mouth and runs from my nose as I bob up again. I spit and cough, gasping precious air before the next wave smashes over me. Above, in a stormy sky, a sliver of moon peeks out between fast-moving clouds. Lightning flashes and rain comes in sheets. I search all around; however, between the intermittent lightning there's nothing but inky blackness. As I rise on the swell, I make out the lights on my husband's yacht vanishing into the distance and yell and scream, waving my arms, but no one will see me. I let out a sob as my husband's pride and joy, the *Laura*, leaves me to die. Panic has me by the throat. I need to swim—but which way? Which way is land?

Something large bumps into my legs and images of sea monsters crash into my mind. Panicking, I scream and thrash about as another wave rolls me into a spin. Dark water rushes up my nose but I fight. My instinct is to survive. I rise to the surface, suck in air and dive below the next wave—I must get away. A shark will take me in chunks and the moment my blood colors the water it will cause a feeding frenzy. I swim hard in the darkness until my chest hurts and I sink again under a crashing wave. This time, bubbles escape from my mouth and I fight to break the surface. Exhausted, I float on my back, riding the waves and gasping precious air into my lungs. I lick rain from my lips but it's not enough to survive. I don't want to die. Not here all alone in the dark. Wind whips up the waves around me and rain splatters my face. I open my mouth, hoping to catch a few more drops to ease my parched throat. I'm lost in the darkness and it's only a matter of time before the next wave takes me to a watery grave. I should have seen this coming. The drugs in my food, the isolation and now this. Someone on the yacht wants me dead—but who, and why? Is it Jack? I guess I'll never know.

TWO

PRESENT TIME

Willow

Unease creeps over me. Allowing Jack to walk on, I look over one shoulder at Laura's portrait and shudder. So, this is how he keeps her alive. I feel inadequate, and will never come close to her. I move and her eyes follow me as if watching me with her husband. It's eerie and raises goosebumps on my flesh. I hurry along a hallway after Jack and feel her eyes boring into my back. My confidence slips away under her gaze and I'm suddenly an intruder. I push back the unnerving feelings and lift my chin. I'm his wife now so why hasn't he taken down her portrait? I shiver. Seeing his shrine to her is darn right creepy.

"This is our space—one of many." Jack leads me into a large bright room.

Overwhelmed, I follow him, my legs trembling. I want to ask him about the face at the window but change my mind. If Laura had seen it and become obsessed with finding the window, knowing I had seen it too might make him doubt my sanity. I force words from my mouth, anything to sound normal and at least a little excited to see my new home. "How many rooms do you have?"

"Eleven bedrooms on the first floor and more on the second and other rooms on the third." Jack grins at me. "The staff quarters are behind the kitchen in a separate section of the house. We have a staff building as well; the house staff live here and the rest have nice apartments in the other building."

The size of the house intimidates me. I've seen too many horror movies to feel comfortable in an old rambling mansion. "It must be a nightmare to maintain."

"Not really, I have a large housekeeping staff and gardeners. Most of the rooms on the third floor are closed as we'll never use them." He walks to a wraparound window with breathtaking views of the ocean. "We have reception rooms, a ballroom, a library and my office. There's a playroom, where the kids watch TV. They don't come in here. There are too many priceless antiques in here to risk horseplay so they know not to enter this room." He holds out a hand to me. "Sue, the housekeeper, will be along soon. Once we've had coffee, I'll give you a tour of some of the house." He chuckles. "We'll explore together. You know, I'm sure there are rooms here I haven't found yet."

Finding that hard to believe, I meet his gaze. "You really haven't explored the entire house after so many years? That seems so strange. Is there a reason?"

"Honestly, I've seen the plans. So I do know there are small rooms on the third floor." Jack waves a hand dismissively. "I don't need to see dust-covered rooms we'll never use. It's a waste of my time." He glances at his watch. "Where's Sue got to with the coffee?"

Before I have the chance to ask about Sue, footsteps clatter in the hallway.

"Jack, at last." A woman in her late thirties wearing a tight pink top and chinos, with brown hair tied at the nape, breezes into the room waving a piece of paper. "Davis has been on the phone constantly. He needs you to okay a deal."

"Not now, Ruby." Jack frowns. "I've just walked through the door."

"I'm sorry but it's urgent." Ruby gives me a dismissive glance and pushes the document at Jack. "You need to read this right away."

I didn't expect the staff to be so cold toward me. It's very disconcerting, as if I'm an afterthought. I do expect Jack to introduce me before speaking to them rather than just ignoring me. I stare from one to the other. Jack had mentioned a few staff live in staff quarters at the house but I gathered they were gardeners and cleaners. He'd never mentioned Sue or Ruby, let alone George. What is George anyway, a manager? Totally lost and feeling like one of his priceless antiques left on the mantel, I sit on a plush sofa and wait.

Moments later, another woman in her thirties arrives pushing a cart. This one has red hair, and is wearing jeans and a T-shirt. The smell of fresh coffee fills the room as she propels the cart toward me and unloads the coffee pot, fixings, and a tiered cake stand with an assortment of sandwiches and pastries to the table before me. Plates, cups and silverware follow. I nod to her. "You must be Sue?"

"That's me." Sue smiles. "Dinner is at seven." She turns and walks out of the room.

Without a word to me, Jack follows her with Ruby on his heels and their voices disappear along the hallway to heaven knows where. My mind is racing. I did see a face at the window and didn't imagine it, but Bill's warning fills me with unease, especially after hearing there are rooms on the third floor nobody visits. What strange things happen in the house? Am I safe here? I try to get a grip and take a few deep breaths. Do I ask Jack or will he think I'm paranoid? Is this the same behavior Laura exhibited before she died? How can I find out the truth?

I pour a cup of coffee into a delicate bone china cup and add the fixings. The trip has exhausted me. Our honeymoon was four decadent weeks traveling the world. Jack is wonderful but why keep all this a secret? I look around a room filled with antique furniture and priceless collectables. I'll never be able to relax here. My hand trembles on the cup. One drop of coffee on the cream rug and it will stain. As I stare at the open door and the empty hallway, loneliness creeps over me. He is the center of my universe and has never been far from my side for the last four weeks. Any business he needed to conduct happened when I took a shower or went to the beauty parlor in the hotel lobby. How life has suddenly changed. The moment we stepped inside Laura's home, I've become an afterthought. I stare into the view, contemplating my future living here. I sigh. "I guess the honeymoon is well and truly over."

I check my watch. I've been waiting for Jack for over an hour. The bread on the sandwiches has dried, the coffee is cold and he is nowhere to be seen. It is a terrible waste of food as the sandwiches are really good and I drank two cups of coffee. I've been staring out of the window for ages, taking in the scenery, but how long can you look at the beach? I'll do my own tour of the house. I really need to find our bedroom. After traveling by air and in the Porsche for some time, the makeup on my face feels like a stiff mask. I need to take a shower and change my clothes.

I push Bill's warning to one side. The house has staff moving around and Jack is here. I have my phone in my pocket. What could possibly happen? I venture outside into the hallway and look both ways. There is no one around, so I make my way back to the entrance hall and, with Laura's piercing eyes staring down at me, climb the stairs to the first level. I reach a wide balcony with hallways leading away in both directions, and decide to take the one on the right. If my sense of direction is correct, the right-hand side of the building overlooks the ocean.

Artwork is everywhere, from the pictures on the walls to the bronze statues placed strategically on pedestal tables, and I have the strange feeling of being inside a museum. A long rug running along the middle of highly polished wooden floors muffles my footsteps. As I walk, I fling open each door. Most are empty guest bedrooms, apart from two which, from the toys scattered over the floor and the posters adorning the walls, obviously belong to the children. Ahead, at the end of the hallway, is a small vestibule with double doors. I head toward it, certain this must be the master bedroom.

"Ah, there you are, Willow." Jack strides toward me, scoops me into his arms and kisses me. "You are so beautiful. I love you so much."

My heart pounds and my knees tremble from his deep kiss. I smile. "I love you too. I've missed you terribly."

"What are you doing up here?" Jack takes my hand. "Our bedroom is in the other wing. Come, I'll show you." He takes my hand and leads me away.

I walk beside him, trying to find the words to explain my problem with the portrait of his late wife but nothing comes. I follow him along the hallway and across the balcony to the opposite side of the house. When he opens the door to a large spacious bedroom, my heart drops at the view. I see the gardens but the view is of other houses, not the opulent vista of the ocean. The disappointment must have shown on my face as he looks at me and shakes his head. I smile and turn away, opening drawers to search for my things.

"I'm sorry I left you alone but it was business and it intrudes on my life frequently." Jack grips my shoulders and his thumbs massage my neck. "Unfortunately, it's going to cause an issue later as well. I need to go into the office and sort out a problem. It can't wait until the morning, I'm afraid. Ruby has been running interference for me for weeks and now they know I'm home—well, I don't need to explain."

I step away and turn to face him. "Who is Ruby? I'd like to know the names of the people living here with us." I fold my arms across my chest. "How many staff do we have?"

"Quite a few and I don't know all their names. They come and go." Jack grins at me. "I love it when you're feisty." He reaches for me. "Come here so I can kiss you again."

I step back. "In a minute. We need to talk."

"Of course, darling." Jack strokes my cheek. "Anything you want. I only want to make you happy. You know that, right?"

I look at him. It would be so easy to just fall into his arms. "Let's start with Ruby."

"She's my PA." Jack leans casually against the closet door. "We've been working together since college. She lives here in the staff quarters. I rely on her and it was difficult not having her around on our honeymoon." He holds up both hands. "Oh, don't look at me like that, Willow. Of course there's no place for a PA on a honeymoon. That's why she remained here but I'm used to her organizing everything for me. Things like dinner reservations, dry cleaning, and the tours we enjoyed during our trip. The itinerary was planned by Ruby. I made the reservations for our meals but only occasionally. The concierges at the hotels where we stayed were very helpful."

I nod. "Go on."

"You've met George and he takes charge of all the staff for me. That includes gardeners, housekeeping staff, both live-in and outside workers." Jack rubs his chin. "Sue is the housekeeper, she has two assistants who work in the house daily— Amy and Lucy—and then there's the chef, Pierre. The gardener you know is Bill and he has many staff. I don't know their names. The nanny is Jenny." He frowns. "I know the kids are old for a nanny but she's been here since they were born and they're attached to her. Keeping her means we always have someone here for them if we need to go out or spend the weekend away." He sighs and straightens. "I'm guessing you'll want to freshen up. When you're done, I'll be in the office. It's four doors down from the room we were in earlier."

I held up one hand. "Before you go, how many bedrooms overlook the ocean?"

"Six on this floor, why?" Jack frowns. "Don't you like this room?"

I stare out of the window and then back to him. "Not really. The sea breeze on the other side of the house would be wonderful and the views are to die for. I'd prefer to have our bedroom overlooking the ocean." I didn't want to cause an argument on my first night but Jack is so even-tempered, I'm sure moving our bedroom won't be a problem. "I won't have too much to do around here, with all the staff and the kids at school. Do you mind if I pick a bedroom and redecorate it to suit my tastes? I gather Ruby organized this one?" I indicate to the roses on the white drapes and the matching coverlet. "Red and white isn't my thing; in fact, I believe it's unlucky, I always have."

"I'll have them removed at once." Jack comes to me and wraps his arms around me. His cologne is a familiar comfort. "I want you to be happy, Willow. He presses kisses on my cheek and down my neck sending goosebumps down my arms. "I'll be sure to tell Sue to order anything you need." He chuckles and his warm breath brushes my ear. "I didn't like them either. I'm not into florals." He drops his hands and smiles. "I'll be in my office when you're done here."

Grinning and feeling warm all over—Jack does that to me every time he's close—I open what I think is the closet door and gasp. There is a room inside. My clothes take up a small area on one side of a huge dressing room. Along the other side suits are lined up covered in plastic, shirts and then casual clothes. I've never seen so many ties displayed in rows. Shoes, boots are along one part of a wall as well. It's like being in a department store and I'm gaping at the room, unable to believe my eyes. Mirrors are everywhere, and when I pull open drawers to a double dressing table, I discover my makeup and my tiny jewelry box. On the opposite side I find a drawer filled with watches, cufflinks, rings and tiepins. From what I'm seeing, Jack has occupied this room for a time. I collect my things and head into the bathroom.

Like everything else in this house, it is overindulgent. A clawfoot bathtub big enough for two is set before a window. The towels are piled up on a shelf, thick and fluffy. Everything looks brand new. I step into the shower and turn on the faucet. Perfectly heated water jets out from various nozzles around the walls. Above me, the shower head is huge. I sigh in content-ment. I could get used to living like this.

I step from the shower and a noise comes from the bedroom. "Jack? Is that you?"

I wrap a towel around me and open the bathroom door. The bedroom is empty but the door is wide open. I walk to the doorway and peer outside and freeze. The hallway is in dark-ness and footsteps disappear into the darkness. "Jack?"

Nothing.

THREE

TWELVE MONTHS BEFORE OUR
ANNIVERSARY CELEBRATION

Laura

I walked into our arranged marriage with my eyes wide open. I consider myself lucky, you see. Jack is everything a woman could want in a man: handsome, rich and powerful, his influential friends include senators and billionaires. People want to know details about our lives and each time we go to a function we make a splash across the society pages. I enjoy going to functions just to show him off. When we're out together, he acts the loving husband. Often his arm snakes around my waist, and he gives me frequent stolen kisses. Our life appears so perfect. So many women want him. I can see why they're jealous but I don't care—he's mine.

Or is he?

I stare at the bedroom door and his words cut deep into my heart. His cologne lingers and I want to grab it and hold it to me but he's gone. I stare at my reflection—what is happening? Suddenly I've lost him. I try to remember what happened. What did I do? I can't think straight. Am I losing my mind or is someone twisting reality? My marriage to Jack has turned into a nightmare. I can't escape because no one will listen to me. I must act the perfect wife to a handsome, wealthy husband, but I'm trapped inside this marriage and slowly dying.

Realization creeps over me. Jack doesn't love me—he never has. To him I'm just the mother of his kids. His pained expression when we discovered I carried a daughter is imprinted on my soul. My life in Newport, Rhode Island, in the esteemed Beauford Manor, went downhill from then. I've been so stupid to believe his smooth tongue—his lies of love and a future filled with happiness. He'd acted like a hero in a romance novel but now I realize, when I'd walked into a marriage of convenience, I'd made a huge mistake. My family name and the wealth that came with me was his reason to go ahead with this farce. I trusted him and we pooled our money for him to invest in his company—and I got an allowance. I've been fooling myself that he loves me. For a time after Ava was born, he'd acted so loving again but now I know it was for only one reason. He wanted another baby.

The second the ultrasound revealed I carried a boy he commissioned a portrait of me. He wanted to capture my pregnancy glow for prosperity—the moment *his son* was conceived, he'd say—as if he truly believed it. From that moment, it was all about the baby. As my pregnancy continued, my loving husband refused to come near me. He made excuses and isolated me inside the house until Noah arrived. The day I came home from the hospital is etched into my memory like a nightmare.

The moment I carried our son into the nursery Jack presented me with a credit card. Was it payment for a job well done? He had his son, and that was all that mattered to him.

I stared at him in astonishment. "Oh, Jack, that's very nice of you, but I won't have time to go shopping with a new baby." I nuzzled my son, inhaling his sweet aroma, and my breasts tingled, although the doctors had forbidden me to feed him myself. I wanted to. "Where is Ava?"

"She's having a nap. There's no need to worry, Laura. Jenny will care for Noah. That's why we hired a nanny." Jack took the baby from my arms and handed him to Jenny. "You're free to do what you want now."

I stared at him in disbelief. "No, Jack. I'll care for him." I went to take my son from Jenny. "Give him to me."

"Don't make a scene, Laura." Jack gripped my arm. "You know it's for the best."

Trembling, I gaped at him, tears stinging my eyes. I couldn't give up my son. I wouldn't. "You can't take my son away from me."

"Laura, stop it." Jack gave me a shake. "Now look, you've made him cry." He looked at Jenny. "Take him to the nursery. I'll be along soon."

Pain gripped my heart as Jenny walked away with my son. I reached out a hand, wanting to run after him, but Jack glared at me, and I lifted my chin, ready to fight. "No! I'm his mom. He needs me. He doesn't know her. Give me my son." I pounded on Jack's chest.

"You're not well, Laura." Jack held me firmly by the arms. "You need to rest, and when you're better, you can do all the things you wanted to when you were pregnant. I know you hated that time, and I'm sorry for it, but Noah is here now, and I won't expect you to go through it again."

The smell of the old house surrounded me. It was decaying like a corpse, but I was the only one who saw it. I shook my head, edging toward the stairs. "I'm fine. You can't keep me away from my baby."

"He's my son too." Jack gave me a little shake. "Right now, you're not capable of caring for him or Ava. I can't trust you with my children." He sighed. "You need more time to recover. It's for your own good."

Tears rolled down my cheeks. I fought to get away, but his hands clasped tighter. I couldn't win. "I want to see my babies. Please, Jack."

"You'll see them." Jack led me up the stairs. "You need to rest, but I'll ask Jenny to bring them to you once a day. We don't want to upset their routines, do we? Now it's time for you to take your meds." He took my hand. "You know it's for the best, Laura."

I stared into the eyes of my portrait hanging above the stairs and wanted to scream. I looked at him. "What if I decide to take my children and leave? You can't hold me here against my will."

"No, I can't, but you'll be leaving alone." Jack turned me to face him. "I'll never allow you to take my kids—not ever."

I dug my feet in. "I imagine you'd prefer if I left you, Jack. You don't want me anymore, do you?"

"Laura." He gave me a condescending shake of the head. "You rejected me, and if you really want to leave, I can't stop you. Be very sure, because I won't chase after you—not this time, not after what you did."

What had I done? I had no idea. I gaped at him. "Oh, you'd like that, wouldn't you? You'd divorce me and remarry before the ink is dry on the paperwork."

"Maybe I would." Jack shook his head. "One thing is for sure—I wouldn't walk back into hell with someone like you again."

FOUR

PRESENT TIME

Willow

After dinner, Jack kisses me goodbye and heads into the office with Ruby. His PA seems like a nice woman and made me feel at home but I did wonder why she sat at the table with us for dinner. When I asked after the children, I discovered Noah and Ava would be spending the next few days with their grandparents, to allow me to settle in. I'm hoping they'll accept me into the family. Deep down inside I have the strange feeling that there's a reason I wasn't introduced to them before we married. They weren't even at the wedding. It was a low-key event because I didn't want a big wedding. I married Jack in a hotel room with my parents and two of Jack's business partners looking on. After a perfect honeymoon, being left alone on my first night in this creepy old house seems so out of character for Jack. I stand as a girl who tells me her name is Amy clears the table. "I'll follow you to the kitchen."

"Yes, of course, Mrs. Hunter." Amy places the dishes onto a cart and pushes it into the hallway.

I follow the squeaking wheels, peeking into as many rooms

as I can along the way. I poke my head inside the library door and inhale the smell of books. The bookcases almost reach the ceiling; leather-bound volumes fill one wall and another has various books of all shapes and sizes. Two cozy leather chairs sit before a fireplace but although the evening is cool, the grate is empty. I guess they leave the fires until winter. The weather here is comfortably warm in the summer and from what Jack tells me the sea offers a fresh breeze. I duck out of the room and run to catch up with the squeaky cart. I enter the kitchen, noticing the doors are like a restaurant, as in two swinging doors with a metal strip halfway to allow carts to push through without damaging the surface.

I step inside and all eyes turn to me. One young woman is stacking plates into a wall cabinet above an impressive marble counter. Like the rest of the house, everything is marble but in here, the high-end appliances are stainless steel. I gape at the refrigerator; it takes up a huge space along one wall and has a glass front displaying the contents like in a supermarket. Above a center island hang pots and pans from a rack.

"Mrs. Hunter." Sue comes toward me wiping her hands on a dishtowel. "Is there something you need?"

I smile at her. "Not right now. I'm exploring the house. Jack didn't have time to show me around. He has an emergency at the office."

"Do you want me to take you?" Sue folds the dishtowel and looks at me expectantly. "It's easy to get lost."

I shake my head. "No, I'm fine. Are there any locked areas I'll need keys to open?"

Furtive glances move through the staff and my stomach clenches. Are there secrets in this house no one wants me to know? I wait, glancing from one to the other. I clear my throat as the question remains hanging. "Another thing. Who decides the dinner menu?"

"That would be Ruby, she knows what Mr. Hunter likes." The chef comes out of a walk-in pantry and smiles at me.

I nod to him. "Yes, maybe she does but I'd prefer to discuss the menus for the week with you from now on, Pierre. I'm sure you can advise me on Jack's favorite meals, although after four weeks with him, I have a good idea of what he likes." I turn to Sue.

I walk to the drinks area of the refrigerator and pull open the door. It is like a store; with everything a person could desire. I select a bottle of water and with a nod continue to explore the house. It's dark now and the drapes remain open with the night pressing against the windowpanes. I admit, I'm scared of the dark and being in this house magnifies it a thousand times. Just going and closing the blinds gives me the creeps. I'll need to tell Sue that I want the drapes closed at dusk.

I make my way to Jack's office and take a pen from his desk. I'll make a list of the things to do and present it to Sue or George in the morning. Where is George? I haven't seen him since we arrived. Maybe he goes to his room on the stroke of five or whatever. I'll need to know who is on duty and at what times. I sit in Jack's comfortable leather chair and inhale the scent of him. How strange I could almost feel him the moment I entered the room. I need a notepad and pull open the top drawer. Inside are neatly stacked notepads and a bunch of keys. I take a pad and lift the keys to inspect them. Five keys, two large old ones, the other three look almost identical. I push them into the pocket of my chinos, but I want copies of all the keys and head back to the kitchen. As I walk past the stairs, the portrait of Laura stares at me as if daring me to invade her sanctum. I keep my eyes averted and keep going. "Jack is mine now. Soon, you'll have a new home in the loft and can keep your dirty looks for the mice and spiders."

In the kitchen, I go straight to Sue. "Now about those keys. I gather there's more than one set for the house? Will you get me a set please?"

"There's always someone here to answer the door, Mrs. Hunter." Sue lowers her eyes to the floor as if trying to hide her expression. "The other keys are to keep the children from the cellar and the loft. There is, of course, the room on the first floor. None of us are allowed inside by Mr. Hunter's orders. I don't have a key. I'll ask Mr. Hunter if I can get copies of the others cut for you in the morning."

She's refusing to give me a key to my own house? What the heck is going on here?

FIVE

SIX MONTHS BEFORE OUR
ANNIVERSARY CELEBRATION

Laura

Jack tells everyone he purchased this house for me. It's a lie. He bought it as a status symbol and tells everyone that will listen it was because it belonged to my uncle and I wanted to live here. I never have, but I keep up the story to make him happy. I spent some time here as a child and it was spooky then and hasn't changed. I swear I've seen a face looking from a window that doesn't exist. I've searched for it and found nothing. Strange things happen here and when I speak to my fast-dwindling circle of friends they figure I'm joking. They're jealous of the house but don't know how difficult it is to live here. Honestly, I look at the carved wood, marble and priceless antiques and my skin crawls. Each day my home is invaded with people, cleaning and making noise with vacuum cleaners. They have that smell, you know, that dusty old-ladies'-house smell, which wafts around for hours once they've been through, and then there's Ruby, Jack's PA. Miss Super-Efficient, I call her, with her tight tops and chinos and perfume that closes my sinuses. I understand he needs someone to do all the grunt work for him but I wish he had a male PA. I'm a jealous woman and I admit I don't enjoy him spending so much of his time with her.

Jenny, the nanny, and Sue—the housekeeper—are plotting against me. I swear they keep moving my things. I'm forever looking for my phone. I put it down for a second and it grows wings and moves to another part of the house. I make requests and, when things aren't done, they insist I never asked them. I figure they're trying to make me look bad in front of Jack.

I'm isolated in this house, no car, no visitors. I'm a prisoner in my own home. I only get to see people when Jack takes me with him to spend time on the yacht. Early in our marriage we threw many dinner parties and he escorted me to his business lunches and socialite parties but things changed when I had Ava. Although during that pregnancy I was allowed to visit my friends and go shopping alone, not so with Noah. From the moment Jack knew I carried his son, my freedom and most of my friends vanished. The staff watch me now as if I might turn into a monster and kill them all. I hear them whispering when I move around the house, sending secret messages to each other as they follow and likely record my movements.

Am I paranoid? Most people would love the lavish surroundings, enjoy having the most handsome and rich husband in town, but every day something else happens to make me question why I'm here. My babies hardly know me, Ava allows me to brush her hair and chats to me, but Noah screams and holds his arms up for Jenny. When this happens, Jack sends the children away and tells me not to become upset. I want my babies—I'm their mom, not Jenny.

I can never discuss anything with Jack. He works most days and when we are at dinner, his PA is at the table. He treats her as if she's one of the family and I often wonder if she is having an affair with Jack. They are always together, even though they leave in different vehicles each morning, her office at his company is right next door. She organizes everything for him right down to what he should wear for the next meeting—all the things a wife should do. I need to do something and take my chance after dinner as Ruby stands to leave. I touch Jack's arm and lean into him. "I'd like to talk to you. I'll refill our coffee cups."

I stand and go to the buffet where the coffee sits in a large pot beside the fixings. The aroma of the fresh brew fills my nostrils and reminds me of the time we sat at a little café in Paris. We held hands and he hand fed me spoonsful of lemon gelati. I believed it when he said he loved me. I sigh; life never turns out as planned, does it? As I fill two cups, I glance into the pink tinted mirror running above the buffet. I swallow hard when a distorted face looks back at me from behind my own reflection. My heart pounds as I turn but no one is peering into the dining room. Is Ruby spying on us? I beckon Jack over. "Jack, come and see this."

He reluctantly gets to his feet and I point into the mirror but of course the other person has vanished. "I'm sure I saw someone in the reflection behind me. Can you see anyone or is my imagination playing tricks on me again?"

"I see you and me, Laura." He stares into my eyes, his expression concerned. "What do you see?"

I laugh, what else can I do? He already believes I'm losing my mind. "Oh, I'm sure I saw Ruby peeking around the door. She doesn't like to miss out on anything involving you, does she?"

"That's because she needs to know everything about me, so she can assist me in my work." Jack takes his cup and sits down at the table. "She is excellent at her job, that's why she lives here, Laura. She takes the extra work from you."

He doesn't understand that saying things like that cuts me

to the quick. I swallow hard and stare at him, trying to keep the hurt from my expression. "What do you mean by that?"

"Most wives of CEOs enjoy organizing and hosting dinner parties. I know you hate doing that kind of thing, so that's why I need a PA." He gives me one of his condescending looks as if he's placating a small child. "Ruby makes sure I'm dressed for the occasion, and organizes my day."

You know that look someone gives you when they figure they've won? The small confident smile? It doesn't work for me. It just makes me angry and I slam my fist on the table. My coffee cup tips over and spins in the saucer, spreading brown liquid over the pristine white linen tablecloth. I love the look of horror in his eyes as he fixates on the spreading brown stain. "Does she take my place in your bed too?"

"I won't dignify that with a reply." Jack leans back and lifts an exasperated gaze at me. "I'll make an appointment for you to see the psychiatrist. I believe your meds need adjusting."

Seething, I grip the edge of the table to prevent me from slapping his smug face. "There's nothing wrong with me. I'm just sick of sharing my meals with the help. I want you to fire her."

"That's never going to happen." Jack places his cup in the saucer and stands. "The meals, well, I'm sure she'll understand because as sure as hell, I don't want any of the staff witnessing your violent episodes." He grips my arm. "I'll walk you back to your room."

We mount the stairs and the musky old smell of the house suffocates me. At least my room overlooks the ocean and I can open the window and smell the salty brine. As we get closer to my prison, the portraits of people I don't know and don't give a damn about stare down at me in judgment. I can hear them whispering. "*Laura's been a naughty girl again.*" I straighten my shoulders and walk tall, not saying a word. I'm not complaining but I refuse to comply. He takes me inside, sits me down and hands me my medication. I push them into my mouth, pretending to sip water and swallow. The moment he leaves, I run to the bathroom and spit them down the toilet.

I'll wait a few minutes and sneak into the nursery to see my babies. My heart breaks as the click of a key turning in the lock dashes all hope. There is no escape from this nightmare.

SIX

PRESENT TIME

Willow

Needing to find a bedroom on the ocean side but not too close to the children's rooms, I make my way to the opposite wing. I walk along the carpet running down the center of the hallway, the floor either side is polished to a high shine. It's darker here than I expect, with only one light glimmering high above. I search the wood paneling for the light switch but the one I find only controls the single light. The row of highly decorative chandeliers must be controlled somewhere else. I make a note to ask in the morning.

Moving on, I open doors until I find a large room. It's perfect but more of a sitting room than a bedroom. It must be part of a suite as the first door I open contains a lavish bathroom. I pause at the window. The view of the ocean will be spectacular in daylight. The glimpse of waves crashing on the sand under a witch's moon is a delight. I turn away and look at the huge double doors with a small vestibule outside. The bedroom must lie behind the splendidly carved wooden doors. I move to the door, aware of the lack of light. Shadows cloak the area as I close my hand around the doorknob but it doesn't turn. Sue's words come to mind. This must be a restricted area for the kids. Why would a bedroom be restricted? It makes no sense to me. Maybe it has a balcony and Jack is concerned they might fall to their deaths.

I dig out the keys from my pocket and try each one. The last key slides inside and turns with ease. I'm not sure what to expect, perhaps another empty room, but my heart pounds as the door swings open. The air is thick, musty but with a lingering hint of perfume. I swallow hard and fumble for the light switch. As light floods a magnificent bedroom, I feel like an intruder. The bed is unmade, headmarks crease the pillow. A champagne bottle and a glass sit on a tray beside the bed. A red negligee lies in a pile on the rug as if someone just stepped out of it. This must be Laura's bedroom.

Across the room, windows mirroring the family room below give a panoramic view of the beach. I turn slowly, unable to understand why Jack has left this shrine to Laura. It's been seven years and he hasn't gotten on with his life at all. I move to the bathroom, and the same untouched condition greets me. The next door leads to a dressing room as big as our current bedroom. Clothes line the racks. Dresses with labels I have only seen in glossy magazines or on red carpets. It's messy, with discarded clothes tossed around. The dressing table spans the width of the room. Open drawers display glittering gold and diamond jewelry, watches and bracelets in a statement of wealth. This woman flaunted her fortune and held a total disregard for her staff expecting them to pick up after her. I look around in dismay. I'd be too embarrassed to leave a room in this mess.

I turn on lights and notice Jack's clothes are there as well but covered in plastic. I venture inside and find a second door. I turn the handle, peer inside and find a light switch. It's a bedroom covered in dust cloths. I stand in a desolate lonely room and try the door to the hallway. It's locked. They had separate bedrooms? How strange, when Jack spends every second of his night with me and hates leaving me each morning. When his wife died was it too painful for him to return here? I can almost piece together the night before she died. Had they left the house after a night of passion and only one returned? I close the door, leaving the sadness behind, and move around the dressing room. I see my footprints evident in the dust and a sudden chill lifts the hairs on the back of my neck. It's as if Laura is watching me, judging me to see if I'm good enough for her husband. I shake my head, dispelling the thoughts. No one has been in this room since Laura died—and no wonder—the room is depression incarnate.

The dressing table is untidy with discarded makeup and dirty tissues all over. The laundry basket is full with items hanging over the edge. Clothes are piled over the backs of chairs as if Laura had been deciding what to wear. My heart pounds. It's as if she walked out and time stopped, freezing this moment. I hear a slight sound and glance over my shoulder just as the door whines and shuts me inside. Fear grips me, I don't want to be trapped inside this mausoleum. Breathing heavily, I drag it open, push it wide and peer outside. No one is there. I'm acting like a fool.

I ignore the overpowering feeling that I'm being watched and I walk to a closet and slide open the door. Inside, Laura's clothes are hanging neatly, covered in plastic. I run my hand along them, seeing an overindulgence of expensive designer clothes from casual dresses to fur coats. Everything she wore is preserved. The shoes number at least fifty pairs. I walk along the rack and feel the silk of an uncovered gold blouse. Why isn't it dusty? Dust coats the bedroom but not here. How strange. Does Jack come here to be close to his wife?

I throw open another closet door and cry out in shock. Inside is a mannequin in a wedding dress complete with long lacy veil. I swallow hard. I need to get out of here and slam the door shut. Rushing from the dressing room, I close the door behind me. I stand in the bedroom leaning against the door, my heart pounding. This isn't keeping a loved one's memory alive—this is an obsession.

SEVEN

With each step away from Laura's room, I feel better. I refuse to look at her portrait. Am I afraid she might smile at me, knowing she's scared me? Heavens above, I'm starting to lose it. I need to get a grip. A hint of fresh coffee brewing reaches me. Needing caffeine, I make my way to the kitchen. Sue stares at me when I enter and sit down at the center island. She raises an eyebrow and glances at Amy who is emptying the dishwasher, and they exchange glances in a secret language of looks between them. I'm an intruder, no doubt, and I don't figure they like their normal being upset. I look from one to the other. I'm lonely and really need the company. If they'll allow me, I intend to make friends with everyone. "I smell fresh coffee."

"Yes, it's ready." Sue takes down a cup and looks at me over her shoulder. "If you need anything, we're all listed on the house phones. You don't need to come down to the kitchen."

My mind is a shambles but I smile and push a long strand of hair behind one ear. "I enjoy chatting with you and would value your insight about the running of the house. I would have asked Jack but he's not here. I lived a simple life before marrying him, and all this is new to me. I feel like a fish out of water right now." I indicate to the mugs hanging on hooks in a line under the above cabinets. "I'd like my coffee in a mug. The bone china cups make me nervous."

"Of course, it's your home. What do you need to know? I'm happy to help." Sue places a mug of coffee and the fixings on the table before me. She gives me a stare from under her lashes.

I notice her mouth tense into a thin line; I guess she doesn't want me to cross the line between employer and employee. Do I make her uncomfortable? I hope not. Maybe I can put her at ease. I indicate to a chair. "Please, join me."

With obvious reluctance, Sue pours herself a mug of coffee and sits opposite me. I look at her, she's in her forties, neat and tidy. I'll keep the questions general and then try and make her reveal the house secrets. "How long have you worked for my husband?"

"Since the day he moved in." Sue turns her cup around in her fingertips. "I'd say it must be nine years by now."

This news is good to know and I nod at her. "So, you were here the night Laura died?" I lean closer, seeing the flash of panic in her eyes. What does she know? I smile. "I know all about what happened but it's such a mystery. I'd love to find out more about it and you were right here at the time. You don't mind, do you? Just between you and me?"

"I guess it's public knowledge now anyway, so no harm done. I was here that night. It was Mr. and Mrs. Hunter's wedding anniversary. They held a party on their yacht and I believe Mrs. Hunter fell overboard. No one noticed her missing. The weather had gotten bad, a storm I believe. They never found her body. Mr. Hunter was devastated."

I add sugar and cream to my mug and stir slowly. It's one indulgence I allow myself. "Has he ever mentioned why he hasn't emptied their bedroom? I went inside and it looks like she just left."

"We received instructions not to touch anything." Sue eyes

me with suspicion. "He keeps the door locked. There's a rumor that she haunts that room. In fact, some of the staff swear the entire house is haunted." She laughs. "I don't and I'm here most of the time but that's what happens in these old houses. People believe they're filled with spirits."

My mind is moving at warp speed. "Do you figure that's why Jack doesn't go inside?"

"I don't know." Sue looks at me over the rim of her cup. I can almost see her shutting down. "You'll need to ask him."

I sip the delicious coffee and sigh. "I've seen Laura's portrait and her clothes. What happened to the rest of her belongings? She must have other things?" I frown. "I hate to ask Jack and stir up sad memories. Can you tell me?"

"I guess so. They were moved into the loft when you married." Sue frowns. "Before that, none of her personal items were touched. Everything remained where she'd left them. Her boots were in the mudroom along with her wet weather gear. Photographs of their wedding, and other personal items, are stored in the loft. I guess Mr. Hunter wanted to keep her alive for the children for as long as possible."

"The thing is—" A woman in her late forties, with brown hair and kind eyes, wearing a summer dress and sandals, walks into the kitchen. She smiles at me. "—they don't have any recollection of her at all. They know the woman in red is their mother but they were way too young to remember her." She holds out her hand. "I'm Jenny, the kids' nanny. I've been here since they were born. Mr. Hunter insists I talk about her to the children. I tell them stories about her all the time, to keep her alive for them, but they aren't interested." She shakes my hand and frowns. "Ava is frightened of the portrait. She says the eyes follow her."

I clear my throat. "How terribly sad."

"I hope you'll redecorate." Sue purses her lips. "Mr. Hunter had the kitchen renovated the week you married. It's only been finished this past week."

"He followed my specifications." The man I assume is Pierre opens the refrigerator and takes out a plate of pastries. He sets them on the table. "There are always fresh pastries, pies and cakes in the refrigerator. Healthy snacks as well. The children have ferocious appetites."

I smile at him. "That's good to know. Please, everyone, come and join us. I'd like to get to know all of you."

"Mr. Hunter would never approve." George blusters into the room, his face beet red and one strand of gray hair hanging over one eye. "The late Mrs. Hunter had strict rules. She didn't like any of us being seen when she had guests, unless we were serving food. I'm sure Mr. Hunter approved."

I turn to look at him. From what I gathered from Jack, Laura was Mother Teresa. "Really? Was she old school, like the mistress of the house?"

"And some." Jenny giggles.

"You shouldn't speak ill of the dead." George frowns. "They say they come back and haunt you."

I lift my chin. "I'm not Laura and I'll enjoy our chats together." I shift my gaze to Sue. "Redecorating is a splendid idea. I used to design stage sets when I was in college. It will be fun. I'll speak to Jack when he gets home. I'd like to take the old master suite but not as it looks now. A complete makeover will remove any ghosts." I chuckle. "You have my word."

By the time I finish my coffee, my notebook has pages of staff names, and their shifts. Those who live in the house and those that come by daily or weekly. I stifle a yawn as footsteps echo in the hallway along with muffled chatter. Beside me, George leaps to his feet and hurries out the door. I raise an eyebrow at Sue. "It's late for visitors. Who might that be?"

"I'd say Mr. Hunter is home." Sue stands and gathers the cups. "I hear Ruby's voice. She'll be calling for a snack."

I stand and a shiver of excitement runs through me knowing Jack is home. I need his company and hope the honesty he promised me on our wedding day proves to be true. There's so much I want to ask him but how do I explain how horrified I am at seeing the shrine—and it is a shrine—to Laura? He's waited seven years before marrying me and he must have moved on—or has he? I need to know. I glance at my watch. It's five after eleven and everyone is up. I look at the staff. "Do you wait up for him every night?"

"Yes, we do." Pierre stretches and replaces the plates of pastries in the refrigerator. "He doesn't work late every night so it's not so bad."

I look at the staff. They snap to attention, shutting down any further conversation with me. I look from one to the other. "I've enjoyed our chat. I'd like to discover more about Laura's time here."

They exchange glances and Sue gives a slight shake of her head. They regret speaking to me and my hope of discovering more information is remote. What are they afraid of?

EIGHT

Trying hard to cool my excitement at seeing my husband, I dash along the hallway and into the sitting room. Jack is handing his briefcase to George and his face lights up at the sight of me. Curled in one corner of the sofa, Ruby has kicked off her shoes and made herself at home. She is a very friendly woman but I need some alone time with Jack. As far as I'm concerned, we're going to be on our honeymoon for a long time. I go to him and immediately his arms come around me, engulfing me in his warm masculine scent. I lift my lips to his and he kisses me passionately. I'm breathless when he finally lifts his head. His eyes fill with love as he meets my gaze. "I've missed you," I say.

"Me too." Jack rubs his nose on mine. "I'm also starving. Ruby has sent for coffee and sandwiches." He stands back and loosens his tie.

I smile and turn to Ruby. "It's been a very long day, I'm sure any shop talk can wait for the morning. I'd like some time alone with my husband—do you mind?"

"Of course she doesn't mind." Jack grins at me. "I'm all yours until Monday. I'll take you to my club tomorrow for lunch. Ruby has made the reservations. I can't wait to show you the *Laura*."

Words freeze on my tongue. "The what?"

"His yacht." Ruby pushes her feet into heels. "The vessel is named after his first wife." She smiles at Jack. "Goodnight, Jack, Mrs. Hunter. Sleep well."

"Night." Jack examines my face. "What's wrong?"

I'm shocked. "You kept the yacht after what happened to your wife?"

"She loved it." Confusion crosses his handsome face. "She wouldn't want me to sell it. I named it after her."

I shake my head. "Jack, she fell from the boat and drowned. I'm sure at the time she didn't like it at all." I watch his expression change from joy to remorse. "Is that why the room upstairs hasn't been touched and her portrait still hangs in the entrance hall? All these years you did this to please a dead woman?"

"At first maybe, but then as time went by, it was a memento of our time together. I'd go inside the dressing room and sniff her perfume. I'd cry like a baby but it was like having her back for a few minutes." He shrugs and stares into my eyes. "We had three wonderful years and two beautiful children together. Part of me still loves her but then I met you. It was like the sun breaking through the clouds after a storm that lasted seven years." He pulls me close and wraps his arms around me. "You're my soulmate and I love you more than life."

I lean into him. "I love you too." I sigh, hesitant to broach the subject of Laura's clothes and upset a perfect relationship. Maybe if I take baby steps, I can ease her things from the house. "When do you think you'd be ready to let go of Laura's clothes? Of course, we'll keep her jewelry for the children and any personal items but Goodwill would make a fortune selling her clothes. I believe it's the right thing to do."

"Let me think on it for a time." Jack can't meet my eyes. "I'm not sure I can let them go to strangers."

Dismayed, I slip my arms around his waist and look at him. "Then we'll move them to another room. It's such a waste having that beautiful room closed. It needs sunshine and fresh air."

"It is a special place." He points up to the ceiling. "It's right above this one and we share the same view. Unfortunately, the second floor has small windows, which makes that room unique."

Is he deliberately not answering my question? This man has the art of the deal in business so he can manipulate people and likely uses his skill many times to get contracts but he's never shown this hard side to me. I decide to change course a little and see if I can make any headway. "Do we really need to go to lunch at the yacht club tomorrow? I'd really like some time to get acquainted with the house. There are a few changes I'd like to make. Would you agree to me making it my own?"

"I've already renovated the kitchen." He looks down at me. "I guess that would be okay but use muted colors befitting the style of the house. I really dislike bold bright colors. Before you make any changes, run your ideas past Ruby. She knows about the renovation restrictions for heritage buildings." He smiles at me. "You're like a breath of fresh air, Willow, but leave all your plans for weekdays. I like to enjoy myself at the weekends. It's perfect weather for sailing. I'll get Ruby to gather some of my friends and we'll spend Sunday on the water. What do you say?"

I almost turn green at the prospect. I shake my head. "I'm sorry, Jack. I get seasick crossing a bridge over a river." I try and read his masked expression. "This is the first time you've mentioned the yacht or I would have told you."

"Okay, okay." He pushes a hand through his hair. "My bad. I can go sailing alone, well, with some of the boys. We do take fishing trips." He nods as if to himself and then looks back at me. "I'm sorry I wasn't here to show you around. Is there anything about the house you need to know?"

I swallow hard. "The staff figure the house is haunted. I find it hard to believe, in this day and age, that people still believe in ghosts."

"Oh, well I do too." Jack stares into space as if looking at something over my left shoulder. "I never did until I saw one myself. I went to check on the kids, like I do every night to make sure they're asleep, and I swear I saw Laura outside our bedroom door. I dashed along the hallway, opened the door and searched inside. Of course there wasn't anyone there. Some of the staff have claimed to have seen her too." He shook his head. "It only happened the once for me and I figure it was her saying goodbye—or was it wishful thinking? I guess I'll never know."

Goosebumps crawl up my arms as I remember the way the door moved and almost shut me inside the dressing room. Had I imagined it too, or was all this talk about ghosts some weird initiation prank to welcome me to Beauford Manor?

NINE

SATURDAY

I can't get the notion of ghosts or wandering spirits out of my mind and after tossing and turning all night, I'm totally exhausted. Honestly, I'd expected Jack to completely deny the fact there are ghosts in the house—not say he believed he'd seen Laura's spirit or whatever. I'm not easily spooked but find myself staring into the shadows, waiting for them to move.

I doze for an hour or so before the first rays of sunlight creep through the window to wash the bed in bright light. I hold up my hand to cover my eyes. From now on the drapes will be closed at night. I sit up and Jack stirs beside me. He always wakes up in a good mood and gives me a smile to melt an iceberg. "Morning." I peer at him from under my hand. "The sunlight is blinding me."

"I'll fix it." Jack jumps out of bed and draws the blinds. "Better?" He glances at his watch and pulls me from the bed and into his arms. "It's almost time for breakfast. Shower with me."

Sometime later as we're dressing, I recall some of the other things that kept me awake most of the night. I understand completely the role of a PA and for Ruby to be with Jack most of the time. He's a busy man and she organizes his day literally down to the second, however there must be a time when she steps away for a while and leaves us alone. I dress with care. Jack purchased so many clothes for me on our honeymoon, I know what he likes and expects from me. At first, I balked at the prices of the outfits he suggested and tried to refuse his generosity. It concerned me that he'd likely gone through most of his savings. I could see it made him frustrated, so when we went shopping, his "buy what you like and don't look at the price" became the rule of the day. If I'd known then how wealthy he is, his actions would have made more sense. The yacht club has polished wealthy clients, so I dress in a white blouse, a beige tailored skirt and a soft blue jacket with matching espadrilles. I glance in the mirror. My skin is tanned from our honeymoon and my dark-blonde hair has sun streaks. I meet his gaze in the mirror. "Is this okay for the yacht club?"

"You look wonderful." He wraps his arms around me and kisses my ear. "You didn't sleep well, did you?"

I shake my head. "Nope. All the talk about ghosts, I expect."

"Ghosts?" Jack chuckles. "I don't recall mentioning ghosts? Maybe you had a bad dream."

Confused but not sure if Jack is joking with me, I turn as he moves away to put on his shoes. "Before we go down for breakfast there's something we need to discuss."

"And that is?" He straightens and glances in the mirror before smoothing his thick dark brown hair.

As his wife I'm entitled to make demands—right? So here goes. I take a deep breath. "I know you've been on your own for a long time and likely needed the company at meals, but we're married now. What I'm trying to say is, does Ruby need to share every meal with us?" I give him a long look, trying to judge his reaction, but he's very good at hiding his feelings when he wants to. "You'll be back at work on Monday and I want to cherish every second alone with you when you're home. Is that too much to ask?"

"Ruby has always been a big part of my life, in fact, since I left college. Laura never had a problem with her living with us." A frown creases his handsome brow. "I rely on Ruby to make sure my day runs smoothly."

I nod. "So, you employed Ruby before you married Laura?"

"Yeah, we couldn't manage without her." Jack shrugs. "She handles everything for me. Laura liked her, they got on well together. I'm sure you will too."

His constant referral to his dead wife is getting annoying. It's as if he figures having her approval means something to me. I turn to look at him. "Did Ruby share meals with you and Laura?"

"For a time, and then Laura decided to keep the staff at arm's length—even Ruby who frankly is more like family." Jack chuckles. "Ruby understood and kept Laura at arm's length too. They rarely interacted at all. This worked well because Laura got annoyed if she spotted Ruby around the house. The only time she expected to see any of the staff was when they were serving our meals or during a dinner party. She tolerated Jenny, the nanny, and would discuss meals with Pierre, the chef, once a week on Mondays."

I lift my chin, feeling a surge of confidence. "That's good to know because I plan to have a few rules of my own. I want to spend as much time with you as possible, so from now on, do you mind if we eat dinner together, just us, no staff? This includes Ruby at our lunches at any of your clubs. That's our time together, business hours is her time. I'll discuss the menus for the week with Pierre. I figure I know your tastes but if there's a specialty he prepares, let me know and I'll be sure to include it."

"I'm good with that." Jack beams at me. "See, you're settling into my world just fine." He clears his throat. "Allow me a few minutes to explain things to Ruby." He picks up his jacket and heads for the door.

Oh, no you don't. I charge after him. "We need to show a united front, Jack. I don't want her to believe it's personal. I happen to like her very much."

"Okay." He pauses in the hallway and offers me his hand. "Come on then."

As we walk down the stairs, he pulls out his phone and calls Ruby.

"I need a word. In my office, please." Jack disconnects and smiles at me. "I'll ask her about the renovations at the same time."

So, he remembers the renovations but not the ghost story? I shake my head, trying to rationalize my thoughts. I recall the dressing room door moving for no reason and closing behind me. It spooked me as not one breath of air had circulated around that room in years. Had that experience made me dream vividly, and I imagined Jack had told me about seeing Laura's ghost? I glance at him as we walk down the stairs and head to his office. "That's good. I'd like to start right away on Monday. I'll need a budget." I squeeze his arm. "Are you happy for me to move Laura's things and redecorate that beautiful room? I'll make it look totally different. It will become our special place. I want to make new memories in that room with you, Jack."

"Don't move anything yet. Just work out what you want." Jack nods as if deep in thought. "You don't need a budget. In case it slipped your mind, I'm a builder. Like I said, run the ideas by Ruby and she'll send the right people to speak to you. I'll give her instructions to be the intermediary if necessary. I'm sure we'll come up with a plan we're both happy with."

Excited, I almost dance along the hallway. We find Ruby waiting in his office, scrolling through her tablet. She's dressed in smart casual clothes. I assume she believes she'll be coming with us to the yacht club. I nod to her. "Good morning."

"Good morning, Mrs. Hunter." Ruby turns to Jack. "You wanted to speak to me?" Her mouth turns down. "Is something wrong?"

"Not at all." Jack shakes his head. "It's just that some things will need to change now that—ah—my wife is here."

I look at him and blink. Did he forget my name? Ruby didn't notice his slip and is looking at him expectantly. I move my attention from one to the other; it's like watching a tennis match.

"I spend long hours at the office, as you know." Jack clears his throat. "When I get home, I need to spend my entire time with ah—Willow. I don't expect you to be beside me for all my waking hours. Willow mentioned that you need some time for yourself too. So, unless some emergency occurs, the weekends are yours from now on, and we will be taking all our meals alone." He smiles at her. "Willow will be speaking to you about renovations for the house. Call in one of our architects to make sure any changes don't contravene any building regulations for historical homes. I'll look over the plans before we begin. I'll be having the final say."

"Okay." Ruby makes a few notes and then turns to me. "Thank you for thinking of me, Mrs. Hunter. That's very kind of you." She smiles. "I do appreciate having some extra time to myself and I'll look forward to discussing the renovations with you." She looks at Jack. "If there's nothing else, I'll grab breakfast before Sue throws it in the garbage."

"Thanks, Ruby." Jack leads the way out of the door. As we enter the dining room, he smiles at me. "That went well."

The aromas of delicious food greet me and I stare at a smorgasbord of dishes filling a sideboard. My stomach groans in appreciation. To think I had a fear of being wealthy. I smile to myself. This luxury I can get used to. Above the sideboard is a long, beveled mirror, the antique finish is unusual and the color a watery pink. As I spoon eggs onto my plate, I glance up and see a face in the doorway. It's distorted and I turn quickly to see who's coming—but there's nobody there. I turn to Jack. "Did you see someone in the doorway just before?"

"No." He frowns and touches my cheek. "Maybe it was one of the staff making sure we're okay. There are people moving around the house all day. Make yourself familiar with them, so they don't concern you. I don't want you having nightmares again."

How can I tell him the face I saw was Laura?

TEN

Although we're going to the yacht club for lunch the plan is to arrive early, so I can take the tour of Jack's yacht. The idea of seeing where Laura died terrifies me but how can I tell him when he is so excited? I try to concentrate on the magnificent scenery. I didn't expect the Newport Yacht Club to be so picturesque. Set on an impressive marina, my gaze is drawn to sleek yachts and sailboats rocking gently in the water. As Jack guides his Porsche to a parking space with his name on a plaque, I absorb the elegance of the club's classic architecture and marvel at the brightly colored flowerbeds. There are even flags on top of flagpoles waving madly in the wind from the harbor.

"It's impressive, isn't it?" Jack slides from behind the wheel. "Wait until you see inside."

I smile at him, as we enter a massive foyer. The glossy wooden floors reflect the lights above as we walk to a counter to sign in. My attention is drawn to wide picture windows that offer amazing views of the marina. A large room to one side with tables covered with crisp white tablecloths and silverware has servers buzzing around preparing for lunch, no doubt. Beside me Jack waves to someone and then we head to a group of tables, where his friends are sitting. Everyone is drinking coffee and chatting. The atmosphere is warm and inviting. I usually feel out of place in these swanky places but everyone is smiling, and I relax and decide to enjoy myself. Everyone looks at me as we approach and I'm suddenly self-conscious.

"Hi, everyone." Jack is smiling. "Let me introduce you to my beautiful wife, Willow." He places a hand on my back to urge me forward. "Willow, these are my friends, Carol and Peter Sutton."

I step forward as he indicates to a woman in her forties, tanned with eyes like a hawk; her husband Peter stands and offers me his hand. He is wearing a blue and white striped polo shirt and white shorts; he is perhaps fifty with a protruding belly and graying dark hair. His handshake is damp but firm. "Nice to meet you."

"June and Martin Cleaves." Jack indicates with his chin. "Missy and Jim Durum."

The men—both Jack's age, lean and good-looking—shake my hand. June is a mousy woman, as in she resembles a mouse, and Missy is younger. She is an example of a plastic surgeon's best friend with her false eyelashes, plumped up cheeks and lips. I blink at breasts big enough to use as a floating aid; she is friendly enough and stands to hug me and welcome me to Newport. I like her. With all her enhancements she seems to be the only real person in the group. They talk about sailing, fishing and the stock market. I'm sitting beside Missy and she leans toward me. I turn in my seat to look at her.

"It must be difficult stepping into Laura's shoes. She was larger than life." Missy frowns and her forehead doesn't move. "I was there, you know, the night she went missing."

My ears prick. I know nothing about that night and lean closer. "Really? How terrible. What exactly happened?"

"No one knows for sure—but I always wonder if Tom was somehow involved." Missy gives me a knowing look.

I frown. "Tom?"

"Well..." Missy leans closer. "There was something going on. I'm not sure of the details but after Laura died, Tom was demoted. He used to live in the house. It screams coverup to me. Jack suddenly didn't want his bodyguard, and good friend since college, living in the house. It's as if they purposely distanced themselves from each other."

I can't believe what I'm hearing but I don't want her to stop. "Did anything involving Tom happen the night Laura died?"

"Yeah, Laura, Jack and Tom were all acting real strange—you know, what's the word—forced. As if they were trying to act happy." Missy raises one perfectly manicured finger and points to the marina. "We were all into our third or fourth bottle of champagne before we even noticed Laura hadn't returned to the party. She'd had an argument with Jack... well, let's say a disagreement. It's very hard to get Jack to argue about anything, he is the coolest man I know."

Intrigued, I look at her. "Go on."

"I gather she told Jack something about one of the staff and he didn't believe her. Laura lost it and Jack told her to go outside and cool down. The next minute, Jack is pushing Tom into the galley to speak to him. I never found out what that was all about. Not long after, Tom went out on deck." Missy leans closer. "Laura didn't take orders from anyone but she told me she needed some fresh air and Jack was being a jerk." She shrugs. "That was the last time I saw her alive. The thing is, Laura could swim like a fish. It's unlikely if she fell overboard that she didn't make it to shore."

I meet her gaze. "They never found her, so that never happened. Do you have another theory?"

"Not really. I blame the champagne but another thing someone mentioned is that one of the life buoys was missing." She gave me a long look. "I guess it could have been washed overboard in the storm. Maybe Laura grabbed it before she fell?"

The idea of being washed overboard horrifies me and I swallow hard. "That leaves a ton of unanswered questions, doesn't it?"

"I'm not saying anything but I find it hard to believe Laura fell overboard." Missy shook her head. "She was a fine sailor."

My gaze moves around the table and cold chills raise the hairs on my arms. "Why would anyone want to hurt her? You were all close friends."

"That—" Missy rolls her eyes "—is the question I've been asking myself for seven years."

ELEVEN

Jack's excitement is palpable as he takes my hand and leads me to the marina. His constant chatter in my ear about the *Laura* reminds me of a small child on Christmas morning. Obviously, sailing is a very big part of his life and yet he concealed it from me during our whirlwind courtship. I'm concerned why something so important to him failed to come out in any of our conversations. As we walk together, luxury surrounds me. I've never been this close to so many huge extravagant yachts. They glisten under the sunlight, each polished to a high shine. It seems everyone is trying to outdo each other by buying the biggest and best. Although I'm impressed by the beauty of each vessel, just the idea of even stepping on board makes me queasy. I have tried to control seasickness; I've taken medication but the second anything moves under my feet I'm gone, and the feeling lasts for days afterward.

"I know you get seasick but have you tried to ride it out?" Jack squeezes my hand and looks genuinely concerned. "I've known people who start off seasick and end up fine sailors after a day or so. Sometimes it just takes a little time to adjust."

I look at him and shake my head. "I know now that sailing is a big part of your life and I'd love to be with you enjoying the ocean. I love the sea, truly I do, but it's something to do with my inner ear. Anything that unbalances me, even driving fast around a few corners, makes me giddy and sick." I shrug and meet his troubled gaze. "I discovered the problem when I went on a cruise. I couldn't get off the ship and spent four long weeks spewing. They gave me seasick pills and they did nothing. The worst thing was it didn't stop when I left the vessel. It took me a few days to come good."

"That bad, huh?" Jack rubs his chin. "It must be terrible being like that."

I stop walking and turn to face him. "I wish you'd have told me about all this before. Now you've married a woman who can't join you in your favorite sport." My heart aches as I look at him. "I guess as marriage is a contract, and I didn't reveal all the details of my life to you either, that's grounds to get an annulment, but I didn't do it intentionally."

"An annulment?" Jack dashes a hand through his hair and stares at me. "It might have helped if I'd told you about my yacht. The thing is, Willow, I was so head over heels in love with you, I didn't want you to believe I was one of those pretentious rich guys. I know this life isn't what you wanted. The one thing I do know about you is you're not a fortune hunter. You enjoy the simple things in life and I appreciate that." He rubs his hands up and down my arms. "I know you want me for myself and all this—" he waves his hand to indicate the marina "—means nothing to you. I know the house isn't what you'd choose as our home. It's way too big for us but, in my profession, clients expect to see wealth and prosperity." His Adam's apple moves up and down as he swallows hard. "Please don't tell me you want to leave me because of a stupid yacht. I couldn't stand it."

Tears burn the backs of my eyes at Jack's distraught expression. "I love you, Jack, but you're right—all this means nothing to me. I'm used to working hard for everything I own. All around me I see waste and overindulgence, while people are sleeping in the streets and kids are going hungry." I fight back tears. "I can't be what you want me to be, Jack. Our honeymoon was wonderful; traveling was something I've always wanted to do. I figured you'd spent all your savings making it perfect. When you said you were in real estate, I thought as in a Realtor, not a real estate mogul." I drag in a breath and try not to cry. "I can't be Laura, Jack. She was refined and sophisticated. That's not me and never will be."

"I've never wanted a replacement for Laura." Jack pulls me into his arms and rubs my back. "To be perfectly honest, I never believed I would find anyone to love again. Laura was the complete opposite to you. She came from wealth and it made her spiteful toward other people less fortunate than herself." He steps away and lifts my chin to look deep into my eyes. "If helping the homeless is something that will make you happy, we can set up a charity. In fact, I could probably build apartment blocks to use as halfway houses until they can get a place of their own." He smiles at me. "Sometimes being wealthy can be an advantage."

I blink, hoping he's not just saying things to make me feel better. "You'd do that?"

"I'll get my legal team on it on Monday." He takes my hand and we continue to walk along the sun-bleached dock. "Once it's established, we can do many things to raise money. I'll start with a sizeable donation and make plans for the halfway houses. You'll need a working board to run all the nitty-gritty but you can be involved in all the decision-making."

Knowing how donations for charities can be eaten up by the paid board members, I stop walking and look at him. "I'm happy to have paid legal counsel and an accountant but I want like-minded people who do this work for charity, not to line their own pockets."

"Okay, so wives of the rich or famous?" Jack nods as if thinking. "I'll ask around." He suddenly smiles. "I've always wanted to be a philanthropist and this seems to be a very good way of starting."

I'm happy he cares about my feelings enough to start a charity. He surprises me with his generosity all the time. I stare at the line of yachts sparkling under the sun and bobbing slightly. Just looking at them makes me giddy. As this club is a big part of his life, I'm glad I offered him a way out of our marriage— although losing him would break my heart, I need to know where I stand with him. He is still so new to me and so is my new life alongside him. His chatter goes over my head as we walk along the dock; my stomach tightens at the idea of stepping onto Laura's yacht. How could Jack still cherish the place where his wife died? Although heat burns through my clothes a shiver runs down my spine and a wave of nausea grips me. I really don't want to go near the *Laura*. In fact, I need to be anywhere but here.

TWELVE

We walk in brilliant sunshine along a dock lined with millions of dollars of the finest vessels money can buy. When we reach his yacht the captain greets us. I must admit the yacht is magnificent and I gape at the seamless blend of glass and polished steel with multiple decks offering panoramic views of the sea. The name "Laura," emblazoned on one side, screams out at me. I nod as Jack introduces me to the staff but I won't be staying long. Even in dock the boat is moving too much for my comfort.

Inside is luxurious and I can see Laura's touch everywhere —not what I would expect to find at all. It's as if Jack's neutral taste has been completely disregarded and Laura's feminine touches have taken over. I personally don't like lace and frills and it seems very strange to me that Jack hasn't changed anything since his wife died. This yacht is his "baby" and yet it resembles a feminine boudoir.

He shows me the decks and the bedrooms. They smell of room freshener and fish. The mixture is doing strange things to my stomach and I turn to head back into the fresh air. As I move along the passageways in an attempt to escape, I can feel Laura's presence so intensely that I expect her to open a door and scream at me for stealing her husband. I'm moving faster now, running until I slow to move down the gangplank and back onto the dock. I bend over, sucking in deep breaths of salty air.

"Willow." Jack is at my side. "I'm so sorry. I had no idea this would happen."

I straighten and look at him. "That boat isn't you, Jack. It's old and not a good representation of who you are in this world. You're a builder." I wave a hand at the yacht. "Inside is the opposite of your tastes. Neutral, you told me, and that is more like a brothel. You should sell it and buy something more appropriate." I breathe slowly, trying to settle my stomach. "You don't need to please me, Jack. Buy something to please you. Yes, I'll miss you when you go fishing with your friends but I'll never stand in your way. We can work this out. One thing though. I would prefer you go out fishing with the boys and not have parties on board without me."

"Oh, that's a given." He smiles at me and his eyes sparkle. "I'm faithful and that's one thing you can take to the bank." He leads me to a bench and we sit down. "Rest for a time until you get your sea legs."

I chuckle. "That will never happen." I turn to him as we both stare at the yacht. "If it's not too painful, what happened the night Laura died?"

"There's not much to tell really." Jack rests one arm along the back of the bench behind me. "It was our wedding anniversary and we had some friends aboard to celebrate. We'd had a great meal and were drinking bottles of champagne. Something had gotten into Laura's craw. She had a problem with a couple of my staff and wanted me to fire them immediately. I asked her to cool down and just enjoy herself and that I'd deal with them in my own time. She flew at me and slapped my face." He shakes his head slowly and sighs. "She had a temper and didn't suffer fools easily. We went through so many staff in the house as she always found something wrong with them."

I want more information and turn in my seat to look at him. "When did she go missing? Was she drunk?"

"No, she wasn't drunk. She'd had maybe one glass of champagne and she always drank water with meals." Jack stares into the distance and I can almost see the memories coming to the surface. "After she yelled and slapped me, I told her to go and clear her head and she went out onto the deck." He points to the back of the boat. "She was heading for the stern when I last saw her. I wasn't concerned in any way because she often went and stood at the railing and stared at the stars. It was her favorite place to be, especially at night. I figured I'd give her a few minutes to cool down and then go and see her but I got into a conversation with the others and lost track of time. I guess twenty or thirty minutes had gone by before I went out to speak to her. She was nowhere in sight. I came back inside and asked if anyone had seen her come in. No one had seen her and then we all searched for her. When we couldn't find her, we contacted the Coast Guard and turned around immediately and headed back the way we'd come. We moved at a slow rate of knots and used the searchlights across the water. It wasn't long until the Coast Guard arrived and we searched all night and the next day. There were choppers and just about everyone I know from the marina out searching but we never found a trace of her."

I frown as he hasn't mentioned the weather or the missing life buoy. "What could have caused her to fall overboard? She was an experienced sailor I assume and familiar with that spot."

"The water was choppy but was it enough to throw her overboard?" Jack turns his gaze back to me. "This fact has played on my mind since that night. You see, Laura hadn't been herself for months. She'd been unwell and I put it down to the medication the doctor had given her for depression. She was never the same after Noah's birth and I blame myself for her death in some ways. I avoid arguing with anyone, it's not in my nature but she kept goading me. This time, I told her to get some fresh air because she was making a spectacle in front of our friends and I knew she'd regret it in the morning. I said it softly and I doubt anyone heard. The thing is, Willow, I should have taken more time to listen to her and maybe help her work out her insecurities." He sucks in a deep breath and lets it out. "She was the mother of my children and I cared for her but our relationship toward the end was difficult. I'd hoped she'd recovered but, when she attacked me, I knew she needed to see the psychiatrist again. Nothing I did helped her. I can't get it out of my head that maybe she took her own life just to spite me."

THIRTEEN

SUNDAY

I stretch and snuggle back under the covers. Tiredness grips me, pulling me down into much needed sleep. The room is dark, the drapes tightly drawn, but slivers of sunlight peek through in places. The scent from the vase of roses on the desk fills the room and I can just make out a fallen petal in a beam of sunlight. I reach out to touch the warm body beside me and sigh. I love having such an understanding husband and don't believe he was any different with Laura. I want to have confidence in him but there are so many conflicting accounts, I'm having trouble getting my head around. Again, last night I had trouble sleeping and just couldn't get Jack's tragic expression from my mind. I know it's been seven years but most people recall a terrible incident in their lives with clarity. What is the truth about Laura's death? Getting one version of the night she died from Sue, then another from Missy and then a slightly different story from Jack makes me want to get to the bottom of what really happened. Did she fall overboard, jump, or was she pushed? I need to know and I'm not doing this for Laura—although it would be good to know if she was a spoiled brat or the mother with postnatal depression that Jack insists. I guess she could be both. If she was unstable, was it because of the ghost stories and the face at the window—or this depressing house? Have I been mistaken about Laura all along? In the portrait anger shimmers from her eyes, it's unmistakable. The problem is I have strange things happening to me too. In her position, I'd want someone to find out the truth or am I going crazy too? I know there are vastly different trains of thought about spirits. Some say they don't exist while others insist they haunt houses for a reason and that's to reveal the truth about their deaths and so lay their souls at rest.

I didn't imagine the door closing or the image in the reflection in the dining room mirror yesterday. I've tried to make sense of it all and the only logical explanation is that Amy or one of the other staff were peeking in to make sure we had everything we needed—but that doesn't explain the door closing behind me in the dressing room. Then there's the conversation I had with Jack about ghosts. I remember it so vividly. Had that really been a dream or had he forgotten he'd told me? It would have been an intimate moment for him, seeing her as if she was saying goodbye. Then again, Jack might believe it shows weakness by admitting he'd seen her. What I can't fathom is, he remembers everything else we spoke about that night. It doesn't make sense to me that he'd forget the bit about seeing her ghost. I sit up in bed and shake my head; perhaps the lack of sleep and exhaustion is causing a slip in my memory—or am I slowly losing my grip on reality?

I'm apprehensive about meeting the kids today and more so Jack's parents. I overheard a heated conversation he had with them just before we boarded the flight to Paris. His mother's outraged voice cut through my happiness like a wrecking ball. She'd heard about our whirlwind romance and marriage from Ruby. Personally, I don't believe it's Ruby's job to inform Jack's family about his personal life. He wanted to tell his parents in his own time. He'd told me his mother believes no one is good enough for her son. I was shocked to discover she'd arranged for him to meet Laura. The fact that he'd liked her was a bonus and he insists he'd married her for love, not for her family name or the old money behind her.

I push hair from my eyes and swing my legs over the side of the bed. I would be the last person she'd pick for Jack. Although I'm educated, I wanted to be an actor and ended up taking any work I could get, mostly in advertising. My agent would send me to the craziest auditions but I was fortunate enough to make a living. Beside me, Jack is sleeping soundly. I head for the shower. I'd like time to speak to the staff before he wakes.

When I'm done, I walk to the kitchen determined to get answers but, before I make it to the bottom of the stairs, I hear Jack calling my name. I turn, try to ignore the accusing stare from Laura's portrait and call back. "I'm on the stairs. I'll wait for you in the kitchen."

"Okay, give me five." The bedroom door slams shut.

I stare blankly for a few moments. Have I upset him? I shrug and hurry down to the kitchen. It's busy with people moving around, Sue is issuing orders and George is just finishing his meal. I figure it's too noisy to ask questions so I get Pierre's attention and make an excuse for being there. "Can I have crispy bacon this morning?" I smile at him. "I love it with pancakes."

"Your wish is my command." Pierre grins at me. "I'll send it right along." He turns back to the stove.

I nod at Sue and notice Jenny entering the kitchen. I wait for her to come to me. "Do you know what time the kids are due home?"

"They should be here by the time you finish breakfast." Jenny glances at her watch. "Mr. and Mrs. Hunter live about twenty minutes or so away. It was convenient as they were due for their grandparents' weekend. It gave you time to settle in."

I consider the implications of caring for another person's

children and lean against the counter. "What is a typical day for them? I'd like to be involved but I don't want to push myself on them."

"Weekdays they go to school. They'll have breakfast with you and then I drive them. I collect them in the afternoon. They have a snack in the kitchen and then I supervise their homework. After that they play until dinner. They have a short time watching TV or playing video games and then they go to bed. It's much the same every day. Weekends vary as to what Mr. Hunter has planned. If he wants some time alone, I can take them to the park or the beach. There are many things to do here. Sometimes they just want to chill at home."

Interested, I nod. "How are they at school? Do you need to tutor them in any subjects?"

"Only with reading at first but they're good students." She smiles. "They attend a very good school."

I hear footsteps in the hallway and push away from the counter. "That's good to know." I head for the dining room.

"There you are, sweetheart." Jack pulls me close and kisses me. "Got tired of me already?"

I gaze into his bottomless blue pools and sigh. "Never. I couldn't sleep so I took a shower and came downstairs. I wanted to ask Jenny about the kids' routine."

"They're set in their ways." Jack shrugs. "They'll accept you easier if you slide into their lives unnoticed. Don't make sudden changes. They're settled with Jenny; she's been a surrogate mother for them since Laura died and, in fact, she was the one that changed their diapers. Laura liked them when they were fresh and clean." He frowns. "Don't judge her, she loved them but that's the way her mother raised her."

I look at the table, set for two, and smile to myself. Moments later Amy glides into the room carrying a covered platter and places it on the sideboard. "That will be the crispy bacon."

Over breakfast, I turn to Jack. "I'm going to spend tomorrow checking out which rooms I need to redecorate. Do you have a floorplan I can use? It's something I'll need if I plan to suggest changes."

"I'll send you the password to my computer and the office files." Jack looks at me over the rim of his cup. "If you type 'Beauford Manor' into the search engine, the blueprints of the building will come up. Print what copies you need. There's been many changes over the years. Laura insisted the house has secret passageways where she used to play when visiting here as a child. The house was in her family for a time. I've scanned the blueprints and can't find anything. I do know part of the house was changed, as in interior walls moved to increase the size of some of the rooms. There are windows on the outside that don't show on any plan I've seen. They don't exist on the inside. It's a mystery."

Intrigued, I open my mouth to reply when footsteps come clattering down the hallway with the unmistakable sound of children's voices. Two dark-haired children run into the room, and a young girl is waving a toy. A smaller boy of the same coloring follows close behind.

"Dad! We had the best time yesterday." Ava threw herself into Jack's arms. "Grandma took us to a place called Save the Bay."

"The aquarium?" Jack pulls her onto his lap. "Yes, I've been there. It's great fun, isn't it?"

"We got to touch the fish and some yucky things." Noah waved a blue shark under Jack's nose. "Grandpa got this for me at the store. I saw a big lobster with huge claws. The lady said we couldn't touch it because it might hurt us."

"I got to touch a starfish." Ava held up a finger. "It was all bumpy and weird. It made my finger stink. Here, smell it." She stuck it under Jack's nose.

"Ava, that's not nice. Haven't you washed your hands since yesterday?" Jack frowned at her. "What else did you do?"

"I did wash my hands but I can still smell it." Ava's gaze left Jack and she looks at me. "Is that Willow?"

"It is." Jack moves around in his chair to look at me. He gently places Ava on the floor. "Willow, this is my daughter Ava and my son Noah."

"She's not ugly at all." Ava looks at me; she is a replica of her mother, right down to the almost black-blue eyes and tumbling ebony curls. She gives Jack a strange look and frowns. "Stepmothers are supposed to be ugly. Grandma read me a story, but Willow is pretty and has hair like an angel."

I grin like a monkey and a giggle escapes my lips. "Thank you. I think you're pretty too. It's nice to meet you, Ava, and you too, Noah."

"Are you staying here now?" Noah looks at me with his father's deep blue eyes. "All the time. Like a real mom?"

I nod and notice just how like Jack this little boy is, right down to his concerned expression. "I am, yes. Is that okay?"

"Yes, I guess so. I can't wait to tell my friends about the—" he looks at Jack "—aqu-er-ium? Can we go again some time?"

"Please, Dad." Ava jumps up and down. "It was awesome."

"Yes, we will, soon." Jack looks up and waves at the door.

"Come on now, you two." Jenny comes into the room. "Help me carry your things upstairs."

As the kids scamper off, an older couple walk into the room. I look at Jack and he smiles at me. My stomach does a backflip. This must be his parents.

"Mom, Dad." Jack stands and hugs his mother. "Thanks for taking the kids. It sounds like they had a great weekend." He turns to look at me and holds out a hand. "I bet you're dying to meet Willow."

I stand and walk to Jack's side feeling like I'm an animal at a show and these are the judges. His mother flares her nostrils and her eyes flash with instant dislike. "It's nice to meet you, Mrs. Hunter." I offer my hand but she doesn't take it.

"Welcome to the family." Mr. Hunter takes my hand in both of his and looks into my eyes. "I hope you'll be happy living in Beauford Manor; if not, I'm sure Jack will build you the home of your dreams." He glances at his wife's stony expression and smiles. "Jack tells me you're an actor." He leads me to the table. "Tell me all about yourself over coffee."

I sit down and the temperature in the room drops to zero. The woman is staring at Jack in disbelief. I smile sweetly at her husband. "Yes, and interior design. I've created quite a few sets in my time too."

"You are a breath of fresh air to this family." Mr. Hunter beams at me. "Isn't she?" He glances at his wife who's standing like a frozen statue.

"An actor?" Mrs. Hunter glares at Jack. "Why is this news to me?"

"Come and sit down, Mom." Jack urges her to the table and pours her a cup of coffee. "I'm sure you have many questions. We have all day. Ask away."

I cringe, waiting for a putdown, and wrap my trembling fingers around my cup. I meet my mother-in-law's cruel expression. "Yes, an actor. It's a well-respected profession and has been for many years."

"If you say so." Mrs. Hunter lifts her chin and her beady eyes move over me. "All the women are fake. They've had so much cosmetic surgery men don't know what they're really getting until the children come along looking like gargoyles."

I meet her gaze. "I haven't had any enhancements. This is my real hair color. In fact, my life is an open book and I have nothing to hide from Jack."

"They all say that." Mrs. Hunter shakes her head and stands abruptly. "Peter, I want to go home—now." She bends to kiss Jack on the cheek. "You need to fix this right away." She straightens and then storms out of the door with her husband on her heels.

I swallow the bile creeping up my throat and turn to Jack. "That went well."

"Well, at least Dad likes you." He shrugs. "Don't worry, Mom is a little prickly at times but she'll come around."

The woman's disgusted gaze is imprinted on my mind. I'd made an instant enemy. "Somehow I don't think so."

FOURTEEN
MONDAY

I really enjoyed our Sunday alone with the children. They are exhausting but so much fun. I believe Ava needs a mom—someone to just have fun with and shop until we drop at the mall. We made popcorn in the afternoon and watched kids' movies. Ava chatted all day and, from what she tells me, Jenny keeps a very close rein on them. Noah is delightful, and when he asked me to give him a cuddle, my eyes became all misty. I figure they've wanted a mom for a long time and they understand Jenny can never fill that role. When we tucked them into bed, I read Ava a story and she smiled so sweetly. I do believe I've made a good impression. It's wonderful how kids accept a person on face value and give their trust without reservation. I admit, I wasn't expecting it but I'm so glad. In a few hours, I'm part of a family. It's surreal.

I dress quickly, aware of the time limit, with the kids going to school this morning. Out of the blue, Jack surprises me by giving me a password to his corporate account. I stare at my phone and then look at him. "Isn't it dangerous to give this information to me? What if I lose my phone or something?"

"Take a look at the message again." Jack slides into his

jacket and gives me a slow smile. "It says, 'here is that number I promised to send you.' It doesn't mention anything about my company or which account it opens. Once you get onto the website, you'll use your name to log in. I set that up for you last night. There's a dropdown file on the left. Go to blueprints and specifications. It will ask you for a password. Use the one I sent you and search for Beauford Manor. There's everything there I have on the renovations over the last fifty years or so but there are documents held at the city clerk's office and they have an online database if you need to go back in time." He smiles at me. "If you need any help, Ruby will be here until ten; she's chasing up clients. Her office is next to the kitchen. Sue will point you in the right direction." He checks his watch. "I gotta go. I wish I could spend more time with you, showing you around, but I guess you have the general layout of the house by now?"

I go on tiptoes to kiss him. "I'll be fine. I have a ton of things to do."

"Great. The kids will be ready for school and I like to be there when they leave." He picks up his briefcase and holds out a hand to me. "They like you. Ava figures you look like a princess in one of her fairy tales."

The children surprised me with their openness. They chatted with me over breakfast as if I'd always been there and asked so many questions. My head is still buzzing from the chatter. "I like them too. They seem very contented. Jenny has done a fine job of raising them; it must have been difficult for all of you when Laura died."

"They were a little confused and Ava asked for her mom but Noah was very young and he spent most of his time with Jenny. Laura loved the kids but Ava was the favorite, she doted on her; and Noah has always been loud. I had his ears tested in case of deafness but he's just loud."

We head down the stairs and meet Jenny and the children

by the front door. I stand to one side as Jack hugs and kisses both kids.

"What do we call you?" Ava frowns and looks at Noah. "Noah wants to call you 'mom' because we don't have one and it would be nice but Jenny says Dad will be sad if we call you 'mom.'"

"I don't want to call you 'stepmother', it's silly." Noah's blue eyes meet mine and his cheeks pink.

"I'd be happy for you to call Willow 'Mom' if that's what you want." Jack looks at me and I see him misting up. "Would you like that, Willow?"

Speechless, I can't believe they want this after just meeting me. I look from one child to the other and then bend and open my arms. "I would love that. Thank you so much." They run into them.

Tears wet my cheeks and then the moment is over. The kids give me a hug and then tear out the door with Jenny and into the Range Rover. I turn to Jack as his arm slides around my shoulders. "I'm stunned."

"I'm not." Jack squeezes me and then drops his arm. "They've been asking when I'll get them a mom for about two years now. I believe with the current high divorce rate the turnover of moms and dads at their school is quite frequent. Changing a parent has become the norm."

I blink and look at him. "I hope that's not why you married me?"

"Oh, Willow. I have Jenny. She's as close as any mother could be." Jack snorts with laughter. "I married you because I love you. If there had been any doubt, I'd have asked for a prenup. Them liking you from the get-go is a bonus I could never have dreamed of." He bent to kiss me. "I'd better go before I carry you back upstairs." He turns and hurries to his Porsche and drives away with a wave.

I watch his car get smaller as it vanishes from sight and then go to his office. I boot up the computer and log in to the company files. I find what I'm searching for and sit scanning the blueprints. There have been many changes to the house over the years. I hear footsteps in the hallway and look up as Ruby sticks her head inside the door.

"Is there anything I can do to help?" Ruby smiles at me. "Did you find the files you need?"

I smile back. After our first hurried meeting, she's been pleasant and helpful. I nod. "I have but I'd like to print some sections of the house plans. Is there a printer anywhere I can use?"

"See that door." Ruby walks over to what looks like a closet and slides open the door. "In here you'll find stationery and printers for large documents or the regular size ones. Just print as usual and the document will be in here. Jack is very organized."

I stand and peek into the room. "That's good to know. I'm hoping to reclaim the main bedroom upstairs and convince Jack to clear out all of Laura's clothes but he has difficulty letting go of her possessions. When he comes around to my way of thinking, I'll need a storage area. Any ideas?"

"I believe he stores some of her personal items in the loft but perhaps one of the bedrooms on the third floor would be more suitable. Maybe if we get someone in to line the walls with closets, the garments can be hung inside?" Ruby taps her bottom lip. "Then he's not throwing out anything, is he? I'll speak to him as well. Maybe if we form a united front, it will work?"

I'm enthusiastic by her willingness to help. "Yes, if you can convince him that would be brilliant. Of course, all her jewelry, I'll make sure is in the safe. We do have a safe, don't we?"

"I believe there are several." Ruby went to a picture and it swung back to reveal a large safe. "There's this one. One in the main bedroom, so maybe there are more of her things in there. One in the sitting room and maybe more. You'll need to ask

Jack. This one is used for contracts and other documents regarding his business and the house. The others, I have no knowledge of the contents. Jack doesn't give me that information."

Excitement at getting things moving spurs me on. I can imagine how the main bedroom would look if I made the changes I require. "Okay, I'll make a list of my proposed changes and run them past Jack."

"No, you won't." Ruby smiles. "He told me to call in whoever you need to make you happy. The architect will talk to him." She indicates to my phone. "May I? I'll add my number and contact email. He mentioned bed linen and drapes as well? Just send a list along of what you prefer and I'll order them." She sighs. "I'll also arrange for the architect to drop by and speak to you. We'll need him to make sure we stick to code. He'll arrange any work that needs doing and all you'll need to do is supervise and make sure it's what you want."

I hand her my phone. "How long will it take to get someone here?"

"We're always busy but I'll make sure to find someone suitable." Ruby thumbs in her details and hands the phone back to me. "Jack will make it a priority so not long at all." She checks her watch. "I have a video meeting in five, I'd better go. Catch you later." She hurries away and her high heels clatter on the floor.

I lean back in the chair mulling over what she said. *Most of Laura's personal things are in the loft.* Jack told me the upper part of the house is never used, and nobody goes there. It's no wonder if the rumors of strange happenings are true. I consider going to search the loft and hesitate. What could possibly happen in daylight? The rooms in the top part of the house are empty or the furniture is draped with dust covers. How long has it been since anyone went to the loft? Yesterday, Jack made it quite clear that going upstairs would be a waste of time—does he know about what happens to people searching the house alone and has kept it from me? I shake off the impending feeling of dread. The loft and its potential secrets are calling to me. What if there are letters or something in Laura's possessions that tell her state of mind? I have a good excuse to be searching upstairs—not that I need one as Jack's wife but gossip can cause problems, so hunting for a room for Laura's clothes would cover me. I need to know what really happened to Laura. There are so many conflicting stories. If I'm ever going to be happy here, I must discover the truth.

FIFTEEN

Laura

I stare at my reflection. I no longer look like me. I'm painfully thin, my clothes hang on me and my face has hollows below the cheeks. I need new clothes and Jack is planning a wedding anniversary party aboard the *Laura*. I can't meet his friends looking like this. Why hasn't Jack taken me shopping? Maybe I should make an appointment with him? Yes, it's that bad. I need to ask Ruby to fit me into his schedule but I'll have to wave her down the next time she flies past. That woman is always busy. I wonder when she sleeps. I go into my dressing room and pull clothes from the hangers but find nothing to wear. I'm not usually a person who lounges around all day in my nightwear but the skimpy negligees Jack used to love are the only things that fit me—not that he comes to my room anymore.

I take a shower and then drag on a gown only because my hair stylist is due soon. She does my hair three times a week. Maybe I can talk to her, at least she can't run away or make an excuse not to answer. I've sent emails to my friends but very few reply. It's as if I've been sent to the naughty corner and that knowing me is social suicide. Although, looking at me now, I'm not surprised. I wrap a towel around my wet hair and grin at my reflection. I don't care. They're all fakes, hanging around Jack in case I catch an incurable illness. Any one of them will jump into my place before my corpse is cold.

Wrapping the gown around me and securing it with a belt, I walk out into the hallway as Jack comes out of his bedroom with Ruby beside him. He's dressed for work in his blue suit and she's Ms. Corporate Fashion, wearing six-inch heels, a jacket, silk shirt and skirt. She has her nose buried in her tablet as usual and is talking a mile a minute. They both stop walking and stare at me as if I've suddenly grown two heads. I smile. "Morning, Jack. I'm glad I caught you." I pull him into my room.

"Are you sick?" Jack examines my face. "Do you want me to call a doctor?"

Surprised by his compassion, I give him my best smile. "I'm fine. I'm getting better all the time but I need new clothes. With the weight loss it seems I don't have a thing to wear. Can you take me shopping in New York? I'll need something special for the upcoming business events and of course our anniversary party."

"That's not a problem." He steps outside and turns to Ruby. "I need to organize a shopping trip. Fit it in ASAP." He looks at me. "There, done."

"We've already discussed this, Mrs. Hunter." Ruby smiles at me as if I'm a small child. "Monday last. I asked Sue to measure you so I could order you some basic outfits. You can't go out in your robe."

I blink, wondering why she is lying to me. I look at Jack. "That isn't true. I only thought about asking you to make time to go shopping just before, so how could I have spoken to Ruby?"

"She did mention something about you needing new clothes, Laura." Jack steps closer and runs his hands down my arms. "Don't get upset. The medication likely makes you forget things. It's quite normal."

I want to shout that I haven't taken the medication for months. Each time he gives it to me I flush it down the toilet. I imagine the sewer rats must all have amnesia by now. I laugh at the notion and catch myself when I see the confused expressions in their eyes. I look at Jack, trying hard not to snigger. "I recall everything else, Jack. Maybe Ruby discussed the clothes with you. I do remember telling her I'd lost weight."

"Your clothes will arrive today, Mrs. Hunter." Ruby looked up from her tablet. "They're coming by courier."

"If you want me to take you shopping for something special, I'll make time." Jack walks me back to my room. "We'll talk about it later." He glances at the stairs. "Ah, here's your hair stylist. I'll leave you to it." He kisses me on the cheek and then hurries away, Ruby following close behind.

I stare after them, dumbfounded. I hadn't spoken to Ruby about my clothes, although I do recall mentioning my weight loss. I can't recall what day it was. I wave the stylist, Joan, into my bedroom and go and sit in the chair in front of the table below the window. Outside, the waves pound the beach, the sky is angry and dark clouds rush across the horizon.

"How have you been this week, Laura?" Joan combs my wet hair and adds product from a large bag she'd placed on the table.

I don't mind her using my first name; we've known each other since I moved into this horrible house. "Fine. Well, not fine really. I'm not sure if I'm becoming forgetful or someone is playing a sick game with me."

"How so?" Joan uses her scissors to trim my long hair.

I explain and she nods. "Do I sound crazy to you?"

"Not at all." Joan takes out the hairdryer and her brushes. "I know it's old-fashioned but why not start a journal? Write down the things you need to remember and things that happened.

Make a note of anything unusual and then you have a record and if anyone is gaslighting you, you'll know."

That makes sense and, if anything should happen to me, I'll have a record for hopefully someone to find. Right now, I don't trust anyone in this house. I look into the mirror Joan set up on the table and smile at her reflection. "What a brilliant idea. I'll use my laptop."

At last, some good advice—if I can trust Joan. I'm no fool. I know Jack is at the end of his rope with me. One more slip and I'll be in trouble. He'd never divorce me, it would cause a scandal, but if I died suddenly Jack would be the grieving widower. I need to watch my back.

SIXTEEN
PRESENT TIME

Willow

As I climb the stairs to the third floor, it's as if I'm stepping into another dimension or time. The long empty hallways seem to stretch out, like endless dark tunnels. Each room I open is dark inside. The drapes are tightly drawn and a musty smell accosts my nose. Although, when I turn on the lights, dust doesn't coat the rooms as I'd expected. In fact, the floors are highly polished and clean. It seems that Sue keeps this part of the house clean and tidy but that doesn't stop the sudden panic that creeps up on me every time I open another door. I assume the scare from the mannequin in the closet is still with me and I try to shake it off. I find a room, with one small window; it's square and wide and would take wall-length closets large enough to house all of Laura's clothes. Job done, I make a mental note of the location and move on.

According to the plans, the loft is at the top of a single staircase in the middle of the house on the top floor. I hunt for light switches along the way but I'm unable to find the main panel for the entire length of the hallway. The only one I locate turns on one single light, the same as on the hallway outside our bedroom. Fighting my fear of the darkness, I move through the shadows until I come to the ornately carved banister and move slowly up the steps. As I climb toward a shadowed doorway, a patch of coldness surrounds me with such intensity, my breath comes out in a cloud of condensation and goosebumps rise on my skin. I feel around for an air-conditioning grate and, finding nothing unusual, hurry up the stairs.

In front of me is a solid oak door and I turn the ornate copper doorknob. I expect it to be locked but the door swings open and a loud squeak and grind of metal breaks the silence. I feel inside the door for the light switch and to my horror my hand sinks into a mess of cobwebs. I cry out and jump back, teetering on the top step. Windmilling my arms, my feet slip and I go down two steps before grasping the handrail. I lean against the banister, panting. If I'd fallen and knocked myself out, I'd be lying here for ages as no one comes to this part of the house. I must be more careful. I hear something and look behind me, staring into the darkness. Was that music? I listen and hear a tinkling sound. It's like a music box but it's coming from inside the loft. Fear grips me, but then I recall a music box I had as a child and how the slightest vibration would set it playing. My stomping up the stairs could have caused the same phenomenon.

Gathering my wits, I pull my phone from my pocket and walk inside the loft. Using the flashlight, I search along the wall. It's not cobwebs; it's a fringe on a wall hanging beside the door. I find the light and listen intently but the music is no longer playing. The loft is spacious and takes up the entire footprint of one wing of the house. The light doesn't penetrate the farthest recesses and shadows cloak the corners. The strange forms hidden in the darkness could be anything or anyone. I want to look around but this place freaks me out. I take a deep breath. I must do this. It's the only way to discover the truth about Laura.

Stale musty air crawls up my nose and dust itches my eyes as I hover at the half-open door and a shimmer of fear washes over me. What if I get locked inside and can't get out? I open the door wide and step into the unknown. Heart thundering, I search around and find a wooden chair. I drag it to the doorway and push the back under the doorknob, pinning it against the wall. Dust motes twinkle like fairy dust in the beam of my flashlight as I turn slowly, determined not to lose my nerve. I suck in a deep breath. It's just a dark room. I can do this.

The house creaks and groans and tree branches brush against the windows in an eerie screeching sound. I try to dismiss the feeling that someone is watching me. Taking a firm grip on my nerves, I use my flashlight to search the immediate area. I notice boxes with "Laura" written on the side, piled up in one area of the loft. I head in that direction and read the labels. They say things like "books" and "photographs" but then I come across one that says "laptop." I take it down and brush the dust from the top before tearing it open. Inside I find a laptop with "Laura" written in sparkly lettering across the top. I lift it out, collect the cords and tuck it under my arm. A laptop tells many things about a person. I've hit gold.

I turn toward the door, remove the chair and turn to take one more look at the boxes. I use the flashlight, flicking it over the walls, and discover portraits of people staring down their noses at me and then something moves. I freeze and my attention fixes on a lit area. It wasn't there before and now I can see a face looking at me—it's moving. I can't breathe and stare transfixed, frozen to the spot. The phone in my hand slips in my damp palm and the figure staring at me lifts what looks like a candle. I gasp and move the phone. Realization hits me—I'm staring into a dusty cracked mirror. I walk backward. I hate this place and need to get away—now. Suddenly terrified, I start to run and hurtle down the stairs and bolt along the hallway to my bedroom. I lean against the door, panting. My instinct tells me there's something bad in that loft and, whatever it is, I sure as heck don't want to meet it.

SEVENTEEN

I place the laptop on the small table in front of the window in my bedroom, plug it in and then stare at it. I pace up and down chewing my fingernails. I'm not sure if I've done the right thing. Opening Laura's laptop is like invading her privacy. Going to the loft has unnerved me. My overactive imagination has gotten the better of me. My fear of the dark goes back to when I was a child playing with my cousins and one of them locked me in a closet. They left me there and went to play downstairs in the garden. I recall the smell of dirty shoes, and the clothes hanging around my ears, feeling like somebody was constantly touching my hair. By the time my aunt came to rescue me, all I wanted to do was go home. It seems that particular fear has never left me.

I shouldn't need an excuse to open Laura's laptop but the little voice inside my head is whispering, *Would you like a stranger to expose your innermost thoughts?* I need a good reason to open the laptop and discover what I can about Laura. From what Jack told me, he's been living with guilt since her death. If I can uncover the truth, maybe it will give him some peace and will shut down his so-called friends' gossip. I didn't like Missy's implications. Did she believe that Jack killed

Laura? I can't imagine him doing such a thing but the seed has been planted and now it's something I need to consider—if I'm to weigh up all the facts.

I recall the way Missy leaned into me to drop her bombshell. She'd taken no time at all to rat on her friends. There's one thing I hate about people, and that's those who speak about their friends behind their backs and make up stories. I'm not sure if it's their weird attempt to be liked, or maybe they just don't have anything in their miserable lives to talk about and so must make something up. I stare at my reflection in the mirror as cold grips my heart. I love Jack and must assume he's telling me the absolute truth about the night Laura died, but the ghost story denial is like finding a worm in a juicy apple.

Taking a deep breath, I sit down at the table and open the laptop. It's working and looks in good shape. I tap enter and at once it asks me for a password. I enter the kids' names and then Jack Hunter. Nothing happens and I have one more chance. I stare at the graffiti all over the laptop. It's childlike. Laura has scratched her name or written it in marker pen over every spare space. It's almost obsessive. This is so unlike how I imagine Laura. She dressed in the height of fashion and from the photographs in Jack's office of her, she appeared to be stylish but was she childlike and uncertain? I take a chance and enter: LAURA. The computer opens and an outdated Windows background greets me but all the icons are familiar. Documents, pictures and the like. My finger is poised over the files.

Where do I start?

The list of files opens and it is a long list. Different file names intrigue me. One is titled "Bones" and when I open it, it contains a journal of sorts. Lists of things Laura didn't like about the staff. The staff have their own sub file with an assortment of complaints. I laugh at the absurdity of the things that upset her. The salt wasn't filled to the top each day or the orange juice wasn't sweet enough. I open another file, titled "Laura" and scan the pages. It's a diary. I lean back in my chair, unsure if I should invade a woman's privacy by reading thoughts written just for her. My cheeks heat and I close the file and move to her emails.

I'm surprised to discover her friend is the one I met at the yacht club.

Laura Hunter

To: Carol Sutton

Tuesday 30th April 2.00 p.m.

I don't know why I married Jack. He suffocates me.

L

Carol Sutton

To: Laura Hunter

Tuesday 30th April 2.05 p.m.

I wish he'd suffocate me lol. What's wrong?

C

Laura Hunter

To: Carol Sutton

Tuesday 30th April 2.10 p.m.

He wants to know everything I do. I figure he's having me followed.

L

Carol Sutton

To: Laura Hunter

Tuesday 30th April 2.12 p.m.

Why would he do that?

C

Laura Hunter

To: Carol Sutton
Tuesday 30th April 2.15 p.m.
He doesn't trust me alone with the kids.
L

There's no response and the emails stop there as if that statement had frightened her friend away—or she didn't want to be involved. I stare at the emails and go back to the diary. I search for the date of the emails and read the pages from the months before she died. I find the usual things that people do. Shopping, buying clothes and trips on the yacht. Then in the months before she died and after Noah was born, things start to change.

May 30

This is the third time this week my phone has gone missing. I know I had it at breakfast. I went to grab a newspaper from Jack's office and when I came back it had vanished. I went to the landline and called it. I found it beside the bed. Another time, I fell asleep in Noah's bedroom and found it in the kitchen. How many times do I go into the kitchen? When I mentioned it to Jack, he says that women often get distracted when they have new babies.

I turn the pages and scan the screen, needing to know what happened next.

June 21

I've heard footsteps in the hallway four or five times and when I go to look, there's nobody there. Jack is late home most nights and I refuse to spend my time with the staff but I'm sure someone is in the house, watching me. Just this morning I caught the reflection of a woman's face in the mirror above the sideboard. I asked Jack and he looked at me as if I'd gone crazy. Have I? I don't know anymore.

I stare at my phone beside me on the small table and breathe a sigh of relief. It hasn't gone missing yet but the other things disturb me. I've heard noises and then there was the face in the mirror. I didn't imagine it either. I don't imagine things. I stand and pace up and down but the diary drags me back. I need to know what happened next. I sit and scroll through a few days of nothing unusual happening and then find an entry about Ruby.

July 15

I don't need to be told what to wear to a dinner party and having Ruby interfering is just too much to bear. She purchased me a ton of what I call house clothes and Jack promised to take me to New York to select evening attire. How dare Jack send her to choose a dress for me to wear? Doesn't he know me well enough to trust me to select my own clothes? It's an executive dinner party, so I'll wear black and white. A little black dress and shoes will do nicely, although they should always drip designer labels, as is fitting for his wife. So, when she arrived with frills and silk, I sent her away and all hell broke loose. Jack came storming into my bedroom and ordered me to take Ruby's advice and to apologize to her for being rude. I told him, I'll do no such thing, so he locked me in my room. At six I heard his car starting and looked out of the window. He'd taken Ruby to the dinner party. A short time later Sue came and opened the door.

July 16

Jack didn't return until breakfast. He said nothing and gave me no explanation. I need space from him and, with Jenny caring for the children, as usual, I take a walk in the garden. I have scissors in my basket to collect flowers. As I walk into the shadows alongside the garden beds, I hear footsteps crunching in the gravel. I turn but no one is there. I move on, and they come again. I chance a glance over one shoulder but see no one. Is Jack having someone follow me in the garden? If so, why?

I swallow hard. The implications of Laura's rambling notes make me wonder if she was of sound mind. Had Jack been coping with an unstable woman? Could this be why he didn't trust her alone with the kids and why he believes she took her own life? I need to know. I close the laptop and slide it into my underwear drawer. Right now, I don't want anyone knowing what I'm doing.

I cast my mind back to seeing the face in the mirror above the sideboard. Laura saw the same face over seven years ago, so why did I see it? A cold shiver raises the hairs on my arms. I've only been living here for a short time. I had a frosty start but now I get along with everyone just fine, so why are unusual things happening to me too? Is someone in the house trying to make Jack believe I'm unstable just like Laura? Why would they do such a thing and what do they have to gain?

EIGHTEEN

I head downstairs and hunt down Jenny. I find her in the laundry, ironing the kids' school clothes. I have no idea what duties she performs. It seems she takes the place of a mom. I'm not sure if I agree with that. As their new mother figure, I should be at least assisting with their homework or reading them bedtime stories—if they still enjoy bedtime stories. Not having children, I have no idea what kids of their age do but I can learn. I see a basket of freshly dried clothes and smile at Jenny. "I've been hunting down a room to relocate Laura's clothes. This house is bigger than I imagined." I take out socks and start to match them into pairs and roll them together.

"It's huge." Jenny glances up at me and returns to the ironing. "I've only gone to the second floor once. Ava decided to run away and made it up there. She was convinced she'd seen a ghost and had nightmares for weeks."

I pile up the socks and nod. "I'm not surprised. It's creepy up there. I gather it's cleaned? Most of the rooms look spotless."

"Once a week, I believe." Jenny smiles at me. "How are you settling in?"

I make piles of underwear on the table and shrug. "I'm fine.

I'd like to be more hands on with the children but I don't want to step on your toes. Is there anything you'd suggest?"

"Maybe start with helping them to get ready for school?" She glances up at me. "Start slow and see how you go." She sighs. "You know, kids go along at their own rate. I'm surprised they wanted to call you 'mom' so soon."

I pull out shirts and dresses and fold them. "I'm very surprised. It's nice though. What do you remember about Laura? Have you kept her alive for them?"

"The truth? Laura was a complicated person and only liked them fresh and clean." Jenny stops ironing and places the garment on a hanger. She glances at her watch. "Time for my break. Would you mind discussing her over a cup of coffee?"

I smile at her. "Sure. I'm famished."

The smell of baking and coffee greets us as I follow her into the kitchen. We collect mugs of coffee and fill our plates with food the chef has already prepared and left in the refrigerator and then head outside to a garden table and chairs. The fragrant garden beds surround the small picnic table and closer to the back door is a large kitchen garden overflowing with fresh vegetables and herbs. The house looms up behind us. It's not pretty this side and resembles a prison. The bricks have many years of moss growing all over and vines climb up the walls and surround the windows. I lean back in my chair to look up and see the many windows, like the eyes on a fly, dark and reflecting.

I dig into a slice of cherry pie and look at Jenny. "So, was Laura always like this or did something happen around the time she died? Please don't hold back. This is between you and me. I just want to know more about her and how she died, mainly to support Jack."

"I arrived here when she was seven months pregnant with Ava." Jenny peers at me over the rim of her mug. "She was diffi- cult to work with and hated being pregnant. When Ava arrived, she doted on her in public and in front of Mr. Hunter but she never changed a diaper and had a strict rule that both children remained in the nursery." She leans back, regarding me as if gauging my reaction. "I remember the fight they had when she discovered she was carrying Noah. It was around the time she'd sat for the portrait. She had her figure back and they were out dancing the night away all the time. Things changed after she had Noah. She became forgetful and spent long hours in her room."

I nod; that tallies with what Laura wrote in her diary. "Jack said he didn't trust her with his children but won't elaborate. I hate to push him. Do you know what happened?"

"I do." Jenny shudders as if remembering frightens her. "She filled the bathtub with water, not much, just an inch or two and placed Noah in the bath and then walked away. She denied it and became angry, saying someone was trying to make out she was crazy but I never saw anyone near the nursery that day. It had to be Laura." She shook her head. "He was only a month old, so tiny. If I hadn't heard him crying, he'd have likely drowned. I told Mr. Hunter and he took Laura to see a doctor soon after and he never allowed her near the children again unsupervised."

I stare at her in disbelief. "But she never tried to hurt Ava?"

"No." Jenny shook her head. "They didn't know Ava was a girl, they wanted the sex to be a surprise, but when she came along, things changed. They argued about everything and when Ava turned one, they became close again until Laura became pregnant. She hated Mr. Hunter for making her pregnant and, after the birth, she practically ignored Noah. I assumed it was post-natal depression and did my best to support her and ease her gently toward caring for him. I didn't believe she'd try to kill him."

I eat my pie, thinking. Nothing in the journal intimates that Laura hated her children. She seemed lost and alone. Jack obviously got help for her. I wonder how long her depression lasted.

I look at Jenny, glad of her candor. "So, the night they went out for their anniversary, was she okay?"

"In front of Mr. Hunter she always acted perfectly normal. When he left for work, she spent the entire day screaming at the staff or locked in her room. She accused everyone of touching her things and one day she insisted I was having an affair with Mr. Hunter. I recall her accusing him of spending too much time settling the kids with me each night." Jenny nibbles on a sandwich. "The night she died, she dressed in the new dress that Ruby had purchased for her and they left to meet their friends on the yacht. She kissed the kids goodnight but Noah turned his head away and buried his face in my shoulder. She waited for her husband to leave and poked her finger at me and said, 'If I ever hear my kids calling you 'mommy', you're fired.' That was the last time I saw her." She stares at me. "Do I try and keep her alive for them? No, not really. They know the portrait is their mother and Ava was upset for a time when Laura went missing but that wasn't because she missed her mom; she reacted to Mr. Hunter's grief."

I sip my coffee and mull over what she told me. "Did anyone tell you what happened on the yacht?"

"Yeah, she fell overboard and drowned." Jenny shrugs. "I hear rumors but they're just that. Her body was never found."

I look at her. "Rumors? What rumors?"

"Most people will tell you, including her friends, that they believe someone murdered her."

NINETEEN

Did someone kill Laura? I can't help wondering if the same person that moved her things around to make her appear unstable put Noah in the bathtub to clinch the deal. Who would risk the life of an innocent baby? I doubt anyone in the house would gain from her death, and, by all accounts, Jack was devastated. My mind is in turmoil. If strange things were happening to Laura, in this house as she claims in her diary, no wonder she became unstable. I need to know more. What was the exact date of the tragedy? I have no idea and feel foolish asking. I head back to my bedroom. I can google the information. The death of Jack's wife would have made the news.

I go to the table but my phone isn't where I left it. I search the floor and pat my pockets. I distinctly remember leaving it on the table. Why didn't I take it with me? I never leave my phone behind. I must be so consumed with discovering the truth I left it somewhere—but where? I check the room again and then head back downstairs retracing my steps; laundry, kitchen and outside but it's nowhere to be seen. I come back inside and go to Jack's office and call my number. I hear my ringtone and follow the sound into the dining room. I stare in disbelief. My phone is on the table where I sat to eat breakfast. I grab it up and slowly head back to the office to disconnect the call. I walk inside, shut the door and lean against it. What is happening to me? I'm an actor, I learn lines and need to know cues and stage direction; I'm not a scatterbrain.

Calm down, so you forgot your phone. It happens. Reading Laura's diary must have disturbed me more than I imagine. I look around the dark walls and aging wallpaper and wonder why Laura insisted Jack buy this place. This old house with dark hallways and spooky corners would disturb anyone. It's daunting and will never be home to me. I wonder if Jack would move. A new life in a different home sounds like a plan—if I can keep my sanity in-between time. *Concentrate on the jobs at hand.* I take three deep breaths and sit down in the worn but comfortable office chair and inhale the scent of my husband. It's imprinted in the leather seat, and his familiar cologne lingers in the air as if he's just left. Feeling him around me makes me feel better.

Determined to get the information I need, I open his computer using the password he gave me. Pages of images and news reports fill the screen. What is missing is any details or interviews with anyone on board. I stare at the screen. After scrolling through the different news items, I find a list of the people on board that night and notice with interest that in Missy's rendition, she mentioned her friends and the crew, but forgot to mention Ruby and Tom Bates. Maybe, as Laura considered them as staff, they weren't invited to the party.

What happened to Tom Bates?

I go to social media and can't find him. Is he Ruby's friend? I'm not aware of Ruby's last name and sit for a few moments figuring out the problem. I go back into the company files and search for a list of employees. It doesn't take long for me to find Ruby Wiseman listed as PA to Jack Hunter. I have her last name and can search for her on social media but I suddenly have a hunch and put Tom Bates into the search engine and discover he works at Jack's company as a security guard. I investigate his employment record and discover he's been with the company for ten years. Why would Jack require his bodyguard with him on his yacht? I haven't seen him with a bodyguard on any of the occasions that I've been with him. I scan the records again and find no indication that Tom Bates has been fired, so he's still with the company. What did he do to be demoted to a security guard?

There is one person in the house who would know, and that's Sue. I shut down the computer and movement in the doorway startles me. "Oh, it's you, Ruby, I figured you'd left for work ages ago."

"I needed to make a few calls and when I contacted Jack, he told me to stay here as he's going to be home early today." She stands staring at me. "I saw you going up to the second floor; did you find a suitable room?"

Glad I'd found one, I stood and grabbed the copies of the blueprints I'd printed earlier. I point to the room I'd selected. "This one will do. It's large enough and very wide. It's perfect for lining with closets. If you could arrange to get someone in to fit them, we can get Laura's things moved. Once we've emptied the room, I'd like to speak to the architect whenever you can get him to drop by. I'll be completely changing the dressing room and bedroom on the first floor. I don't want any memories of Jack's past life creeping up on him when we're alone."

"I'll run it past Jack but I doubt you will ever get Laura out of this house." Ruby indicates behind her with her thumb. "That portrait is a constant reminder. I doubt very much that Jack will remove it."

I'll run it past Jack? Really? As we'd already discussed making changes, I wanted to say, "Well, you know him better than I do." But I wouldn't give her the satisfaction. She'd been kind to me and I didn't want to sound ungrateful but I couldn't help feeling like an outsider. For some reason Ruby made me feel superfluous, like the new puppy someone brings home and interest wanes after a few days when it pees on the expensive rug. "We'll see. I'll speak to Jack about the changes and then call you." I tap my bottom lip. "Who do I see about changing the drapes and linens when they arrive? Is it Sue or George?"

"George handles the running of the staff and Sue handles everything else." Ruby crosses her arms. "Is there anything else I can assist you with? I have a few calls left to make."

I so want to ask her about Tom Bates but bite my tongue. I have no idea if they were close friends and if he was in any way involved with Laura's death, but I need to keep that revelation to myself. I stand and shake my head. "No, not for the moment. Thank you for dropping by. I'll call you after I've spoken to Jack."

I go to the door and watch her walk back to her office. I follow at a discreet distance and slip into the kitchen. Luckily Sue is there and she turns to look at me. "Hi there."

"Oh, Mrs. Hunter, I apologize. I completely forgot about asking Pierre to prepare your lunch." She looks at me with an aghast expression. "He won't be back until four."

I smile at her and shake my head. "That's okay, I'm sure I'll find something in the refrigerator. I don't eat much for lunch." I go to the refrigerator and swing open the door. As usual the shelves on one side have a selection of grab food. I take out egg salad sandwiches, wrapped in plastic complete with the date and time they were made. "Goodness, this is like living in a delicatessen."

"If you'll go into the dining room, I'll bring you a cup of coffee or whatever refreshments you require." Sue turns away to refill the coffee pot.

I place the sandwiches on the island and sit down. "I would rather sit here if you don't mind? There are a few things I need to ask you."

"Sure." Sue turns and leans her back against the kitchen counter. "What can I do to help?"

I slowly unwrap the sandwiches and Sue instantly gives me a plate. "Thank you. There's a couple of things I need to speak to you about. One of them is the furnishings for the new main bedroom. I'm not sure what the protocol is here for purchasing drapes and furniture. I'm not sleeping in the same bed as Laura, so everything in that room will need to be replaced."

"Have you spoken to Mr. Hunter about changing every-thing? He doesn't like me to touch the bedroom at all. I am only allowed to go in and dust the dressing room." Sue pushes hair behind her ears in an almost nervous gesture. "He wouldn't throw out any of her things. I collected everything she'd left around the house and stored it in boxes in the loft. I did this because seeing her things made him upset."

I nibble at the sandwich and stare at her. "Yes, I have. I understand you never went back into her bedroom after the night Laura died."

"That's right. He didn't either, as far as I know. He wouldn't sleep in his room. He slept on the couch in his office until a new bed arrived, which he had placed in the bedroom that you're using now." Sue takes down cups and then smiles at me and collects a mug from a line of pegs under the above cabinets and fills it with coffee. "He asked me to gather three sets of clothes for him from the dressing room. The next morning his new wardrobe arrived, along with his tailor. He had new suits on order so he'd replaced everything in his closets upstairs within a week." She hands me the mug and places the fixings on the table. "Have you asked him if he'd like to go shopping for new furniture? It might be something he'd enjoy."

I smile at her. "I will, that's a great idea." I add creamer and sip the coffee and then lift my gaze back to her. "Have you met Tom Bates? I believe he is, or was, Jack's bodyguard. Is that true?"

"Yes, he was until Laura died." She frowns. "I hope you don't mind me calling her Laura; it's just easier to distinguish between you and the last Mrs. Hunter."

I nod. "That's fine. Then we all know who we're talking about." I take another bite of the delicious sandwich. "What do you know about Tom Bates?"

"Ah, well." She glances at the kitchen door and drops her voice to a conspiratorial whisper. "I did hear he became involved with Ruby, and Mr. Hunter has a no-fraternization policy in his firm. He still works there but, after Laura died, Mr. Hunter wanted to fire him. Ruby pled his case and he ended up demoted and works in general security, as in he takes care of the building."

I stare at her, dumbfounded. "Can you recall when this happened?"

"Vividly." She leans closer. "It was when Mr. Hunter, Ruby and Tom arrived home after Laura fell overboard. I didn't hear exactly what went on as they were in the office but Tom stormed out, packed his belongings and left. That's the last time I saw him."

I swallow the sandwich and stare at my plate. "I wonder what really happened on the yacht that night."

"That's what we've all been thinking for the last seven years." Sue's eyes rounded as Ruby walked into the room but she gathered herself well. "Ah, Ruby. Great timing. Did you smell the coffee?"

TWENTY

I wonder if Ruby was eavesdropping in the hallway and, if so, what will she do? Hiding a smile, I add another spoonful of sugar to my mug. I love the rich brown sugar that Jack prefers. I stir it slowly, waiting for Ruby's reaction.

"Mrs. Hunter... or may I call you Willow?" Ruby smiles at me. "I'm not sure Jack would approve of you eating in the kitchen with the staff. Would you like me to carry your meal into the dining room?"

I'm sure Jack has explained that I'm not from his usual circle of society friends and Ruby is only trying to be helpful. She must figure I'm a trophy wife without a brain in my head and must be told how to behave. As she calls my husband "Jack" and seems to be beside him every waking moment, I must assume she's of great value to him. Although I feel the rebuff, which it is—even heavily disguised, it's her attempt to pull me into line—I notice there is a hierarchy within the staff. Although Jack informed me that George oversees them, it's clear that Sue runs the house, and it doesn't take a fool to see that Ruby lords over all of them. I don't intend my place in this house to be controlled by a member of the staff. "It's Mrs. Hunter, if you don't mind, Ruby, and I just happen to like Sue's company but thank you for your concern. While I have you here, can you tell me who was on the yacht the night Laura died?"

"Jack and Laura, of course, the Suttons, Cleaves, Durums and the crew. I believe we had six people on board to serve drinks and a chef, a couple of cleaners, and the captain and second mate." Ruby crosses her arms and I wonder if it's a tell that she's lying. "It's a long time ago."

I stir my coffee slowly and look at her. "You were on board as well, weren't you, and Jack's personal bodyguard? What was his name? Ah, yes. Tom Bates. Whatever happened to Mr. Bates?"

"Yes, I was on board with Tom. He is still working at the firm." Ruby's eyes sweep the table. "Jack doesn't employ a personal bodyguard now."

I sip my coffee nonchalantly. I need to keep the conversation cordial. "Do you remember what happened the night Laura went missing?"

"It's not something anyone could forget." Ruby turns to the counter and pours herself a cup of coffee and then turns back and sits down opposite me. "It started out a wonderful evening. We had a great meal and everyone was sitting round chatting and drinking champagne." She stares blankly over my shoulder for a few seconds. "Everyone was talking. The men were discussing recent fishing trips and the women were chatting about a fashion show they'd all attended the previous week. I went to the bar to get a drink of water and overheard Jack and Laura disagreeing about something. They weren't having an argument, but it was obvious that Jack had discovered I was seeing Tom."

I glance at Sue and she raises an eyebrow. "Yes, I'm aware you were involved with Tom. I assume that didn't go down too well with Jack as he has the no-fraternization policy for his staff?" I met Ruby's troubled gaze. "You knew that, didn't you? Why would you risk losing your position?"

"We'd become friends working in such close proximity, and it just happened." Ruby shrugs. "Office flings happen all the time. Although, I do understand Jack's rationalization for introducing the clause, but it's not realistic, not when we both lived in the house as well. People fall in love."

I shake my head. "I disagree. The clause is designed to protect workers. Vulnerable young people can be taken advantage of by superiors." I don't wait for her to comment. "What else can you tell me about the night Laura died?"

"She was saying something about having one rule for me and one rule for everyone else." Ruby turned her coffee cup around in her fingertips and then ran the tip of one finger around the rim. "She was very possessive of Jack. In her eyes every woman was a threat to their marriage. As I work very closely with him, I was always in her sights but it wasn't always me, his secretary and other office staff came under fire as well and were moved around frequently for no other reason than Laura was jealous of them."

I lean back in my chair observing her. "How come she wasn't jealous of you?"

"I made a point of flying under her radar." Ruby sighs. "Jack understood her unfounded jealousy, so made sure I didn't interact with her. There was one time, when she needed new clothes and I spoke to her about getting Sue to measure her so she could order online. Laura had been ill and lost a lot of weight but apart from that, I was invisible to her. She didn't like me, so to keep my job, I kept my distance."

I need to get the conversation back to the night Laura died. "So, what happened on the night she died?"

"Laura went out to get some fresh air." Ruby blows out a long breath. "The next second, Jack is in Tom's face and he fired him. I went to plead his case and then followed Tom out on deck and we stood for a time watching the ocean."

Interest shivers up my spine. "Did you see Laura?"

"Yeah, she was standing by the railing in the stern, staring at the stars." Ruby sips her coffee. "She did that all the time."

I nod. "What was the weather like that night?"

"The water was a little choppy and the wind was cool." Ruby places her cup on the island and sighs. "I only stayed outside for a few minutes before I went to my cabin. At the time, I didn't feel like rejoining the party. I needed to think of a way to prevent Tom from being fired. He didn't deserve that just for having an affair with me."

I scratch my head, unable to understand Jack's reasoning. If they both broke the rules either give them a warning or fire them both. Jack always acts fairly, so what made his decision different this time? "Was Jack upset with you too?"

"No." Ruby lifts her chin. "I've never seen Jack upset. He is the most even-tempered person I've ever met. He said, 'You know the rules. You are both pivotal parts of my company. I rely on both of you. I can't have either of your minds wandering. In your case it would mean a breakdown of communication, and for him safety. I can do without the safety. I can look after myself. I only hired him in the first place because Laura insisted.' I said I would end the affair and begged for Tom's job. He demoted him to a position on the security team but is paying him at the same wage. Since then, Jack has promoted Tom and now he is running the entire security for the firm."

I hold my mug up to Sue who refills it and then settle back in my chair. "So, what happened next?"

"I don't know." Ruby pushes both hands through her hair. "I heard shouting and went out on deck to see everyone hanging over the railings staring at the sea. Then all hell broke loose. There were helicopters and the Coast Guard. We were awake all night and the next day searching for Laura."

I nod. "So, the water was choppy. Did the weather cause a problem searching for her?"

"Not that I recall." Ruby finishes her coffee and places the cup in the saucer decisively. "That's all I know. I need to finish up in my office." She stands, goes to the refrigerator, grabs a packet of sandwiches and a bottle of water. "Jack said he'll be home before three."

I sit for a few moments mulling over Ruby's story. She mentioned the water was choppy, as did Jack, but Sue said there was a storm that night. I pick up my phone and search for historical weather and it sends me to the National Oceanic and Atmospheric Administration website. They have a database of historical weather. I stand and smile at Sue. "I'll get back to my renovation plans."

Once in Jack's office, I close the door behind me and find the website. I enter all the information I have about the night Laura died into the database search engine and wait. It only takes a few minutes. I print out the results. The weather is in detail and measured in hourly increments. From what I understand, from the wind gusts, the water was indeed choppy from the time they climbed aboard. A violent storm blew through the area between ten and ten-thirty but it rained heavily for four hours. From the media's accounts, Laura was last seen around ten and they checked on her before eleven. How come nobody mentioned the rain or the storm? How could they miss it sailing on the ocean? It makes no sense and, if they're lying about the weather, what else are they covering up? I lean back in Jack's office chair and stare at the picture of Laura and the kids on his desk; beside them is another of her in the infamous red dress.

There isn't one of me.

TWENTY-ONE
TUESDAY

This morning I'm going shopping with Jack and I'm so excited. When he came home yesterday, he went through my closet, checking my clothes, and decided I need a completely new wardrobe again. Apparently, he has dinner parties and other social functions to attend and needs me by his side. I want to argue, the clothes I have are fine. I wave a hand at the closet. "What's wrong with these clothes? They look perfectly fine to me."

"Most of the functions are in New York." Jack smiles at me. "It's a different world."

I'm nervous as we head toward the helicopter, its rotors spinning slowly. I climb inside, and Jack makes sure my seatbelt is secure and I have a headset to listen to the conversation in the cabin. "Where exactly are we going?"

"New York, I like to shop on Fifth Avenue. We'll be landing in Manhattan at the East Thirty-Fourth Street Heliport." Jack smiles at me. "You'll have a ball. Laura loved to shop for clothes. I'm sure you'll be the same once you get used to spending money." He gives me a long look. "I've never met someone as frugal as you. Most women would go crazy with the allowance I give you."

I'm not most women. I look at him and shake my head. "Actually, I don't like having an allowance. It makes me feel as if I'm one of your employees rather than your wife."

"Oh, I see." Jack runs a hand down his face and stares at me. "Laura needed an allowance. I would put a certain amount of money into a bank account for her and she had a debit card. She knew she could spend everything in that account over a period of one month. She came from a wealthy family and was given carte blanche when it came to spending. Giving her access to a joint account would be like giving the inmates of a sanatorium the keys to the place."

I shrug. "You told me on our wedding night that everything of yours was now mine. Why would I want to or need to spend so much money? I'd bankrupt you and that doesn't make any sense. Yes, I'm frugal, but that works to your advantage, doesn't it? There's no way I would run through huge amounts of money without discussing it with you first. I'm not made that way and you should know that by now." I sigh. "I wish you would stop comparing me to Laura, because we're completely different people."

"Okay, okay." Jack chuckles. "I'm sorry, I didn't realize I was doing that. It must be very frustrating for you."

I nod and drop the subject. "Have you considered my ideas for changing the bedroom you shared with Laura?"

"I have, and it's not going to happen." Jack gave me a solemn look. "I can't possibly go into that room again. I can feel her in there; her scent lingers everywhere. It's soul-destroying." He takes my hand. "I've come up with an alternative plan. We move the kids' bedrooms over to the opposite side of the house. They'll love that because the rooms are much larger. Then we knock both their rooms into one huge bedroom. We can add a picture window that will blend in with the same design as the one in the living room and my old bedroom. It will pass scrutiny. I've run it past my architect, and he assures me it can be done without doing any damage to the historical value of the house. This will mean you will have an entirely new room. Somewhere you can make your own, without any ghosts of the past." He squeezes my fingers. "How does that sound?"

Slightly dumbfounded, I blink a few times. "It sounds like a great idea but what do you intend to do with Laura's things? Keeping them in situ like that isn't healthy. It's almost as if you are obsessed with keeping them."

"Let me think on it for a while." Jack leans back in his seat and stares out of the window.

The conversation is over. Have I hit a nerve?

I wait a few minutes before I ask the big question. "Jack, why do you keep Laura's portrait? Isn't it a constant reminder of the pain that you suffer? You've moved on by marrying me, so isn't it time to put that painting in storage?"

"No." His head swivels toward me. "That portrait is there to remind the children who their mother is. They may choose to call you mom, but I won't allow them to forget Laura. Having the painting there is a constant reminder."

I nod. "Fine but a few photographs would do the same thing and wouldn't be so obtrusive."

"Do you believe it should be your portrait hanging there?" He gives me a long stare and one dark eyebrow raises.

I shake my head. "No, I don't. A nice landscape of the gardens would look better." I take his hand. "How do you imagine it will look to your friends the first time we hold a dinner party? They'll believe that, in your mind, I'll never be good enough to be your wife and that I'm just a companion."

"They won't." He shrugs and pats my hand. "You've been on edge ever since we arrived. Don't you like my house?"

I meet his gaze and my cheeks grow hot. "Honestly? It's not something I would choose for myself. I prefer new modern places with white walls, black leather furniture and tons of stainless steel and marble. You could build me the house of my dreams."

"It was Laura's dream house." He sighs. "The kids are happy there. You wouldn't want to take them away from everything they know, would you?" He pats my hand in a placating manner. "You'll be happy there too. Just give it time. If, after six months, it doesn't grow on you, I'll build you a house."

It's an inch in the right direction so I smile at him and hold up my phone. "While we're out today, I'll take some selfies so you can have photographs of us together on your desk. I believe that would be good for the children to see as well. They weren't old enough to see the relationship you had with Laura. It's time for them to see what a normal, loving family looks like."

"I'd like that." Jack's blue eyes wash over me. "I'll have some photographs taken when we're at the dinner parties as well. I'll have them framed and placed on the mantel." He indicates with his chin out of the window. "Manhattan looks wonderful from the air, doesn't it? You're about to have the time of your life."

A wave of uncertainty hits me, and my stomach clenches. I'm moving into his world and I'm so not ready for this.

TWENTY-TWO

We land and the wind lashes me as I step down from the chopper. From here I can see buildings rising all around me, packed in without any space in between. It's like a forest of bricks and chrome.

"I've made an appointment for us at Saks. You'll love it. It was Laura's favorite store." Jack takes my hand as we leave the building. "We can walk from here. I would have had a car waiting for us, but with the traffic being as it is, it's faster to walk, and it's not like we need to carry anything. I'll have everything delivered by courier."

I look at him and wonder if he realizes what he is doing. The constant comparing of me to Laura is jarring—no, it's downright unpleasant. It is as if I'm a replacement or he wants to create me in her image. "I hope to discover the stores I like. I don't feel comfortable walking in Laura's footsteps."

"You're nothing at all like Laura." Jack frowns at me as if confused. "You've seen her photographs and the portrait. That was Laura, dressed in the height of fashion, and she never put a foot outside the door without having her hair and makeup perfect. We employed a stylist. They lived in the staff building and attended her whenever she needed them." He smiles at me. "It's how she was raised. Old money and a family that goes back generations."

Does he even realize his comment is a putdown? I swallow the distaste crawling up the back of my throat and feel like Orphan Annie. "Well, everyone's family goes back generations, Jack, or we wouldn't be here. I guess it's been difficult for you to make the switch from old money to a lowly actor."

"They say love is blind." Jack chuckles as if it's funny. "When I met you, I didn't care where you came from or your profession. It was love at first sight."

I consider my answer as we walk. "I've met quite a few people from old money, as you call it, and most of them didn't have a brain in their heads."

"You can be so delightfully naive sometimes, Willow." Jack stares straight ahead. "It's never about brains—it's about money."

I stop walking, and he turns to look at me. I raise my chin. "It wasn't for me. I didn't marry you for money—far from it. You told me you were in real estate. I figured you sold houses, and I know that job can be lucrative, but most people just scrape through on the few sales they make. The cream of the real estate sales usually goes to the owner of the company." I clear my throat. "You didn't look like this then, did you? I mean, wearing a thirty- or forty-thousand-dollar suit, and I had no idea you owned the company who wanted the commercial. I was just auditioning. You could have been one of the crew for all I knew."

"Hey, don't get yourself tied in knots over who we were when we met." Jack cups my cheek and shakes his head ruefully. "It's who we are now that matters. My friends love you. You made a good impression, so now you'll have the confidence to move into my business circle."

I want to say, I don't need confidence. I'm an actor. I can

play the part he wants me to play, but it won't really be me—will it?

We come to the end of the block, and I see the Fifth Avenue street sign. It's like stepping into another world. High-end fashion stores line the sidewalk. I feel so tiny as I stare up at the skyscrapers that seem to lean in toward the street. They dominate the entire landscape. As we walk along Fifth Avenue, tall light-gray buildings line each side of the street. The aroma of fresh coffee leaks from the cafés mixed with hot dogs from the vendors' carts. It's noisy, with vehicles moving up and down packed together, snake-like, as they crawl along the blacktop. Horns honk and street vendors raise their voices to sell their wares. Bright-yellow cabs, buses, and riders on bicycles weave in and out of the traffic. There are so many people rushing in every direction. I cling to Jack's arm as he strides along in absolute confidence, head held high. I believe his attitude was one of the things that attracted me to him in the first place.

We arrive at Saks. It has an impressive façade that appears as if it's draped in long, wide purple ribbons. A doorman greets us, and we step into Aladdin's cave. Jack leads me through the store and the scent of perfume envelops me in a miasma of fragrances, not one stronger than another. I'm mesmerized by the lavish interior and wish I had the time to explore. It's as if Jack is on a mission as he leads me through the different departments. He knows where he's going, and soon we arrive at a women's designer fashion area.

A woman wearing a neat, tailored cream suit glides out to greet us with another close behind. They speak to Jack, not me, about what I require and then guide us to a private shopping area. Jack sits in a gold velvet chair as, shellshocked, I stare at the chandeliers spreading a soft light over the cream carpet. Racks of clothes are set in alcoves under the designer names. The magnificence of the place is daunting. I'm a fish out of water, and as the assistant stands looking at me, hands folded in front of her and with an expectant expression, my nerve almost deserts me.

I glance at Jack, who is staring at me, supremely confident as usual. I can't let him down. He's known here and has a good reputation. I inhale and decide to play my best role ever. I lift my chin and act as if I own the place. I indicate to a designer I admire, and we head in that direction. "I need everything. My wardrobe hasn't arrived from LA, and I'm stuck here without a thing."

Both women exchange glances, and I smile at them. "New York fashion is so different from LA. I'm sure you'll be able to guide me."

"Of course." The oldest of the two removes dresses from a rack and holds them up for me.

I touch the fabric, and it runs through my fingers like silk. There is no price tag. I assume if you need to ask the price, you shouldn't be in the store. I nod and give them my size. "Yes, I like that one, but I have many dinner parties both day and evening to attend. I'll need everything, as I said, from gowns to shoes and accessories. Bring me anything you consider suitable." I can almost see the commission dollar signs flash in their eyes. I play the performance of my life and try on outfits and display them to Jack as if I do this all the time. I see his eyes light up as he nods his approval. I can't believe it; acting the part of the rich and famous is even fooling him. Maybe he's seeing his beloved Laura in me, and the thought chills me to the bone.

"I like this one." Jack stands and points out a black dress, with a low backline. "Try this on next."

In the changing room, I stare at my reflection and my blood runs cold. I press both hands on the mirror, trying to breathe. I've seen this dress before in the pictures taken on the yacht. The dress is exactly the same as the one Laura wore the night she died.

This morning, I spent time with the children, getting them ready for school. I enjoy every second with them and the chatter is uplifting. After sending them off with Jenny, I walk Jack to his Porsche and kiss him goodbye. I have many things on my mind. The inconsistencies in the stories about Laura's death are starting to niggle at me. I wonder who is telling me the truth and who is gaslighting me. If I am to believe Jack and Ruby, I must consider that the information about the weather is incorrect, or perhaps it didn't rain where they were at the time. I've known it to rain on one side of the street and not the other, so anything is possible. Inside I want to believe my husband and his personal assistant. I can find no reason why Ruby would lie to me about the weather when she has been so forthcoming about her affair with Tom.

I make my way to the kitchen and find Sue loading the dishwasher. "Morning, Sue. I'll just grab a mug of coffee and then I'm going to work on my plans for the new bedroom."

"That will be exciting." Sue smiles at me over one shoulder. "I can't wait to see it."

I take down a mug and pour myself a coffee. "Me either. I'm

sorry to be harping on Laura again, but do you recall who told you about the accident?"

"Ruby." Sue raises her eyebrows as she looks at me. "She was standing right there where you are now. When she returned home with Mr. Hunter, they were both exhausted from being awake all night."

I stir cream and sugar into my mug. "How did they look? Were they wet or dry?"

"They resembled a pair of drowned rats." Sue shook her head. "Both of them had wet hair and their shoes were soaked through. I suppose that's not surprising considering there was a storm that night."

I nod. "So did they mention a storm?"

"Yes, they both believed that's how Laura got tossed overboard." Sue's eyes narrow. "Have you heard something to the contrary?"

I straighten and smile. "No, I know about the storm. It's a huge yacht so people can easily move around without being seen. I know Laura left the others to get some fresh air, and she was seen by Ruby and Tom. The thing is, I'm surprised they were on deck during a storm. From the weather report it was bad with high waves and, if Laura fell overboard, I doubt anyone heard her scream. If it was a bad storm, as the reports say, I couldn't see her lasting long in that swell. I'm just surprised her body didn't show."

"The Coast Guard searched for a full week." Sue swallows hard. "Likely a shark ate her. They didn't find so much as a shoe."

Head spinning with the conflicting stories, I sip my coffee. I must keep my composure although inside my stomach is twisting. So many different versions that I can't keep my head straight. I need to get away and think. I stand slowly. "That's awful." I frown. "I'd better get a start on these ideas. Ruby will have the architect here before I'm finished." I smile as I leave the kitchen and carry my mug up the stairs.

As I climb the stairs, I'm acutely aware of Laura's eyes following me from the portrait. The uneasy feeling remains as I make my way to my room. Even in the daytime the hallway is still dimly lit and, as I walk, the hair on the back of my neck stiffens. I stop and look around. I'm sure someone is watching me. A loud bang comes close by. It frightens the heck out of me and I spill hot coffee over my fingers. Heart pounding, I lean against the wall, scanning the hallway. As I turn, one of the bedroom doors moves and a sliver of light cuts across the hall carpet. I'm frozen in place, staring at the door, but nobody emerges and everything is eerily silent.

No one should be here. The rooms along this hallway are furnished for guests but the furniture is covered. I can think of no reason why light would be coming from that room. When I looked inside just yesterday, the blinds were shut tight. The door creaks and moves again, sending more light into the hall-way. Panic grips me but I listen, trying to hear over the pounding in my ears. A clicking sound comes from the room but no footsteps or voices. Gripping the mug before me like a pistol, I watch the door moving back and forth. The mug trembles in my hand and I place it on a delicate highly polished table beside a vase of fresh roses set on a lace doily. I don't recall seeing the table before and why are the flowers here outside this particular room? The door whines again and I shrink back, heart thundering in my chest.

This is supposed to be my home so why am I so afraid? I'm no threat to anyone. Taking a deep breath, I push leaden feet toward the door, place one palm against it and thrust it open. I flinch as someone runs toward me but it's only the long white silken curtains billowing out from the window like two women dancing in long white gowns. The window is wide open, pushed up on a sash and the thick drapes either side are gathered back and secured with gold ropes to rings in the wall.

Reluctantly, I step inside and scan the area. The bed and everything else are the same. Goosebumps prickle up my arms but I push through the fear and walk across the room and shut the window and secure it. I search the garden below and see Bill tending the flowerbeds. I leave the drapes open and move slowly through the room. The ever-present feeling of being watched hangs about me in a shroud of uncertainty. Why would someone want to observe me? I move my attention around the walls, searching for cameras, but shake my head. The technology these days could mean a camera might be hidden anywhere in anything and appear like a speck of dust.

Opening closets has become a challenge since seeing the mannequin but I suck in my breath and throw open the doors. A wave of old wooden closet smell fills my nostrils and a light flickering inside illuminates a figure. Alarmed, I jump back but it's just a coat. I laugh at my stupidity and close the doors. I walk out, leaving the bedroom door wide open. The light streaming into the hallway is welcome. I gather my courage and make myself check the second bedroom but it is the same as it was the first time I peered inside.

The feeling of being observed clings to me and I hurry to my bedroom. I'm glad to get inside but somebody has been here. The new curtains of a beige velvet and the matching bedspread are welcome additions. The room has been made up and is sparkling clean. I close the door, turn the key and then sink onto the bed. I should feel comfortable in my home and yet it's as if I'm in a five-star hotel. I'm not sure if I'm happy about strangers going through my belongings and setting things straight. It seems like an invasion of privacy. All the strange happenings since I arrived are unsettling, especially when my phone went missing. It's as if everything around me is slipping from my control. Is that what Laura felt like living here? Am I starting to parallel Laura's time in this house?

I remember my mug of coffee and go out to retrieve it. I stand and listen to the creaking of the old house for a few seconds and then turn back to my room. My mind is in turmoil and small insignificant things have become giant problems. This just isn't like me. I've always been strong but, right now, after the conflicting stories about Laura's death, I don't know who I can trust. It worries me that Jack gave me the same story as Ruby's and yet differs on the weather from the original one Ruby told Sue when they returned home that night. So how come they both gave me a different version? A storm at sea is a crucial detail to forget as it offers a rational explanation of how Laura could have fallen overboard—so why the cover-up? Or was Tom involved—if so, why would he want to kill Laura? My attention moves to the bottom drawer of the dresser where I've hidden Laura's laptop. I wonder if Jack knows that Laura wrote a diary. If so, was he aware of the unusual happenings she experienced in the house and just dismissed them? Should I ask him or keep the diary to myself? I stare at the drawer, unable to drag my eyes away. I must discover more about Laura and can tell no one. Someone is lying about that night and I need to find out why.

TWENTY-FOUR

I can't stop thinking about the diary. It's becoming an obsession. I need to know what happened to Laura. The diary and what's inside are like a box of chocolates you keep in the refrigerator and make a rule to only eat one each day, but then you go back multiple times until you take the box and eat them all. I open the laptop and scroll through the pages. After reading for an hour, I'm at the entries written a few weeks before Laura's death. Unusual things happened to her and I need to spend more time reading every page but, from my quick scan of the entries, I can tell Laura was getting more and more paranoid about everything happening around her, but there's one thing she mentions that catches my attention. I read it through and then again to make sure I'm not mistaken.

August 1

Is anyone out there reading this? I discovered something disturbing about Jack, before I had Noah. At first, I dismissed it as a bad dream but I'm sure it led to Jack sleeping in a separate room. Although we shared a dressing room, once I mentioned it,

Jack never came to my bed again. You see, Jack talks in his sleep. More than once, he mentioned a woman by the name of Caroline. When I confronted him about her, he was visibly shocked but just said, "She's someone who died."

I couldn't let it go and recalled him mentioning that he kept every newspaper article published about his life in a trunk in the loft, and one day he'd find the time to make them into a book. The loft is a place with way too many family secrets and ghost stories to feel safe exploring but I needed a reason for Jack's evasiveness. I waited until he'd gone to work, grabbed a flashlight and headed upstairs. Once inside, I found the trunk and then hunted through the newspapers and found Caroline. Now I need to confront him and discover the truth.

Swallowing hard, I sit back in my chair. What had she found? Was it enough to have her murdered? Is my wonderful caring husband a killer? I picture his face and the way he holds me with tenderness and can't believe it. I suddenly need a drink of water and take my mug to the bathroom, wash it and fill it from the faucet. Meticulously, I scan the last entries but find nothing more about the mysterious Caroline. The following entries are rambling and it's as if she'd forgotten about her. There's no option. I need to find the old trunk in the loft.

I check my phone and it's fully charged. I stand and head back along the hallway and stop dead. The door to the bedroom is now closed and the flowers on the table are missing along with the soiled doily. It was silent in my bedroom and the floorboards creak in the hallway. I'd have heard someone walking by outside—wouldn't I? I stare at the door, uncertain if I should open it and look inside. Panic rises but I push it down, grasp the doorknob and turn. The door swings open. The room is in darkness and the blinds tightly shut. I close the door and walk back toward my room. I open the next bedroom door. It's the same as before. I head downstairs and march into the kitchen. "Sue, who was upstairs just before? They removed a vase of flowers from the hallway outside my room."

"No one. Amy cleaned your room when you were down here. I don't recall seeing her with any flowers." Sue frowns. "She's been here since you went back upstairs. She just went out to the vegetable garden."

I nod but confusion cramps my belly. "The gardener for the vegetables. What's his name?"

"Bill does the kitchen garden as well." Sue smiles. "He potters around but the landscapers and garden service come by twice a week."

That doesn't explain who moved the flowers and why. I frown. "Does he come inside?"

"Bill? No. None of the outside staff come in here. They deal with George. He has an office in the terrace."

Trying to act nonchalant, I meet her gaze. "The terrace?"

"That's what we call the line of outbuildings—the staff quarters." Sue indicates vaguely toward the back of the house.

More confused than ever, I walk back to the stairs. I didn't imagine the flowers, did I? Were they there when I retrieved my mug of coffee? I can't recall. I keep my head down to avoid Laura's piercing gaze and make my way to the second floor. Each step fills me with apprehension. As I get to the hallway, I search the wall with the flashlight on my phone for the hidden panel Jack insists is there on each floor. Euphoria grips me as I find it and pop it open. Inside are light switches and I flick them on. The hallway lights up as chandeliers glisten, their crystal teardrops sending rainbows dancing across the walls.

I make my way to the stairs in the middle of the floor. The light hasn't penetrated this far and I use the flashlight app on my phone and take the stairs. Cold penetrates my clothes, raising goosebumps on my flesh. This time I stop and use my light to search for the source and discover a mesh grid on each side of the staircase. I don't enjoy going into dark dingy places but I must; I open the door. I find the light switch easier this time, and placing the chair under the door handle again to keep it open, I search the room.

It's huge but I figure the oldest things are at the back. I discover that the boxes are divided into personal effects. The children have boxes filled with old toys and pictures from kindergarten. It seems that either Laura or Jack kept everything. I find an area belonging to Jack and discover boxes with items relating to his childhood. Under a stack of suitcases, I spot an old trunk. This must be the one mentioned in Laura's diary. Dust billows around me as I move each suitcase to another spot in the well-organized mess. I drag the trunk under the light and sit on the dusty floor. The lid opens easily enough and inside I discover stacks of newspapers, each inside a plastic cover.

It isn't too difficult to find the newspapers containing articles on Caroline. Each plastic cover has a notation across the front. I collect the four newspapers and, with care not to damage them, spread them out on the top of the trunk and go through each one. I estimate the dates on the newspapers come from around the time that Jack attended college. Even then with his family background he made the social pages of the newspapers. From what I'm seeing he and heiress Caroline were college sweethearts. As I go through each one, I discover more. They were engaged and then—Oh, my God! They were married?

I can't believe my eyes. My hands tremble and my pulse thumps in my ears as I turn the pages. The wedding has a full spread and I see Ruby right there with the guests. My heart races. Why didn't Jack tell me about Caroline? Maybe he believed I'd think twice about marrying him if I'd known the truth—Hell yeah, I would. I'd want to know every small detail. I'm no fool and he likely knows it even after only being with me for a short time. I pull the next paper from the plastic and turn the pages like a maniac, heedless of the damage now. I swallow hard at the headline sprawled in bold letters:

WIFE OF JACK HUNTER FOUND FLOATING IN RIVER

Unable to breathe, I scan the report of Caroline's death. She fell from a trail and went over a waterfall during their honeymoon. I read the article twice and then find the report on her funeral. It's depressing and the young woman's smiling face on her wedding day dances through my mind. A shiver runs through me as I fold the newspapers slowly and return them to the trunk. I cover them with the other items I'd found. As I push the trunk back into place and brush the dust from my hands, I stare at my wedding ring. My husband had two wives, and both died in accidents. I lift my gaze and meet my reflection in the cracked mirror. Will I be next?

TWENTY-FIVE

My first instinct is to confront Jack but by the time I get back to my room and take a shower, I've devised a different plan. Maybe it's better if I keep my discovery to myself for the time being, and ask Jack more information about himself. I'll ask him about college and his sweethearts. I figure that would be a normal topic for a couple to talk about. In the meantime, I need to make a list of everything that's happening around me. The way Laura did so she could keep track of everything. I need to talk to people to discover the truth. I realize how isolated I am in this house. If I want to leave I can't. I don't have a vehicle or phone numbers of anyone apart from Jack, Ruby and of course my family, but they're in LA. My only form of online communication is my phone unless I use Jack's computer in his office—but any emails I send can be read by Jack or Ruby. No doubt she knows his passwords. He trusts her with everything. I sit at my dressing table, brushing my hair, suddenly feeling trapped. There are people I would like to speak to. Jack's friends who were on the yacht the night Laura died, and Tom Bates. I need to know if any of them met Caroline and what was the true story behind her death? Will any of them tell me the truth?

My attention moves to the bottom drawer where Laura's laptop is hidden. Now I know the secret of Caroline, I'll be able to understand the entries in her diary. She would be feeling the same turmoil as I am but I guess she wasn't as strong-minded as me. I lock my door and pull out the laptop. Moments later I've found where I left reading. I can feel Laura's confusion in every word.

August 6

I went to see the psychiatrist today. Her name is Doctor Ladley and she is quite nice but I don't trust her. After our sessions I hear her whispering to Jack in the waiting room. This gives me no confidence in her confidentiality. I always believed what was said between a doctor and a patient was sacrosanct, but she gives him instructions on how to keep me medicated. I haven't been taking the meds that Jack thrusts into my hand each night but lately I've been sleeping like death and waking up with a mouth so dry I can hardly speak. My brain isn't working right and it takes me most of the day to wake up. Someone in the house is drugging me. Last night at dinner, the moment Sue placed my plate in front of me, I asked Jack to go and look outside because I was sure I saw someone looking at me through the window. It was a lie, of course. I just needed him out of the way for a few seconds so I could switch our plates.

When Jack didn't come down for breakfast, I knew I'd been correct and Sue or Pierre are involved in drugging me. I can't trust anyone. I don't have any friends and my parents live overseas and wouldn't believe me if I told them. I need to take my life into my own hands. I can't leave. I've got nowhere to go and I'm watched every second of the day but I do have a debit card and this laptop. I plan on ordering meals from my favorite restaurants and having them delivered. It's the only way I'll be able to survive.

I stare at the entry and push both hands through my hair, clutching my aching skull. I'm not sure what to do. Am I reading the ramblings of a woman who is mentally ill, or is she the victim of a coercive husband? I consider my time with Jack. The honeymoon was bliss and we spent every moment together but since he's been back at work, I've been literally housebound. Okay, so I don't have any friends to go visit but I should have a vehicle of some description. Most people in my position wouldn't be content to sit at home every day. I need a car to go visit the local stores, go shopping and drive around the neighborhood to get the feel of it. Am I slipping slowly under his coercive control without realizing? I think over my time since I arrived. I've spoken to most of the staff and they've been very co-operative with me and, in fact, I can't find fault with them. Although I do find them a little intrusive, I guess having all my meals cooked for me and my bedroom cleaned is the usual way for rich people to live.

I return the laptop to its hiding place. I need to limit my exposure to Laura's unstable ramblings before she drags me down with her. What she writes is very unsettling and what if it's true? My resentment for her has now gone, replaced by sympathy for a woman in a terrible position. Like me she had no one to go to for advice and no one she could really trust. The room suddenly becomes unbearably small, oppressive and suffocating. I fling open the door and step outside. The feeling of being watched is overpowering and as I head down to the kitchen I scan the walls for any sign of surveillance cameras. Am I getting paranoid? If I am being recorded, perhaps it's just a security measure but I need to know. Where would I find the hard drives connected to a CCTV? Would they be on Jack's computer?

As the clock in the hall chimes telling me it's one o'clock, I walk into the kitchen. Sue has proved to be a font of information but how much of it is secondhand? If she was willing to drug Laura, can I even trust her to tell me the truth? The people in this house could be rehashing a well-rehearsed fabrication of lies. It would make sense to have a deviation from the original story after so long. Maybe I need to have a chat to George and Bill as well? There are so many things to consider and I make a mental list of things to do. First is to find a suitable notebook. I'm so used to working on a tablet that using pen and paper is going to be strange. I frown, recalling what happened to my tablet. I was lounging under a huge umbrella by the pool during our honeymoon, answering emails from my friends. A shadow loomed over me and Jack smiled, plucked the tablet from my hands and tossed it into the pool. I believe he is jealous of anyone or anything taking my attention away from him. I remember the credit card in my purse. Maybe it's about time I purchased a new tablet online. I smile. I need to become a little more self-sufficient.

I walk into the kitchen and Pierre is there. "Ah, just the person I need to see. I'm starving. What do you recommend for lunch?"

"Spanish omelet, served with French toast?" He smiles at me. "I've read your menu suggestions. Do you want a specific meal on a specific day or do you want me to surprise you? Mr. Hunter has some desserts he likes as well. Is there anything on his list you don't like?" He takes a list from a drawer and hands it to me.

I read down the list of delights and shake my head. "I love all of them, and yes, to the omelet." I turn to Sue. "I'll eat in the dining room today. Could you find George? I'd like a word with him."

"He was just here for lunch." Sue pulled out her phone. "I'll call him."

I leave them and head to Jack's office. Inside I go to his supply cabinet. I find a nice hard cover notebook with his company logo emblazoned in gold on a blue cover. I select two silver pens and walk to the dining room. By the time I place the book and pens on the table, George is knocking on the door and giving me an inquiring stare. I grip the pen so he can't see my hands trembling. I'm an actor and this is just a scene of the mistress of the house talking to a subordinate. *Action.* "Thanks for coming, George. Sit down, I'd like to speak to you."

"How are you settling in?" George rests his clasped hands on the table.

I look at him. He is the man Jack trusts to run the entire estate. "Fine, thanks. May I ask how long you've worked here?"

"Must be over twenty years, I figure." George nods and smiles at me. "I'm guessing you want to know about the previous renovations? They were completed during my time here, although I'll never know why they decided to section another part of the house for staff and then changed their mind and built the staff buildings. It seemed like a waste of money."

I blink, trying to allow the information to sink in. "I didn't notice any other staff quarters on the blueprints Jack gave me to work from. Are you sure they were completed?"

"I've seen them with my own two eyes." He rubs the end of his nose, and his small brown eyes fix on me. "Mr. Langly, the owner at the time, gave me a tour when it was done. The bedrooms were small but there was a sitting room, and a nice kitchen. The entrance was downstairs; it takes up half of the cellar and has steps leading upstairs. It was never used because Mrs. Langly figured she could hear people talking. She didn't want the staff hearing her private conversations, so it was locked up and never used." He frowned. "Some time later, they renovated again and expanded the rooms. They took out the staff quarters. Like I say, a waste of good money."

Mind spinning, I stare at him. "Does Mr. Hunter know about it?"

"I can't say." George scratches his cheek and leans back in his chair. "I've never spoken to him about it. I heard from Sue about the renovations you'd planned and assumed you wanted to speak to me about it. I don't know why it's not on the blueprints. The door is still there. I don't know how much inside remains."

I stand. "Could you show me?"

"I don't have the keys." He lowers his gaze to his hands resting on the table. "Mr. Langly took them from me. I've never seen them since. Perhaps he decided it would reduce the chance of selling the estate if anyone knew about the changes and then had a new set of blueprints created?"

Dismay rolls over me. I sit down and see he is just as confused as I am. "I guess so. How strange. Anyway, while I have you here there are a few things I'd like to know. How is the security here? I don't see any security guards. Do we at least have CCTV surveillance?"

"Yes, we do." George blows out a sigh as if relieved. "Outside and the front gate."

I frown. "What about inside the house? Surely the entrance hall at least is covered?"

"I believe so, yes." George nods. "I recall Mr. Hunter arranging for them to be updated when you married and we do have a security team. They patrol the estate regularly and have an office in the staff quarters."

So, someone is watching me. "To what extent is the house covered by the cameras?"

"All over including the hallways, front and back doors." George ran a hand through his thinning hair. "Outside, the gardens and driveway as well as the gate."

The idea that strangers watch my every move is disturbing. "Where does the feed go to?"

"I believe Mr. Hunter can tell you." George frowns and his eyes shift uncomfortably. "I would imagine he has the house feed either sent to his office or his home computer. It's stored in the Cloud as far as I'm aware. It's only in case anyone breaks in but with the security system that would be remote."

I force my expression into one of relief. "That's good to know." I meet his gaze. "Has anyone ever discussed the night Laura died with you?"

"Well, yes." George opens his hands wide. "It was a topic of conversation at the time. There was a storm at sea, she went out on deck to get some fresh air and a freak wave knocked her over-board. No one knew she was missing for over an hour. They never found her body. It was a tragic accident." He sighs. "The coroner ruled it as an accident and pronounced her dead. Lost at sea."

I shake my head. "How sad. Did you get along with Laura? I heard she could be quite prickly at times."

"She was set in her ways." George stares into space as if thinking and then shifts his attention to me. "She had a habit of mislaying things and often made me question the staff about them. I figure she believed we were playing tricks on her as the things always showed after a few hours. Of course we weren't. Why would we? Mr. Hunter pays us a higher salary than just about anywhere else. We all like working here but, in truth, at times it became difficult."

I clear my throat and smile as Sue arrives with my meal. The aroma is mouthwatering. "Thank you, George. You've been a great help."

I stare at my plate, not a Spanish omelet but slices of crispy duck with fried rice. It looks delicious but it wasn't what I ordered. I look at Sue who places a glass of orange juice on the table. "What happened to the Spanish omelet?"

"Spanish omelet?" She frowns at me and raises one eyebrow. "The duck was planned for dinner. Mandarin duck is one of Mr. Hunter's favorites but Pierre said you insisted on duck. He has two ducks prepared."

I shake my head. *What exactly is going on here?* "You were

there when he suggested the omelet. This looks delicious but I didn't order it." I sigh. "It doesn't matter; tell Pierre I'm happy to have duck for dinner. I like it too."

"Is there anything else?"

The way Sue's mouth puckers reminds me of a cat walking away and I bite back a laugh. I pick up my silverware. "Yes, I'd like a mug of coffee please. Thank you, Sue."

I watch her leave and wonder why the deception about lunch. Why the different accounts of Laura's death? I eat slowly, trying to get my head around everything. I'm no threat to the staff. What game are they playing with me?

TWENTY-SIX

After lunch, I go straight to Jack's office to view the blueprints and find nothing on any of them about renovations. I recall Jack mentioning the state archives. I have a list somewhere on his desk. I can search their online files. It takes two hours but I find the original plans used when the property was first built and a second set with the additional renovations. I print the document and stare at it, seeing how a good portion of the back of the house has been modified. How strange no mention of it was made to Jack. I hear footsteps in the hallway and Jack comes in. I glance at the clock. I hadn't expected him until later. He sweeps me from the chair and kisses me soundly. I catch my breath and smile at him. "I'm pleased to see you too."

"What have you been doing all day?" He glances at the blueprints. "What are these?"

I turn to look at the copies spread across his desk. "These are the original plans for this house and the others are the renovations. I spoke to George about our plans and he mentioned the house was altered considerably twenty years ago. I wanted to compare the plans is all."

"You know, Laura mentioned secret passageways and

mysterious faces at windows. She hunted for the windows but couldn't find them. She insisted they were there when she visited her cousins here. I showed her the blueprints but she was sure she hadn't imagined the rooms. To be honest, I figured it was an overactive imagination as a child. Like an imaginary friend, some things can seem real at the time." He sighs. "I wish she could have seen this. Is it still there, do you think?"

I shrug. "I have no idea. I doubt it." I point to the recent documents. "There's no mention of it here. Who else has been here for a long time?"

"Old Bill." Jack scratches his cheek. "Thirty years, I believe. He started here during the time Laura's uncle owned the estate. She remembered him." He smiles at me. "He was pottering around when I drove in. Do you want to speak to him again?"

Excited, I gather up the copies of the blueprints and nod. "Yes, I most certainly do."

"I figured you'd say that." Jack takes the documents from me and indicates with his chin to the gardens. "He was picking roses." He raises an eyebrow. "For you, I assume?"

I follow him from the room. "Yes, I love fresh flowers and we have acres of them."

"I like them too." His fingers link with mine as we walk to the front door. "They made Laura sneeze."

Trying to ignore the savage stare from Laura's portrait, I lean into Jack and smile. If Laura's ghost or whatever still lingers in this house, she needs to know he belongs to me now. "I'll fill the house with flowers and it will rid us of that awful old house smell. It reminds me of a locker room. It needs to be aired. The windows are always closed and it's beautiful at this time of year."

"You're in charge, Willow." Jack winks at me. "Tell the staff what you want and they'll do it. That's what I pay them for."

I'm not surprised when Jack takes over the conversation with Bill. I notice the man's hesitance to say anything and I look at him and give my head a little shake. I want to convey I haven't spoken to Jack about the face in the window, or Laura's instability.

"Do you recall the renovations to the house about twenty years ago?" Jack unrolls the plans and holds them up for Bill to peruse. "Apparently, they built staff quarters and never used them. I can't find them on the current plans. Do you know what happened to them? Was there another renovation I'm not aware of?"

"Yeah, I recall the renovations but I never got to look inside." Bill drops a rose into a basket and turns to look at us. "I only remember the builders being here that one time. The last renovations were the ones you had here to the kitchen and bedroom, I believe."

"I recall Laura telling me she played in secret passages as a child." Jack narrows his gaze. "There must have been a way inside."

I squeeze Jack's arm. "I know where the door used to be. George recalls it being in the cellar. He said the previous owner locked it and no one was allowed inside."

"Well, the previous owner sold the property to me." Jack frowns. "He died a few years ago, so we can't ask him. I don't remember seeing a door in the cellar but it's not somewhere I visit."

"There's a door." Bill pushes back his straw hat. "It has steps leading up to it. I use the cellar to store my tools."

I turn to Jack. "Can we look?"

"Sure." He leads the way around the side of the house.

I follow, our shoes crunching on the gravel path. "We don't have a key to get inside though, do we?"

"That's what locksmiths are for." Jack pulls out his phone as he descends the steps into the cellar and his flashlight moves around a surprisingly neat and tidy room. He moves the light around. "There it is."

I follow close behind and stare at the door in dismay. There's a door alright but it's behind a wrought-iron gate that's been welded into a frame set into the wall. "Oh, a locksmith isn't going to get that open. How disappointing."

"I'd say, as a builder, that was done because whatever is behind that gate isn't safe." Jack turns back to me. "They likely re-extended the rooms inside the house as the measurements fit the plans I have. As children played in there, it was likely sealed to prevent them being injured." He sighs. "From what Laura told me, she said secret passages, not rooms or staircases. Imagine her uncle discovering his kids had been crawling between the walls? There'd be no way of getting them out if they got trapped, so he sealed the entrance."

I nod. "Yes, that makes sense. I guess you could open it and see for yourself?"

"I believe that's a waste of time. There's nothing on the blueprints." Jack stares at me. "I'd rather leave it. We're just buying into Laura's obsession. I'm not going along that path."

As we walk back to the house, I stare at the windows and count to where I saw the face. In the morning, I'll look for the mystery window myself. Third floor, the sixth window across. Three and six, that's easy to remember. A sudden sinking feeling grasps me. What if someone *had* been stuck inside the walls and died? What if they never got out? Is that the face at the window no one can find?

TWENTY-SEVEN

Over dinner I decide to slide into the subject of our time in college, to see if he tells me about Caroline. "I had so many boyfriends in college, but none of them affected me like you did." I smile at him. "What about you? Who were the great loves of your life?"

"Oh, I had a few." Jack winks at me and his eyes dance with mischief. "I dated all through high school. I admit being on the football team helped. The girls loved us jocks."

I nod. "I dated a few in my time too." I take a forkful of fried rice and almost moan in delight. The food is amazing. "No one special. I've never had that rush of emotion I had when meeting you. The day after, I couldn't stop thinking about you and saw you on every corner. It was the strangest sensation. When we said goodnight that first day, it was as if I was leaving part of me behind."

"I felt the same way." Jack sighs. "It's as if I've known you forever. I missed you the moment you left me."

I glow inside; Jack has a wonderful effect on me, like I'm being hugged whenever he's around. I'm not sure if this is normal. It's never happened to me before. I need to steer the conversation toward Caroline and Laura. I want him to tell me everything about himself. I keep my eyes on my plate. "You've been married before. Did Laura have the same effect on you?"

"With Laura no." Jack sips a glass of white wine. "The spark we have was never there, I'm afraid. We were never soulmates. I found her very attractive and after we'd gotten along together, marriage seemed like the next step. My parents encouraged me to marry her. They kind of pushed us together. It all worked out okay. I believed I loved her but it's not the same as I love you now." He takes my hand and squeezes it. "I didn't believe that could happen twice in my life."

I disengage my hand and cut into the sumptuous duck. This is the moment I've been waiting for. I lift my gaze to meet his and see pain in his eyes. "Who was the first and why didn't you pursue her?"

"I did." Jack blows out a long breath. "I should have told you about Caroline but it's painful to recall and I've pushed her out of my mind for my own peace." He holds up a hand to prevent me from speaking. "Caroline was my first wife of two weeks. I met her in college and I loved her so much it hurt. The same as I love you, Willow." He stares into space and winces. "She loved to hike in the forest so on our honeymoon I arranged for a party of our friends to set out on a mountain trail. We stopped for a rest and Caroline went with some of the others to collect wildflowers growing alongside a waterfall. She slipped and fell into the river."

I take his hand and squeeze. "Oh Jack, that is so tragic. I'm so sorry."

"This is why, when I met Laura, I was content with a good friendship more than the animal attraction I had with Caroline." He shrugs. "I did grow to love her."

I rub my thumb over the back of his hand. "Did she love you?"

"She was possessive, so I guess so." Jack shakes his head

ruefully. "She was jealous of anyone who took my attention away from her. That portrait is her, larger than life, dominating and what I'd describe as an alpha female. It was difficult living with her the year before she died. She became reckless, spent money like it was going out of fashion, and then she became irrational and delusional. The day she died was the only time in almost a year she appeared to be back to her old self."

I clear my throat. "Did you try talking to her?"

"Oh yeah, but that ended up in her throwing things at me." He rubs his chin. "She'd tell me about outlandish events she claimed happened to her and about how everyone was against her. She believed people were watching her and other crazy things."

I want more and lean closer. "What crazy things?"

"She went up to the third floor searching for a room that wasn't there." He looks away and sucks in a breath. "I've installed a door to prevent anyone going up there now. That part of the house is old and decrepit. There's no power. It's a useless space. The bedrooms are too small to utilize and as the loft is huge, I couldn't be bothered restoring it." He looks at me. "Don't be tempted to go up there alone. It's likely covered in mold by now."

I stare at him, uncomprehending. "You're a builder, why don't you renovate it? It seems a little odd leaving it like that. You should make it safe. One day you'll want to sell this place and it will be impossible to sell, if it's as you say."

"You're right, I should renovate it. If it makes you happy, I'll look into it. I honestly haven't wanted to set foot there since Laura died." Jack ran a hand down his face. "She had a morbid fascination with the place. I figure it was the trigger that pushed her over the edge."

I take back my hand and push my plate away, no longer hungry. "Did you find her help? It sounds to me like she was suffering a breakdown of some description."

"Of course I did. She was under the supervision of a psychiatrist but toward the end she refused to speak to her." He rested his hands flat on the table. "The last couple of weeks before she died, I honestly believed she'd recovered. She'd started to care about her appearance again and came out of her room. To me she seemed to be back to her old self. She was over the moon when I told her about the party I'd planned. The week before she died all she could talk about was sailing. It was a dramatic change, as if she had discovered something that settled her. I have no idea what happened to turn her around and never will. The next weekend she was lost at sea."

I have a thought and turn to him. "The group of friends that were with you and Caroline, were they the same people on the yacht the night Laura died?"

"Some of them were, yes." Jack's brow wrinkles into a frown. "I've known most of the guys since college, the women too; well, at least two of them: Carol Sutton and Missy Durum. Caroline wanted to spend the second week of our honeymoon in a mountain resort and she didn't want to get bored so we had everyone along." He smiles at the memory. "You may not think so, but it was very romantic. Our friends weren't with us all the time."

I stare at him in disbelief. The same people? My mind is working overtime. "That's good to know. Thanks for sharing that with me. It would have been a shock to discover you've had two wives and not told me."

It isn't only a shock. This is a revelation. The same people, in the same place, at the same time two tragic accidents occurred is a little far-fetched for coincidence. Was Caroline murdered? Do all of his wives end up dead?

TWENTY-EIGHT

THURSDAY

I'm getting along well with the children. Last night I sat and encouraged them with their homework. I made up a study hour with drinks and snacks. I've been telling them about my struggles at school and how I overcame my shyness. It all went well and when Noah or Ava wrote a correct answer, I cheered and clapped. It was one of the most rewarding hours I've spent in a long time. This morning, I brushed Ava's hair and tied it up with a ribbon. I believe she enjoys the girl time with me. Noah is very much his dad's boy. He likes to wear *his* hair in the same style as Jack. Seeing Jack with his kids is heartwarming. There's never any rush, he spends as much time as they need, even with Ruby breathing down his neck to leave for the office. We stood side by side as Jenny left with them for school.

Last night, after the children were in bed, I spent a wonderful hour or so with Jack on the internet selecting furniture for our new bedroom. He instructed me to make a list of the items and Ruby would make the purchases through the company account—probably for a tax deduction or something. After breakfast I handed her the list along with a color printout of each item from the online catalogue. "I'm sorry to add more to your workload but Jack wants these items ordered through the company account. They're for our new bedroom."

"Oh, no trouble at all." Ruby peruses the items and smiles at me. "Very nice. You have great taste. I'll need to make sure they're not delivered until you need them. The architect has already spoken to Jack. They should be starting the work soon. I'll let you know the date when they come back to me."

I blink. "Jack has already decided on everything?"

"Well, yes, he has." Ruby frowns. "Hasn't he told you?"

I recover from the shock without allowing her to notice. "I guess he wants to surprise me. I love surprises." I head for the stairs. "Thanks, Ruby."

I take the stairs two at a time, keeping my eyes averted from Laura's gaze and dash to our bedroom. Inside, Jack is selecting a jacket for work and comes out of the dressing room, smelling of cologne. He looks so handsome that he takes my breath away. How could I possibly be angry with him? "Ruby tells me you've already decided on the renovations for the new bedroom. You're waiting to speak to the architect before going ahead?"

"Yes, they're the basic plans for what we decided. Two bedrooms made into one large one and a dressing room. You wanted a large window overlooking the ocean to match our sitting room." He lifts my chin and stares into my eyes. "I only did what we discussed. I'll bring home the plans, and any extras you need, we'll add then. The other stuff is just basic; I didn't want to bore you with it." He sighs. "You'll have time, we'll need to submit our plans for approval as the house is listed on the National Register." He lowers his head and kisses me. "I regretfully must go to work. I have a meeting this morning. Taking a month vacation for our honeymoon has everyone in panic mode. I'll be home as soon as I can."

I run my hands through his hair and sigh. "I know you will. My laptop should arrive today and I'll spend all day setting it up but I really need my own vehicle to explore my new home. I'd like to be able to go to the stores and meet people for lunch."

"Okay." Jack frowns at me. "I'll talk about suitable vehicles when we get home. In the meantime, ask Jenny if you need a ride. I'm sure she has time to take you to the store." He kisses me again. "I've gotta go. See you tonight." He dashes out of the door.

I watch him go and close the door behind him. The secrets on Laura's laptop call to me again. I wait until I hear Ruby leave and then when Jack's car roars away, I take out Laura's laptop. I need to know more about her and what happened before she died. From what I gathered from our conversations, Jack noticed a decline in her sanity. He didn't say as much but he intimated there was a problem. I'm nervous as I wait for the files to load and when I open them, I scan them slowly, making sure not to miss anything important. I need to discover more about the window she tried to find and if it was the trigger that sent her off the rails. Was it significant enough to mention it in her diary? My heart pounds as I read and find nothing in the next entry. Surely, she'd have written something about the window? Moving through the files haphazardly isn't working. I need to follow the timeline and discover exactly what happened to her in her last year. I scroll back through the pages and go back to the beginning to step into Laura's mind.

July 15

I dreamed I was pregnant again and woke in a cold sweat. I ran to the bathroom and spewed. I can't possibly be pregnant. I must have a bug. I hated being pregnant. I became so fat and bloated I couldn't go anywhere for months. The birth was horrendous especially when everyone told me the second time would be wonderfully uplifting. It was, in fact, the most painful and embarrassing thing I've ever experienced. Noah is a beautiful child, and I love him in my own way but I have no motherly instinct. I didn't want to feed him or change his diaper. Heaven forbid. I'd spew if I went near one. In any case that's what a nanny is for, right? I'm glad Jenny took over. Now the kids are older, I can show them off to my friends but I keep Jenny close. She is much better with them than I am. After Ava was born, I spent months exercising to get back in shape and then I was pregnant again. Jack was thrilled and engaged an artist to paint my portrait; I needed to look spectacular but I was angry. I never wanted another child and Jack knew it. Most of the painting was done by photographs and then the artist came to finish it in the house and I needed to sit for hours. I overheard a visitor to the house mention that the expression in my eyes looked as if I wanted to kill someone. Maybe he was right?

This is another side to Laura I hadn't seen coming. Leaning back in my chair, I shake my head. How did Jack cope with such a self-centered woman? He says he loved her. Perhaps he didn't know she had no motherly instinct and that her time with the children was just a show she put on for everyone. I feel sorry for her in a way. For me, carrying my husband's child would be a gift not a burden. Not that we've discussed children. Maybe it's something I should ask him?

I read on and the next entry is two days later.

July 17

Last night, I dreamed again of being pregnant. I was so glad to wake up and find it was a nightmare. I say nightmare because that was what it was like carrying Noah. When I told Jack I was pregnant, he picked me up and swung me around. He was so happy and I got angry and slapped his face. We argued, way into the night—well, in truth, I screamed and Jack just stared at me as if I'd lost my mind. It's so infuriating when a man won't fight back, so I took my car and hightailed it to Missy's house. She had my back and told me leaving was the right thing to do. Early the next morning Jack arrived on the doorstep. Jim had called him because he'd overheard me talking about having an abortion. Jack never loses his temper, and is the calmest person I know but this time he was mad. He spoke in a quiet voice and told me if I murdered his child he would divorce me, and as we have a prenup, I'd leave with the clothes on my back. He would make sure he had custody of Ava.

I recall thinking it through on the drive home, and told him it was a one-time deal. I insisted on getting a plastic surgeon to fix my mommy tummy, so I looked good. I made it clear I didn't want to see the baby when it was born. When I spoke to the surgeon, I asked to be sterilized. If Jack wants me, there can never be any more kids.

The day I told Jack I was pregnant was the changing point for everything that's happened since then. Jack hasn't touched me since that night. When we go to dinner parties he rarely sits with me and spends his time with his friends. I need companionship and will need to seek it elsewhere.

I lean back in my chair, allowing the implications of Laura's words to sink in. The loving mother Jack told me about was a sham. Jenny's impression of Laura was true but she didn't know the facts. Was Laura contemplating an affair? If so, did she write about it? I skim over the pages but find nothing. Most of the entries are rambling, so I move back to August and find an entry about the window.

August 10

I saw a face at the window today. I told Jack and he laughed at me. Every time I tell him weird things are happening to me, he just shakes his head. He wants to take me back to the shrink but there's nothing wrong with me. I know what I saw and when I went back inside, I checked on all the staff and everyone was having lunch. I must find the window and see if the dust has been disturbed but I don't like going to the third floor alone. I recall stories as a child of strange sounds and footsteps coming from up there. Jack says it's just the house moving and that's what old houses do. He has no plans to open the third floor. The lights are dim and it hasn't been opened for many years. It's a place time left behind.

I went outside again and stared at the windows. The one where I saw a face was the sixth window on the third floor. I went back inside, found a flashlight in the kitchen and went up the stairs. It was dark and musty on the third floor. The hall-ways are covered in a thick coating of dust. It was cold and the floorboards creaked with each step. I counted the bedroom doors, five doors not six. I went back and counted the doors again. Five doors. I went to the fifth door, opened the room and shone my flashlight inside. It was like stepping back in time. Old moldy furniture covered in a thick layer of dust greeted me. I moved the light around and counted only one window. I closed the door and walked along the hallway, tapping the walls, and found no trace of another door. The sixth room is missing.

August 1 1

I asked about the missing room and Jack showed me the blue-prints of the house. There was no sixth room. So how come there's a window? We went outside and counted the windows. Six. He told me one must have been boarded up to extend a room many years ago. Today I went back up the stairs and tried the door again and it was locked. All the doors were locked. I asked the staff who locked the doors and they all insisted no one had been up to the third floor. I spoke to Jack and he said he didn't have keys for the doors upstairs and he had no idea they were locked. After speaking to him, I'm confused. Many things confuse me lately. I blame the drugs the shrink gave me. Since then, I've experienced weird things. This is one of them. Am I losing my mind? Did I see the face in the window and imagine opening the fifth door? I sat for a time, trying to recall my time here as a child. I did see secret passageways but I don't recall a window. I need to spend some time away from his house. I wish Jack hadn't purchased it now. It's becoming more like a prison than a home.

Suddenly needing clarification, I slide the laptop back into its hiding place. I collect the bunch of keys Sue had cut for me and, grabbing my phone, head along the passageway and up the stairs to the next floor. There are two wings to the house, both separated by a balcony in the center. The back section behind the kitchen is the staff quarters. Where I'd seen the face was definitely on the left side of the house. I climb the stairs and hear Bill's warning words echoing in my mind. He's been working here for many years. What had he really heard about the previous occupants? Which one of them apparently boarded up a room or a window and didn't mark it on the plans? Why would they do that?

Many things speed through my mind as I climb. My few excursions alone through this massive house haven't worked out so well but I figure most of what unnerved me is in my head. I really shouldn't watch horror movies as they're twisting my mind. Jack and the kids have lived here for a long time and nothing weird has happened to them. I'm not unstable and I'm not crazy Laura. I'll be fine.

At the top of the stairs is a huge oak door. It fits in well with the rest of the décor and I'd never have known this led to another hallway unless Jack had told me. I take out the bunch of keys and try any that look compatible. On the fourth try, the key turns, and with a push the door whines open. Ahead of me is a long dark hallway. The house has a different feel up here; like Laura said in her diary, it's as if time has stopped. I use the flashlight on my phone and shine the beam into the dark abyss. The wallpaper is old, brown and peeling in places. I see portraits of people from maybe a century ago, although they're so dust laden it's hard to tell. I follow the beam of light and wonder what this separate floor was used for in days gone by. Why does the staircase to the loft go from the second floor and not the third? It makes no sense unless this part was servants' quarters, but then most servants had the bottom floors, not the top.

It's creepy in here and I take a few steps inside and stand for a moment, examining the people in the portraits. This, I imagine by the dress, was the family who occupied the home in the early 1920s. My light disturbs spiders hanging in cobwebs and they all seem to run and hide at once. It's cold here, a bone-chilling cold that sends shivers down my spine. I'm afraid but curiosity alone makes me step forward, farther along the hallway. Here the air is old and musty, and my light picks up dust motes dancing like fireflies in the beam.

I'm halfway to the first door and hear a creaking sound as if someone is following me and the floorboards are complaining. Heart racing, I turn quickly but all I see is my footprints in the substantial layer of dust on the worn hall carpet. I reach the first door and turn the handle. It opens and I stand back. Inside the dim room, it's amazingly clean; dust covers are over lumps, which I assume is furniture. I move into the room and lift a dusty sheet and peer underneath. I find a very old-style chair but of good quality, undoubtedly antique. I turn toward the window and pull aside one of the drapes. Even through the murky glass, I can see the garden below and the path where I stood looking up at the house.

Without so much as a creak, the door slams shut behind me,

the sound like a gunshot in the silence. I cry out, fear has me by the throat and I move my flashlight around the room. Terror grips me but no one is in the room with me. Frozen to the spot, I drag in stale air as my attention flashes from side to side. Nothing moves but the house moans and a cold breeze brushes across my legs. Where is it coming from? I turn to the window but it's closed and the glass is intact. I need to get out of here, now. My bravery slips away and I go to the door. I turn the doorknob but the door doesn't open. I'm stuck inside, and nobody knows I'm here. Terrified, I hammer on the door. "Hey, let me out of here. What game are you playing?"

Nothing. Not one sound comes from the hallway. Another cold breeze brushes across my bare ankles in an icy caress and I turn my flashlight toward the hearth. I stand panting, trying to get my senses. I have my phone and can call for help. If I knew anyone inside the house's number. In fact, I don't even know the house number. Why didn't I think to add it to my contacts? I stare at the door, uncertain what to do. What is wrong with me? Am I losing my mind like Laura?

I refuse to be like her, and take a firm grasp on the door handle and pull. Nothing. I try again, this time pushing one foot against the wall for leverage. The door releases so fast I stumble back and sit down hard on the dusty floor. I jump to my feet to dash through the opening but it hits me in the back, pushes me out into the hallway, and slams shut behind me. It's as if the room didn't want me inside. I stand breathing heavily and staring at the door. Jack's warning echoes in my mind. What is it about the third floor that makes him hesitant to renovate it? What isn't he telling me?

I move my flashlight along the hallway and regain my courage. Sure, the room unsettled me but I'm determined not to allow my imagination to run riot. I need to see the fifth room for my own peace of mind and walk to the end of the hallway, my light bobbing in front of me. I find the fifth door and open it with ease. As before, the furniture is covered but just as Laura mentioned in her diary, there's only one window. I'm not going inside. I'm not that stupid. I shut the door and stand in the hallway, moving my flashlight around. At this end of the hallway, the dust is minimal. I go to examine the walls where a sixth bedroom should be but a strange grinding sound stops me in my tracks. Maybe that's the tree branches scratching the windows or rats living inside the walls?

What is moving the dust and slamming the doors? I figure the wind is likely blowing down the chimneys—but there's no fireplaces in the hallway. I walk to the ornate oak panels and run my hand over them. They also look clean. How strange. I scan the carpet. No one has been here or they'd have left footprints like I did. I shake my head. Bill told me the house isn't haunted. Even so, I don't like being here and I'm about to head back downstairs when I hear someone singing. I stop midstride and all the hairs on my body stand on end. The sound is gone in a second. Did I imagine it? Are Laura's words twisting my mind? Maybe, but what if someone doesn't want me investigating her death and believes that frightening me is a way of making me stop?

TWENTY-NINE

Unsettled, I wait for the children to arrive home. I really want their chatter to wash away the memories of the third floor but Jenny has taken them to visit their grandparents. It's a regular event that happens every Thursday that nobody mentioned to me. I stare at Sue in disbelief. "Don't you believe I should be told when the children are going somewhere?"

"I'm sure Jenny would have mentioned it." Sue gives me a dismissive look. "Maybe it slipped your mind?"

This isn't happening. Are they gaslighting me and, if so, why? I glance from her to Pierre. "I assume you know as well?"

"I do." He glances at me over one shoulder. "It's a regular visit."

A regular visit and Jack didn't think to mention it? What's going on? I can't believe he or Jenny mentioned it and I was so wrapped up in Laura's diary I forgot something so important. Or did I? The question hangs in my mind, unsettling me. What is it about this house that sends everyone crazy? No—not everyone—Jack's wives. Who could possibly benefit by killing his wives? I see the staff staring at me and passing knowing looks between each other as if I'm just another of Jack's wives that's lost her mind. Dammit, I won't allow them to get away with it. I shake my head. "A regular visit, I should be responsible for. I'm their stepmother. I'll speak to Jenny when she gets back. What time is she expected?"

"Before eight. The kids have dinner with their grandparents." Sue checks her watch. "It's some time before dinner. Would you like a mug of coffee?"

She's placating me with coffee. How long will it be before someone starts to drug my food too? I try to relax. I'm aware someone drugged Laura and I won't be such an easy target. I'll stand and watch her pour me a mug. I nod. "Yes, thanks." I can't ignore the sudden coldness from my two employees and it irks me. "Is there anything else I need to know about the children's movements?"

"You'll need to speak to Jenny." Sue lifts one shoulder in a dismissive shrug. "She'll have all their appointments listed, I'm sure."

I take the mug and add my own fixings. "I'll be sure to get a copy to avoid any misunderstandings in the future." I take my drink and go outside. I find a bench and sit and look at the sea. I need time to think.

When Jack arrives home and asks me what I've been doing all day, I tell him about visiting the left wing on the third floor and he is visibly annoyed. I want to explain the reason I went against his advice. "I needed to see for myself, Jack. You know, to put my mind at rest."

"You should have waited for me to get home." Jack shakes his head. "Not that I enjoy going up there. It's better to lock the door and forget it exists. No one has been there for ages. I can't even imagine what it's like now."

I shiver, recalling the harrowing experience. "There's dust everywhere and spiders. It took all my courage to step inside the hallway. I went into the first room and the door shut behind me and I couldn't get out. I panicked for a time and almost called someone to come and save me but calling the cops or fire department would be a little heavy-handed." I smile. "As you can see, the door eventually opened and I made it out okay."

"Oh, Willow. That must have been terrifying for you. I'm glad you're okay. I'd really advise you to keep away from that floor." He slides his phone across the dining room table and looks at me with a serious expression. "There could be rot in the floorboards or anything. It might not be safe. Grab all the contacts you need from my phone. Did your laptop arrive?"

I smile at him. I'd spent all afternoon playing with my new toy and downloading the software I require. "Yes, it did. I sent a few messages to my friends in LA, asking them to forward their email addresses, but we do everything by text these days anyway. We'll chat on FaceTime when they get home. It seems as if everyone is on vacation overseas at the moment. At least, they replied with messages like: *Busy having fun, will be in touch soon.*"

"Jet-setters, huh?" Jack tucks into his meal.

I finish my meal and collect the contacts I need and then lean back in my chair, staring at my half-eaten food. I notice Jack's gaze slides to my plate and gives a little shake of his head. "What is it?"

"You're not eating." Jack searches my face. "Laura stopped eating too and then she took sick." His gaze never leaves me. "It's this old house. It's depressing. If I hadn't purchased it, Laura would still be alive."

I gape at him in disbelief. If she hadn't died, he'd never have met me. I'm not sure how to take that comment but I feel as if he's just slapped me in the face. I can't stand his faux feelings for her. After reading Laura's diaries, this house was the complete opposite of the Camelot he tried to make me believe it was. "Well, you did buy the house but I can't see how this old house caused Laura to fall from your yacht. This is just one more reason why you should buy another house, a modern house. Nothing here belongs to your family history; all the portraits apart from Laura's are strangers. It's pointless living here. You really need to consider moving and making a fresh start."

"Maybe." Jack pointed to my plate. "Is this house discussion to take my attention away from the fact you're not eating?"

I shake my head. "Don't be ridiculous, Jack. You know as well as I do that the house is unhealthy. Can you imagine a health inspector coming here? It would be condemned. For the sake of our family's health, we need to start afresh."

"Okay, darling." Jack shakes his head and his mouth curls into a smile. "You've made a very good point. Now eat your dinner before it gets cold."

I push my plate away and look at his stubborn expression. "I don't clean my plate because the portions are way too large for me. I'll need to ask Pierre to make them smaller. I had a huge lunch and I always leave room for dessert." He doesn't reply so I wait for him to finish eating and sip my water, deciding what else to say about my trip to the forbidden zone upstairs. "The sixth window, on the third floor of the left wing. Why isn't it attached to a room?"

"Why is that window always such an issue?" He leans back in his chair and wipes his mouth on a napkin. "Laura was obsessed with it and now you go into that filthy hole to look for it as well. As a builder, I'd say it's there for cosmetic reasons. In my opinion, the left wing on the third floor makes no reasonable sense. Why have five tiny rooms? Why not two large useable rooms or one large one like in the right wing? The ballroom is there and it has six windows." He gives me a withering look. "About the sixth window. I figure they added another window on the left side to balance the appearance of the house. It goes nowhere and backs onto the brick as far as I'm aware. Laura told me she saw a face at the window. It must be a trick of the light because it's impossible. I asked the window cleaner and he told me inside was painted black. I guess that was done to make it look the same as the others."

I nod and say nothing as Amy clears the table. When she leaves the room, I lean forward. "It's spooky up there and if you insist on living here, it needs to be renovated. If there's mold it could be spreading throughout the house and that's a health hazard. You really can't risk the health of the children, Jack. Now I've seen it, I really believe you should turn it into a useful space. Are you aware that Ava loves to dance? You could make a practice room for her up there and maybe an art studio. Did you know I like to paint? Three windows would give the room a ton of natural light."

"Yes, I know Ava suddenly wants to be a ballerina. Jenny will be taking her to dance classes once a week starting in August." He clears his throat. "I'm sorry, I should have told you. Although, I'm not sure how long this fad will last. She wanted a pony a few months ago. I took her riding and the next day she'd changed her mind. She said her legs were so sore she couldn't walk properly." He grins at me. "I do listen to them, you know. Last year she wanted to be a dragon rider."

I chew on my bottom lip. I need to talk more about the third floor. "Kids, huh? I wanted to fly." I pause, staring at my hands. "I must tell you. When I was up there, I could hear strange things. A creaking sound and for a moment there I could swear I heard music."

"Willow." Jack rolls his eyes to the ceiling and he barks a laugh. "All the chimneys in this house are connected, so in any room with a fireplace you can hear things from other rooms. Sometimes voices travel through the ventilation grates in the hallways as well. Someone could have been walking by singing and you heard them." He waves a hand toward the window. "Look at the weather; a storm is brewing and it's windy. Branches rub against the house, the house moves. Nobody is there." He takes my hand. "Has that put your mind at rest? I don't want you becoming obsessed with trying to find something that doesn't exist."

I look into his eyes and see sadness there. Is he remembering Laura's mental decline? Am I mirroring her delusional behavior? I'm sure what I'm seeing and hearing is real, but now I'm doubting myself. The lunch confusion the other day, the moving flowers, my vanishing phone all make me more than a little confused right now. How can I tell him I feel trapped inside the house? Seeing his reaction, I decide not to concern him and shake my head. "I'm not obsessed with anything but you, Jack, although I would like the ability to explore the neighborhood and make lunch dates with your friends—I mean *our* friends."

"That's good to know." He cups my cheek. "I didn't mean to trap you here. I know how independent you are. We'll look at cars this weekend—okay? The kids will love it."

I nod and smile like an automaton but inside I feel something is off-kilter. This house drove Laura mad or was it just a stepping stone? I need to read more of her diary and discover what else she had on her mind.

THIRTY
FRIDAY

I need to get out of the house but once again the diary lures me. Once everyone leaves, I run up the stairs to my room and set it up. As the weeks count down to the accident on the yacht, Laura appears to be falling deeper into a delusional state.

August 15

I can't sleep and feel as if I'm drifting between dreams and reality. I went to sleep in my bed last night but woke in one of the spare rooms. I'd even removed the dust cover from the bed. I have no idea how I got there. It frightens me if I've started walking in my sleep, as stairs are everywhere, and I could easily have fallen and broken my neck. From now on I'll lock myself inside my room. I'm convinced there's a conspiracy going on against me in this house but I need proof. I'm trying to get my head straight by re-reading the old emails from my friends. I'm trying to remember what was happening around the time of the emails and I find that I have blanks in my memory. I've tried very hard to prevent anyone drugging me but, somehow, they manage to slip something into my food each day.

Another strange thing happened to me today. My children are still babies and need to be supervised outside. Today I sat in the sitting room staring out of the window at the garden and watched two young children playing on the lawn in the distance. The children must have been around six and eight years old. I immediately wondered who the children belonged to as we don't have any married couples with young children working at the estate. When Sue came into the sitting room to bring me a pot of tea, I asked her about the children and she insisted they were mine. I understand that some days I'm not very clear in my head but I do know the difference between Ava and Noah and the school-age children in the garden. It was pointless to argue with her but I decided to take a photograph of the children to show Jack later when he came home. I wanted him to clarify that those older children are not ours and then go and talk to Sue and tell her she was mistaken.

When I reached for my phone, which I'd left sitting on the table beside the chair, the phone was gone. I searched all over and even called it from the house landline but the phone is missing and I have no idea where it's gone or who took it.

A shiver skitters down my spine; I'm not being drugged and yet some of the same things are happening to me. I'm starting to doubt my own sanity. Laura was obviously not of sound mind but could reading her diary make me believe the same things are happening to me? The idea is ludicrous but I don't have any other solution. Should I read on? I must. The answer to what really happened to Laura and why, must be hidden in these pages.

August 16

My head is clearer today, which is good, as Jack is taking me to purchase a gown for our anniversary celebration aboard the yacht. My phone is still missing and Jack has ordered the staff to search the house for it. After I selected a suitable gown, Jack sent me home with Tom. I like him as he has always been very nice to me and not like the other members of staff. He is more like Jack's closest friend and I feel like I can trust him. I confided in him about the strange things happening to me and my fear of the house. He was very understanding and when we arrived home, I asked him to come and check my room to make sure I was safe. I'm not sure how it happened; one moment I was crying and he was comforting me, the next moment I woke, wrapped in his arms, as the sun crept above the horizon.

I don't feel guilty. I feel liberated.

I stand so fast the chair tips and tumbles to the floor. I can't believe what I've read. Laura was having an affair with Tom Bates! Mind reeling with the implications, I close the laptop and stare at it as if it's on fire. Two and two come together and possible scenarios rush through my mind. Did Jack find out? Was the argument with Tom not about him dating Ruby but about his affair with his wife? Jack wouldn't be able to stand the humiliation of knowing his wife had cheated on him with his best friend. A memory slips into my mind. Didn't Missy tell me Tom would do anything for Jack? Did he toss Laura from the yacht? I'm shaking and pace up and down my room. I need to think. Jack's friends are loyal to him and so is his staff, so to confuse me, it makes sense that everyone would give me a slightly different story—if they were covering up a murder.

THIRTY-ONE

It takes me some time to calm my nerves but I head downstairs. I'm not Laura and I'm not crazy—well, not yet anyway. My day must proceed as normal as if I'm blissfully unaware of the web of lies around me. This morning, I made Jenny aware that I intend to spend more time with the children and will be going with them next week to visit their grandparents. I also requested a list of their movements so I know where they are each day. It's obvious Jenny isn't too happy with me taking over. She even mentioned the hostility I might receive by going with her. I'm aware Jack's parents don't like me and that's just too bad. Next week, I'll be with the children and showing everyone I'm here to stay. The thing is: are they all working against me? Perhaps my inquiry about the night Laura died has set everyone on edge or maybe it's because I'm mentally exhausted and reading things into situations that don't exist.

Lying awake each night is becoming a habit, and lack of sleep is making it hard to concentrate. I should be sleeping like the dead. Jack is an exhausting lover, but all night I just lie there staring into the darkness and listening to the waves crashing on the beach. All I can think about is who killed Caroline and

Laura. Did Laura believe Caroline was murdered too? Had she come close to the truth and needed to be disposed of? Did Jack know and is he covering up for someone?

Where are Caroline's wedding photographs? Most people have albums. Did Jack have photographs taken on their honeymoon? I must find them, and his wedding to Laura too. I need to know who was at both weddings. Everyone there had the opportunity to kill them. It will be easy to narrow down who was at both murder scenes. I'm not sure what to do if I discover the murderer. Keeping away from them will be the first move, the second will be having a nice chat with the local homicide police.

I walk out the front door and follow the path to the rose gardens; my head is so filled with information, I figure it will burst. So many ideas spin around in my mind, making it difficult to make a decision. This is not like me. Maybe it's because I've always had a job and sitting around all day doing nothing is making me crazy. Now that's a dirty word around here and I try and center my thoughts. Having a mission to discover the truth will keep me sane. I pull out the notebook from the pocket of my cargo pants. Having clothing with a ton of pockets is essential in this house. I'll be able to always keep my phone and other things with me. I sit down on a bench beside the fragrant beds. All around me, the heads of the peach-colored roses still carry the morning dew. It's peaceful here and my head clears. I make a note to look for the wedding albums and then wonder if Jack has kept his yearbooks. He seems to hoard everything from his past. I'll need to go back to the loft and search but that can wait for a couple of hours.

First, I need to pick up where I left off in Laura's diary. It's starting to get interesting and her story of what happened before she died is essential, if I'm to discover the truth. I put away my notebook and head back inside the house, closing the front door silently behind me. I hear voices whispering in the hallway. When I hear my name mentioned, I stop and slide into the office doorway to listen.

"I overheard them talking over dinner." Amy's voice drifts toward me. "He hadn't told her about Caroline."

"Then we must make sure she doesn't discover the entrance to the storeroom." George clears his throat. "I'm not sure why Mr. Hunter brought all her things to this house. He is obsessed with his dead wives. It's not healthy." He sighs. "What else do you know?"

"She went to the left wing on the third floor as well." Amy shifts her feet. "I don't think she looked around too much. One thing is for sure: I'm not going up there to move anything. I doubt she'll go back either. She got locked inside a room for a time and told Mr. Hunter she was terrified."

"Good to know. It will keep her from snooping around." George rests his hands on his hips. "I don't want Mr. Hunter to end up with another unstable wife. Make sure you stay close to her and report back to me."

"I'll do my best." Amy crosses her arms over her chest. "At least she's not like Laura. She scared me."

"She did most of the staff. Now get back to work." George steps out into the hallway. "I'll let Mr. Hunter know if she keeps snooping around." He turns and his footsteps vanish into his office.

So, Amy and George can't be trusted. Who else is spying on me and why does Jack need to be informed? Did he tell them to watch me? Anger shimmers over me. Does this mean I can't trust my husband? Why could I possibly be a threat to him? What is so secret he has it locked away, where I can't find it? I need to do something about this right away. I step out and head after George. "George, is that you?"

"Yes, Mrs. Hunter." He gives me a bright smile. "Did you enjoy the rose garden?"

I nod. "Yes, I did. It's wonderful." I meet his gaze. "Do you have your keys with you?"

"I do." He narrows his gaze. "I thought Sue had a set cut for you?"

I smile. "She did. Do you know how many people have copies of the key to the third-floor door in the left wing?"

"Four of us, I believe: me, Sue, you and Mr. Hunter." He frowns. "Is there a problem I should be aware of?"

I shake my head. It's been a long time since Laura died but now, I need to be in charge of my house. "No. Not at all. Give me your key."

"Why?" His neck grows red and his cheeks flush.

I look at him. "Because I'm Jack's wife and, just like Laura, I'll be overseeing the running of my house, George. I'm sure you understand. Please, give me your key."

I wait with my hand palm up for him to give me the key. He looks uncomfortable and has trouble removing the key from the bunch. He eventually hands it over to me with reluctance.

"Thank you. That's all for now."

I need Sue's key before she has time to make another copy. Whatever is hidden on the third floor, I want to make sure nobody moves it—and where is the storeroom? I dash back into the office and grab Jack's keys and then run along the hallway and into the kitchen where I see George in deep conversation with Sue. They stop talking abruptly the moment they see me. "Ah, Sue. I need your key to the left-wing door." I hold out my hand and wait for Sue to comply.

"How many keys do you need?" George peers at me with limpid eyes. "I was just asking Sue to give me hers so I could make a copy. I'll need a key. What if there's a fire?"

I take the key and slide it inside my pocket. "Jack told me there's no power in the left wing on the third floor so the chance of a fire would be minimal. In any case, I'm here to open the door if needs be." I turn to Sue. "I see you're busy. Send Amy to the office with a mug of coffee for me please and some cookies if you have any."

"Right away, Mrs. Hunter." Sue turns to Amy. "You heard her."

Keeping my head high, I walk out the door and go to the office. Inside, I locate the blueprints and spread them over Jack's desk. Where are the storerooms? This house is huge and there will be storerooms all over, but where do I find a place that's hidden? I long to call Jack and ask him. Surely there's a simple explanation but as more days go by in this house, I discover his open trustworthy façade hides a weave of deception. I drop into the office chair, smell his cologne and my heart tears apart. Why did he marry me and bring me here and then lie to me?—no, not lie—he hasn't lied to me yet. He just didn't tell me everything. A second dead wife is a big thing but I have things in my past I'd rather not discuss with him too. Surely most married couples keep a few secrets—or maybe not. I'm not experienced enough to know if this behavior in a husband is considered normal.

I glance up as Amy brings my large mug of coffee and sets it on a chest of drawers. "Wait a minute." I lean back in my chair staring at her, not too sure what to say. "Who asked you to spy on me? Was it George or Mr. Hunter?" I see her stare at her shoes and fidget. "I overheard you speaking with George so please tell me, I need to know."

"Before you arrived, George told us that we mustn't mention Caroline, Mr. Hunter's first wife." She lifts her gaze to me. "He said Mr. Hunter had made the request. He didn't want you to know; he had all of Caroline's possessions locked in the house along with her portrait. It's as big as Laura's."

My mind reeling, I stare at her. "Caroline has a portrait too? Where did it come from? I mean, Jack didn't own this house when he met Caroline and you'd need to own a mansion to place one of that size on the wall. I didn't figure Jack came into his fortune straight out of college although it's not something we discuss."

"Oh." Amy's cheeks reddened. "It's not for me to say, Mrs. Hunter."

I glare at her. "If you know, spit it out." I wait a few moments and then lean forward. "It's no secret I've only known Jack for eight weeks. Yes, I married him after a whirlwind courtship but I didn't know he had money."

"I see." Amy twists her fingers. "I can only tell you what I've been told and that is he inherited a fortune in stocks and property from his grandfather. The company was started by his grandfather and, since his father has no head for business, everything went to Mr. Hunter. His father lives on a trust fund."

Astounded that the help knows more about my husband's finances than I do, I lean back in my chair. "So where is this storeroom?"

"I can't tell you." Amy avoids my gaze. "George says you're not to go inside."

I stand and lean on the desk. I want to tell her this is my house and I can go where I please but I figure she'll shut down and say nothing. Right now, I so want to fire her and George—maybe I'll fire the entire staff. I can't trust any of them but firing them right now won't get me anywhere. "Point out where it is on the blueprints. Then he won't know, will he?"

I show her the blueprints. "Which floor?"

"The third floor in the right wing beside the ballroom." Amy stares at the blueprints as I get the correct page and then she points. "Right here. All the storage rooms are set into the wall, as in you can't see a door. They're part of the design. No door handles, you just push on them and they pop open."

I trace the hallway with my finger and nod. "Okay, and no more snooping on me. You're not here to tell George everything I say to my husband. Confidentiality is part of your job. If that's a problem for you, I'll find someone else to take your place." I move my gaze to her. "Have I made myself perfectly clear?"

"Yes." Amy flees from the room, and her footsteps echo away along the hallway.

I roll up the blueprints and return them to the documents tube and then grab my mug from the bookcase and sit down to sip the coffee. I nibble on the homemade cookies, savoring each delicious bite. I don't intend to go rushing to find the storage area just yet. I'll wait a bit and then go. I'm not sure why I gave Amy the chance to redeem herself when no doubt she is telling George everything that transpired between us. This is the thing with trust. Once it's gone, it's gone forever.

I wait, listening for movement in the house, but hear nothing. I stand and move to the door and peek outside. There's no one lurking around. I step back and facepalm my head. Stupid, stupid woman. I've forgotten about the CCTV cameras. I sit back at Jack's desk and soon have his computer humming. I scroll through the mountain of files and then go to the program files and search for cameras. I find the software program for a security firm and then trace it to the correct files. The program named Beauford Manor Security opens and the screen breaks into multiple images of areas of the house. Right now, no one is in the hallways, so Amy has kept our conversation to herself.

I have no idea if George has access to the camera feed but I can't risk him seeing me. I'm no computer expert by any means but turning the cameras off and on is simple. I turn off the cameras from the stairs all the way to the third floor. A complete blackout. When I'm done, I'll turn them back on. I take a deep breath and head into the foyer, up the grand staircase as if heading for my bedroom and then continue up the stairs to the third floor. This time I turn right and walk along a sumptuous hallway. I open one side of a huge double door and peer inside. A polished floor reflecting the light from a line of windows greets me. There is a bandstand at one end, beautiful antique chaise longues in peacock blue silk along one side and chande-liers glitter along the center of the ceiling. The drapes are blue velvet, tied back with gold ropes. "So, this is the ballroom."

I close the door and walk along the passageway. I find bath-rooms suitable for several guests but can't find the storeroom. I keep walking to the end of the hallway and stare at the ornate carved oak wall panels. I go to each one and press them. The third one along clicks and pops open. I find a light switch beside the door and a white glow floods the room. A small chest of drawers holds clothes and a jewelry box. I see a photo album but the covered painting draws my attention. I pull back the cover and stare at the face. The young woman so lovingly portrayed has long blonde hair, cornflower blue eyes—and my face.

THIRTY-TWO

Disoriented and confused, I fall against the wall. My heart hammers with shock and I can't breathe. What is happening? The implications rush through my mind and it's too much to bear. I must get out of here. I grab the photo album and after closing the door behind me, I run back along the passageway and slip on the stairs, barely grabbing the handrail to prevent my fall. The photo album flies from my fingers and slides to the bottom of the steps. I stand panting for some moments and then move more slowly. I pick up the scattered images and stuff them back inside the folder. With the album gripped tightly under one arm, I somehow make it back to the office. I fall into the chair, panting, and quickly turn the cameras back on and close the computer. I must act normal and walk slowly to my bedroom. My mind is racing so fast and I can hear Jack's words in my head. How much he loved Caroline and how no one came close to his first love until he met me. No wonder—I'm her doppelgänger. Did he marry me as a substitute for Caroline?

Once inside my bedroom, I sit at my table and flick through the photo album. There are images of Caroline and Jack at college, their wedding and honeymoon. They look so happy.

The perfect couple. Jack is so young and happiness spills from the images. I resemble her but we're not identical, although the painting looks more like me. In the back of my mind, I wonder if Jack intends to place Caroline's portrait in the foyer and pretend it's me. Is that why he took so much trouble to prevent me from seeing it? Is my marriage a lie? Uncertainty boils in my veins. Does he even love me? I pull my phone from my pocket and call Jack. The call is diverted to his secretary, Julia Hunker. "This is Mrs. Hunter. I need to speak to Jack."

"I'm afraid he's in a meeting." Julia pauses for a beat. "He should be through by lunchtime. Do you want me to leave him a message to call you?"

The room seems to close in around me. I'm trapped in this house, surrounded by people I can't trust and now I can't speak to my husband. Trying not to lose it, I grip the phone so hard my hand hurts. "I know he had a meeting today but this is urgent. I want you to put me through to him now."

"Mrs. Hunter, when Jack asks not to be disturbed, I don't disturb him." She sighs. "I'm sure you understand? He is meeting with a high-profile client to sign contracts for a new development."

Panic curls in my stomach; it's as if I'm falling in an out-of-control elevator. I suck in a breath. "If you want a job tomorrow, I suggest you put me through to my husband—now!"

I wait and hear clicking on the line. Julia is obviously telling Jack I'm being a problem. I break down when his voice comes on the line.

"Willow, what's wrong?" Jack's voice is like a soothing balm. "What is it, darling? Has something happened to the children?"

I'm crying, tears are spilling down my cheeks. "Jack, why didn't you tell me?"

"Tell you what? Are you crying?" I hear footsteps on tile. "What's happened?"

I tell him about the conversation I overheard between

George and Amy and about my visit to the storeroom. "Why are they checking up on me and why didn't you tell me I look exactly like Caroline? Am I a replacement for the only love in your life? Do you think of her every night we're making love?"

Silence.

Anger wells and I want to disconnect, pack my bags and go back to LA but I stand my ground. "Well?"

"I wish you wouldn't go through the storerooms or the loft when I'm not with you." He clears his throat. "There are many things in my past that might need explaining, I've never said I was a monk. Willow, your resemblance to Caroline is just a coincidence is all. She was a long time ago. This is our time now. Please don't allow this to upset you." I hear a door close and Jack lowers his voice. "You're nothing like her and no, I rarely think of her and never when I'm with you. I married you because I love you, Willow, and for no other reason. I have no idea what George and Amy think they're doing but I'll speak to them when I get home." He takes a breath. "I need to get back to my client. This is a multimillion-dollar deal and I just walked out on him mid-sentence."

I swipe at my tears with my sleeve. He is trying to soothe my ego but I can't erase my suspicion that something is very wrong. How come I'm the only person seeing it? Two wives die in accidents, with the same people at the scenes. The staff are plotting against me with my husband and he didn't even try to deny it. What else is he hiding from me? I'm trembling but this call is getting me nowhere. It seems I need to go it alone to discover the truth. "Okay. I'm sorry to disturb you."

"Don't be. I understand and I'll be home soon." He disconnects.

I'm staggered by his evasion but I'm more determined now to keep going. I need the photo album to match up the faces of the people involved over the time both Caroline and Laura died. I go through the album and, using my phone, copy the group images. Now all I need to do is find the same information about Laura. Will I find photographs in the loft or secreted inside Laura's boudoir? The thought of going back inside that room sends chills down my spine. I really have no choice. I must discover who was involved because next time it might be my neck on the line.

THIRTY-THREE

I don't care if anyone sees me running up the stairs. This is my house and it's about time I took control. Those people work for us and, if they keep spying on me, I'll insist that we either move or fire them. I am prepared to see inside Laura's room this time; I unlock her door and fling it wide and then take the small table from outside and push it against the door. No one is going to shut me inside this time.

Without hesitating, I walk straight to the dressing room and open the door. I find the light switch easily and making sure the door is wide open I take the chair from in front of the dressing table and push it under the doorknob. Anger at being deceived surges through me as I scan the room. I try to put myself in Laura's place. Where would she keep her wedding photographs? As they are not something a person would look at daily, I assume they would be tucked away in one of the closets. Meticulously I open each door, moving piles of sweaters, and then I shake my head and turn around slowly. A chest of drawers is against one wall and I slide out each one; there, right at the bottom, is a pearl-white box, with the names Laura and Jack printed in gold, and underneath the date of their wedding.

As I stare at the box, the musty smell of the room and Laura's perfume envelops me and anxiety grips me with a ferocity that's unnerving. I stare at the closet that contains the mannequin wearing Laura's wedding gown, and the need to be far away from this room rushes through me. I pick up the box and, without bothering to shut any of the doors, I dash out into the hallway and head back downstairs to my room. The smell of Laura's perfume clings to me and, after dropping the box onto the table, I dash into the bathroom and thoroughly wash my face and hands. I pace up and down my room. One part of me wants to discover their closest friends, while the other part of me fears what the truth might reveal. How far would a close friend go to protect Jack if he is responsible for the deaths of his wives?

What if I'm wrong?

A wave of exhaustion washes over me. Am I thinking straight? Has moving into this horrible house and having to compete with a dead woman altered my normally sound judgment? How much of what I'm feeling is an overreaction? I lean on the table and stare out of the window, trying to gain perspective. I've never allowed people to get to me like this before and, trust me, in my business people are trying to walk over the top of you all the time. Being an actor and having to constantly join the line of others auditioning for the same part has shown me sides of people I didn't know existed. Perhaps I've been too critical on the staff here. After all, they have been working for Jack for many years and are obviously loyal to him. To them I am an outsider and it would be normal for them to be protective toward him, especially after dealing with Laura's unstable personality.

I picture each staff member and recall the variations they gave me of the night Laura died and shake my head. I'm convinced there's been a cover-up, and nothing that's been happening since I arrived here will allow me to come to any other conclusion. I glance down at the white box, take a breath and remove the cover. I lift out the leather-bound volume and flip over the pages. To my surprise, the sparkle in Jack's eyes is drastically different to when he married Caroline. He smiles at the camera, but it seems false. I've seen him smile with happiness. He told me he loved Laura—he's made this house and her belongings into a shrine to her memory—but the man in these photographs tells me a different story. I pass over the usual bride and groom images to look at the friends and family. Using my phone camera, I copy as many of them as possible.

I download everything I can find of Laura's and Caroline's weddings onto my laptop. I include the newspaper articles listing the names of the people at the wedding. I line up the pictures on my screen and, even though there is a time difference, it's easy to make out who's who. The group of people we went to lunch with at the yacht club have been close friends for many years and most of them from college. I notice Laura in a few of the socialite events but she isn't with Jack but obviously moved in the same circles. The newspaper clippings I discovered about their marriage were written after the fact, more as a mention than a society event. I scratch my head, trying to make sense of it all. My marriage to Jack was very private and, as far as I know, it never made mention in any of the newspapers, so I must assume that was the same with his marriage to Laura, although she didn't seem the type to agree to anything else but a full-on wedding with all the trimmings.

I returned to the wedding album and went through it again. Why didn't I notice it the first time I looked? Usually photographs taken at a wedding have images of the couple dancing or cutting the cake and often driving away to their honeymoon but not Laura's wedding. All the shots in the album were taken at the church. I consider this anomaly and the false smile on Jack's lips and wonder if he'd been pressured into marrying Laura. If he had been forced into marrying, would that be a reason to murder her?

My head is spinning. The group of people around Jack now have been with him for many years. They were at his weddings, with him on the honeymoon trip when Caroline died, and just happened to be on board the yacht when Laura accidentally fell overboard. On the yacht there were other people. The captain and his crew, the staff and Tom Bates. I notice Ruby in the background of all the other images. Jack mentioned she'd be with him forever, and had been his PA since he first started in business. I did notice at his wedding to Laura that Ruby was on the arm of a man who didn't show up in any of the other photographs. I can only imagine that he was her plus one for the wedding. She would know everything, but getting her to talk would be like squeezing blood from a stone. I'll need to have a long talk with Jack when he comes home, and ask him about his marriage to Laura. This time I expect him to tell me the truth.

THIRTY-FOUR

Jack arrives home early and, as I come downstairs, I hear him in his office. He is speaking in hushed tones but I slide up to his office door and wait outside. He's speaking to George and Amy.

"I asked you to keep an eye on my wife." Jack's voice is just above a whisper. "I didn't tell you to make her believe you were spying on her and reporting back to me. Willow isn't Laura, and she doesn't need constant supervision. My orders were to make sure nothing happened to her if she went upstairs to explore the top floor. You know it's not safe up there. Now she doesn't trust you and that just won't do. I'll try and smooth things over with her. You may go."

Ducking away silently, I head to the kitchen and ask Sue to serve dinner if it's ready and then go to tell Jack. I need explanations and expect to get them. I smile at him. "I'm sorry for calling your office. It's just that seeing Caroline's portrait disturbed me."

"I'm so sorry." Jack pulls me into his arms. "I should have told you, Willow. I know that now but I didn't want to frighten you away. I love you so much. I just couldn't risk it. From now on, I'll answer all your questions." He rubs my back and his eyes glide over my face. "I promise."

I circle his neck and fall into his eyes. "Being honest with me is all I ever want from you, Jack. I don't care about the past. We need to make our own future together."

"That's all I ever wanted." Jack drops his arms and takes my hand and leads me into dinner. "I hope you'll eat more tonight. I worry about you."

I sit at the table and chuckle. "You shouldn't. I eat cookies when you're not around."

"Well, then, don't eat so many; they spoil your dinner." He rolls his eyes. "Oh, now I'm talking to you like a father. That's not my intention. I just care, Willow."

I break a bread roll and butter it. "I know you do."

"I've spoken to George and Amy." Jack leans back in his chair. "They won't spy on you again."

I nod as Sue delivers the meals. "That's good because I need to discuss a few things with you."

A condemned man is allowed a final meal, so I wait until Jack clears his plate. He has his tablet at the dinner table and is showing me a selection of expensive vehicles. I remember my old Jeep that I left sitting in a friend's garage in LA. It had taken two years to pay the loan and I'm proud of owning a four-thousand-dollar vehicle. I scan the screen. "What one do you like?"

"This one." Jack indicates to an SUV. "It's a BMW, top of the range, and we could use it for family outings."

I nod, trying not to look at the price. "I like it. Do they come in silver? I've always wanted a silver car."

"Really? Silver?" Jack looks at me and barks a laugh. "I called earlier and asked what the dealership had in stock. He told me it takes about ninety days to get a new car. So, I asked him what he had on the showroom floor. I told him I'd pay an extra ten thousand to get one this week. He told me the list of available makes and models he had in stock. One of them is a silver BMW." He gave me a long look. "It's basically brand new but a demo model. One they use to show prospective buyers and they have three: black, white and silver. He said he could sell one of them." He pulls out his phone and scrolls through the contacts. "Joe, it's Jack Hunter. I'll take the silver BMW." He looks at me and smiles. "Yeah, sure, send the banking details to Ruby." He pauses a beat. "I'll have the ten thousand cash delivered to you personally first thing in the morning. Thanks, Joe." He disconnects.

The idea of a new car, any car, excites me but I haven't forgotten my mission. "You sound as if you've known Joe for a time."

"Yeah, we have a fleet of company vehicles and I do business with him all the time." Jack takes my hand and brushes his lips across my knuckles. "I might forget dessert and head straight for bed."

I shake my head. "Dessert is my favorite part of a meal and I never know what delights Pierre will serve." I sigh. "In any case, I need to talk to you."

"Are you bored with me already, Willow?" He stares into my eyes as if seeking the truth.

I laugh. "I can't get enough of you but if you want me to be happy, I need to clear up anything that might spoil our happiness."

"What could possibly spoil our happiness?" Jack's eyebrows raise. "I know you hate the house and I've been thinking about that lately. You're correct that it's a moldy old building and in need of renovation. I could change anything you require within the limits of the heritage listing but I don't believe that would make you happy. It seems to me anything to do with Laura makes you question our life together or perhaps my feelings toward you. I'm right, aren't I?"

I can't believe that he is actually considering renovating the house. "If I'm being perfectly honest with you, I hate this place.

I really can't see what Laura saw in it unless it held special memories from her childhood." I squeeze his fingers. "The gardens are absolutely beautiful but I don't live outside. Inside there's a sadness that seems to seep out of the walls and it makes me depressed." I look into his eyes. "The thing is, Jack, you go to work each day and are only at home weekends when the house is full of life with children running around and everything seems wonderful. I've spent my time in the house virtually alone. I honestly believe if I stay here much longer, I'll risk my sanity. Things happen here. Either it's the staff or because the house is falling down around us. Or maybe it's because of the mold. It isn't healthy here."

"I see." Jack's brow creases with concern.

He looks devastated and I hate to keep going but it's necessary to clear the air once and for all between us. "The main reason I wanted to speak to you tonight was because I want to know the absolute truth about your marriage to Laura. I know that Caroline was the love of your life but you didn't wait very long after she died to marry Laura, did you? I find that very strange because most people that have lost someone that they love deeply will at least take a few years to mourn their loss, and yet you romanced and married Laura within six months." I give him a long look. "I don't believe for a second your time with Laura was like a romance novel."

"Things happened." Jack takes his hand from mine and dashes it through his hair.

I take a deep breath. "I know she apparently left Noah alone in the bath and about drugging her meals. What I want to know is why you married her in the first place?"

"How did you find out about Noah? And yes, she was on medication because, after that happened, I realized she was unstable, and so I had her under the supervision of a psychiatrist. I couldn't risk leaving her alone with the children again. You must remember they were only babies at the time."

He is getting irritated and leaning back in his chair, glaring at me. I shake my head. "Jenny told me what happened to Noah and the other information I discovered myself." I sigh. "So why did you marry her? You didn't love her, did you?"

"My grandfather encouraged me to date her." He leans forward on the table, clasping his hands before him. "As his sole heir he wanted me to be well established in his business, married with a child of my own. He and Laura's father were close business associates. She was wealthy in her own right and marrying her would ensure the joining of two building magnates." He takes a breath and blows it out between his teeth. "I'd met Laura in college and made sure I was attending the same functions. To this day I believe that she had been instructed to marry me by her parents. My grandfather told me that no matter who you marry, love would come eventually, and as Laura was a striking woman, I figured it might happen. So we had a short courtship and a very private wedding. She invested all her personal wealth into the business and was given an allowance, which she didn't appreciate."

I can't believe he's being so candid with me. "Then what happened?"

"She was quite normal until Ava arrived." Jack drums his fingers on the table. "She had gotten into her head that I didn't want a girl; that I'd only accept a boy. No matter how many times I tried to convince her, she refused to believe me. It became necessary for me to move into my own bedroom. I took the one the opposite side of the dressing room and spent most of the next few months trying to show her how much I cared for her and Ava. It seemed the moment that she allowed me back into her bed, Noah was on the way. I commissioned the portrait because Laura looked so beautiful. Pregnancy agreed with her but she hated me again. You see she'd just regained her figure and didn't want to have another baby. We had a row and she told a friend she wanted to have an abortion. I know she was angry and just wanted to hurt me. To be honest, I believe Laura regretted marrying me. Once she'd had Ava, she believed she'd fulfilled her part of the bargain. Her threats concerned me, and as I couldn't watch her every second of the day, I thought it best to restrict her to the house."

I wipe a hand down my face. "You kept her prisoner in the house?"

"Not really, Sue took her anywhere she needed to go. I just took her car away." He stares into space as if remembering. "I told her it needed repairing. I lied to her to save my child. She went through the pregnancy without a hitch but had post-natal depression when Noah was born. She became unstable and needed treatment. The medication worked but it took time. When she eventually improved, I planned a party aboard the yacht. She seemed like her old self apart from the weight loss and so we went shopping to buy her what she needed. It was like old times."

I swallow the bile creeping up my throat. "And then she died. You believe she took her own life, don't you?"

"Yes." His sad eyes move over my face. "She did it to spite me."

I want to shake my head and disagree with him. Most of what he's told me is the same as what Laura has written in her diary but she didn't hate Jack enough to take her own life. "That's why you've kept her alive in this house, because you feel guilty."

"I guess so." He gives himself a shake. "Let's not talk about this any longer. Laura was seven years ago and I'd rather be talking about you right now. How was your day?"

If I tell him, he'll never believe me.

I'm enjoying playing tennis with Ava and Noah. I had no idea the estate had a tennis court. What we're playing doesn't resemble tennis in the slightest but we're having fun. I laugh. "I believe the idea is to hit the ball over the net and not at your brother, Ava."

"It's much more fun." Ava giggles and bounces a ball on her racket. "Maybe I've invented a new game?"

"I'm hot and thirsty." Noah hands me his racket and wipes a hand over his face. "Can we go back now? Sue is baking chocolate chip cookies."

I look at Ava. "How does that sound to you?"

"It sounds just fine." She walks beside me, swinging her racket as we exit the court. "Do you think we could go to the beach one day as a family? Daddy is always so busy but I'm sure you'll be able to convince him to come with us. Every time I ask him, Ruby comes up with something else for him to do."

I keep one eye on Noah bounding along in front of us, swishing his racket back and forth at the bushes, and smile at her. "It's Ruby's job to make sure that your dad doesn't forget to do important things and sometimes those things run into weekends, I'm afraid. He runs a big company with many employees and needs to keep on top of things even if it means taking some time away from us. I asked him the other day to give Ruby weekends off but I imagine if something important comes up she must tell him."

"So will you ask him?" Ava looks at me, her eyes filled with anticipation.

I smile at her. "Of course I will. Or maybe we can go for a drive tomorrow? My new SUV will be arriving today and we can take it for a spin."

"I hope not." Ava looks at me aghast. "I don't figure I'd enjoy spinning in a car."

At the house I wait for the children to stow the rackets into a closet and we all head into the kitchen for cookies and milk. I smile at Jack as we walk past his office and he jumps up to join us. "If my car arrives today, can we take the kids out tomorrow? It would be a lovely family outing just the four of us."

"I'd like that. I rarely have time to go out these days." He leans over to brush a kiss against my lips. "I've forgotten how to enjoy myself."

"Eww." Noah pulls a face. "Boys don't kiss girls. Mrs. Downey said boys must shake hands with girls until they're twenty-one."

"Well, we're both over twenty-one, so I guess it's okay?" Jack ruffles Noah's black curls and grins at him.

The kitchen is empty and I take down glasses and then find the freshly baked cookies and place them on the table. I wave the kids to the sink. "Wash your hands."

While they're busy, I fill the glasses and pour cookies onto a plate from the cookie jar. The kids sit around the table and I get a warm fuzzy feeling with us all being together. I feel like I belong with these three people. I want this feeling to last. I look at Jack and a surge of love rushes over me. *Oh, please don't let him be a murderer.*

"We could go to the beach." Jack turns to the children. "Can you swim? You know, I've never asked Jenny."

"Doh! Dad, of course we can swim." Ava rolls her eyes. "Jenny has been taking us into the pool since we could walk. We swim just fine."

"That's good to know." Jack dips his cookie into his milk and then pops it into his mouth. "I used to get into trouble for dunking my cookies as a kid, so I do it now just because I can."

I shake my head. "Don't go jumping off any buildings like a superhero now, will you?" I smile. "I gather that is another rule we all had drummed into us as children?"

"Jack." Ruby walks into the room and surveys the happy scene. "I'm sorry to disturb you but we need to discuss the Bond contract. It's due to be finalized by Monday."

I place a hand on Jack's arm as he begins to rise and look at Ruby. "We have new rules for the weekends, Ruby. You're overworked, and so we want you to take the weekends for yourself."

"Jack, you know this is impossible." Ruby lifts her arms and drops them at her sides. "Your clients are worldwide; we often need to liaise with them at weekends."

"Maybe that was possible before I remarried but I must consider Willow's happiness and I need to spend more time with the children." Jack shakes his head. "The contract can wait."

Ruby is work-focused. It can't be healthy not to want time to herself. I can see anxiety flash across her eyes. I lift my gaze to her. "Please take some time for yourself, go shopping, visit friends. Jack will manage just fine without you for the weekends. We've decided from now on family comes first. Weekends are family time and tomorrow we're going to the beach. I'm afraid the Bond contract will need to wait until Monday." I look at Jack. "I assume if you're finalizing it, they've already agreed on terms."

"Yes, we have." Jack nods. "The lawyers in the office will have the final contract on Monday."

I look at Ruby and smile. "I'm sure you understand we'd like to have time together with the children this weekend. Mr. Hunter will give it a final read through at work on Monday." I look at Jack. "Does that work for you?"

"Yeah." He leans forward in his chair, takes another cookie from the plate and nods at Ruby. "Thanks, Ruby. I'll see you at the office on Monday." He smiles at her. "Go and have some fun."

"Is that true?" Noah looks from one to the other of us. "Are you really going to be at home every weekend now?"

"I intend to be unless something very important comes up." Jack smiles. "I'll give Jenny the rest of the day off and tomorrow as well, while we're at the beach."

"Oh, good." Ava laughs. "We usually do our homework on Saturday afternoons."

"You'll still need to do your homework." Jack frowns then. "If you dash and do it now, you'll have time to do what you want for the rest of the day."

"I'm playing games." Ava punches the air, and grins at Noah. "Coming?"

"We don't need any help, Mom." Noah looks at me. "We've got this."

"I'll be checking later." Jack waves them away.

I turn to Jack. "I guess they'll get plenty of exercise tomorrow."

"I guess they will." He gives me a long considering stare. "I didn't know you knew anything about contracts?"

I sip my milk and wish it was coffee. "I'm an actor and my life was surrounded by contracts. The one with my agent, and contracts for any work I performed—all contracts. I know the process and how to read one to make sure I'm not being screwed. Trust doesn't come into it in business; it all comes down to the bottom line." I smile. "I had my agent to make the negotiations but I made sure I read everything and paid a contract lawyer to look over each one for me before I signed."

"Beautiful and smart." Jack stretches and then stands and holds out his hand. "It's a beautiful day. Walk with me in the rose garden."

He leads me outside. I loop my arm through Jack's and lean into him. The scent from the roses is like a wall of perfume that subtly changes as we move from bed to bed. The colors are glorious and, if they didn't have thorns, I'd like to walk through them and touch their delicate petals. The sun is warm on my face and the grass soft and springy beneath my shoes. As we walk an idea springs into my head. There is one other player in the game I haven't spoken to: Tom. How can I get to him? "I know how busy you are at work but can I drop by on Monday, maybe just before lunch, and take a tour of your building?"

"I'll be in meetings all morning, I'm afraid, but I'll organize a pass for you, so you can at least see the building." He frowns. "I'll give you the code to the parking lot too. I might be able to squeeze in a lunch date with you, at a little bistro next door." He snaps his fingers. "I know, I'll get Tom to show you around and, when you're done, we'll have lunch. I'll get Ruby to book us a table at one o'clock. How does that sound?"

I can't believe my luck. "Tom? Is he the same person who had a relationship with Ruby?"

"Oh, you know about that?" Jack raises both eyebrows. "It was a long time ago, water under the bridge. He is my head of security and I trust him. Who told you about Tom?"

I lean into him. "Ruby. She mentioned the argument you had with him the night Laura died."

"I'd almost forgotten about the argument. It was inconsequential when Laura went overboard." Jack stops walking and looks at me. "Laura caught them kissing in the galley. She figured it was inappropriate, Tom making out with Ruby when he was supposed to be watching my back. I could see her point and spoke to him. It got a little heated but it was seconds, not drawn out. I fired him." He draws in a breath. "I thought it through later and Ruby said it was just a spur of the moment thing that happened. It meant nothing to either of them. I rehired him but insisted he move out of the house and I demoted him. He runs the security team now, so that's a long-time job. Personal security isn't something I need. I can take care of myself. Hiring him was Ruby's idea and it was a mistake. Thinking back, I did it because he was a friend since college, someone I thought I could trust."

I nod. "Do you still trust him?"

"Yeah, I do. He runs the security team well and I've never had a problem." Jack stares up at the house. "You're right about this house. I figured it was a status symbol but my companies are that and more. I will consider moving into a new place or something modern as long as it overlooks the beach. This place holds bad memories and I want my life to go forward with you. Finding a suitable residence to house all my staff will be difficult but leave it with me. I'll contact some of the people I know. Building a new one is an option but will take forever. I'm sure I'll find a house we'll both like." He smiles at me. "Would that make you happy?"

I stare at him a little dumbfounded. One mention of the night Laura died and suddenly his position on everything has changed. I smile broadly. "That would be wonderful. We can make a fresh start with no bad memories."

"That's the plan." Jack looks deep into my eyes. "It's time to leave the ghosts in Beauford Manor."

THIRTY-SIX

MONDAY

Jack has left for work and I take out Laura's laptop to see if she'd written anything more about her affair with Tom. A sudden thought grips me as I scroll through the pages. Has Jack read these entries? Did he know that Tom had an affair with Laura? I consider the implications if Jack knew about the affair *before* the anniversary party on board the yacht. What if he found out that night? Would it be a motive for killing her? If he isn't aware of the diary on the laptop, it leaves me with the moral dilemma of whether I should tell him. The problem being that it would likely destroy Tom's life, because I have no doubt that Jack would fire him again. He mentioned in the garden that he trusted him and that trust would be shattered.

The other part of the puzzle is whether Ruby knew about the affair between Laura and Tom. Has she been keeping a secret all these years to protect Jack from the truth or make sure he had no reason to be suspected of Laura's murder?

As far as I'm aware there was no police investigation into Laura's death until the coroner's report came down seven years later to say she was lost at sea. I can only assume that, when the accident was reported, law enforcement didn't consider foul play. The witnesses on board must have convinced them that Laura fell overboard. Why wasn't there an investigation? I'll ask Tom when I see him and hope that he's honest. I find the file and scroll through the pages. Laura must have been desperate to have Tom in her bed with Jack sleeping right next door. If Jack was giving her meds each night, who did she believe was drugging her food? He'd be at work during the day. I'll ask Sue before I leave if she administered any daily medication to Laura. If she didn't, who did... unless someone else was involved? Who would gain from keeping Laura in a drugged state? Then, what if everything was in Laura's mind and she wasn't drugged at all?

August 20

With Tom on my side, bringing me meals and occasionally sharing my bed, I manage to avoid most of the drugs. Although my phone is still missing, no doubt to keep me isolated, I've stopped asking the staff to search for it. I'm becoming sneaky and now I'm watching them. They have no idea I've been listening to Jack whispering to them about me in the hallways. Each day I'm getting stronger. Having Tom living in the house is a double-edged sword. Our attraction is strong but I'm sure the staff are becoming suspicious. It concerns Tom that one hint of anything between us, Jack will ruin him for life and kick me to the curb.

I read the entry twice. Maybe she was feeling better because of Tom's attention and not because she wasn't being drugged? The next entry is five days later. I can almost feel Laura's confusion. She's spiraling out of control.

August 25

I've ended my fling with Tom. A few things he said to me didn't add up and now I don't trust him. I'm starting to believe his so-called attraction toward me was part of a plan. I'm sure our affair was to give Jack an excuse to divorce me and take the kids. Looking back, it's obvious to me now. Even so, ending the affair hurt me. I cried for days and I'm fighting overpowering depression.

I know Jack is involved in this charade as he keeps Tom close but hardly looks at me. I'm spiraling out of control. Days go by and I don't notice. I have blanks in my memory and the worst part of it is that, now, Tom is turning his attention to Ruby. He figures I don't know but I've seen them sneaking around together.

I need to fight back and stop them feeding me drugs. So I have started ordering takeout. Not one person questioned me about that but now my medication arrives three times a day and Sue stands and watches me take it. The little pills are easy to hide and they all go into the toilet.

The question of Tom comes up again. Is he involved as another facet of Laura's delusions? I'm glad my question about the meds is answered. If she'd been given medication to help her condition and not taken it, it would account for her rapid deterioration. I lean back in my chair and stare out of the window. In some ways I feel sorry for Laura. It seems to me that she pushed people away and ended up with no one to turn to. What I need to determine is whether my husband is guilty of her death or innocent. I'm torn between the Jack Laura portrays in her diaries, and the man I know. Although he admitted he married Laura out of duty rather than love, I honestly can't see him being cruel to her like she insists. Even after she almost killed their son, he didn't divorce her but remained by her side and sought professional help for her. It must have been terrible for Jack, watching his wife slide into insanity.

I shake my head trying to avoid the doubt and confusion sneaking into my mind. I'm making excuses for Jack because I love him and I can't allow my feelings to cloud my judgment—my life might depend on it. I slowly weigh up every piece of information I've gathered. I need to speak to Tom before I come to any conclusion because he is the last player in this tragedy. Did Jack discover Laura was having an affair with Tom—or did he plan it? If not, it would give Jack a motive to kill her, but would he dirty his own hands or ask Tom to do it? After all, money was no option. But what if it was an unplanned affair? I know Laura informed Jack about Ruby's affair. I believe jealousy drove her to do it and she wanted to hurt Tom—a woman scorned and all that. How far would Tom go to prevent Laura from telling Jack about their affair? Laura had no love for Jack, she despised him, so hurting him wouldn't be in the equation, but she'd know Jack would ruin Tom. In Laura's state of mind, it would only be a matter of time before she twisted the knife and told Jack—it would be the ultimate victory—two lives destroyed in one go. So now, I'm sure, either Jack or Tom murdered Laura. She didn't fall from the yacht; she was an experienced sailor. I've no doubt someone pushed her.

I collect the keys for my silver BMW, tell the GPS where I want to go and set off. My car has that new car smell and drives like a dream. I follow the coast road enjoying the sights of my new home. I try to make mental notes of the different stores and features along the way but the opulence of the area is a little overwhelming. As I enter the city the traffic is horrendous and it takes longer than I expect. Relief floods over me when I spot the glass and metal building. I follow the ramp to the underground parking lot and punch the code into the panel. A metal gate grinds open and I drive inside. As instructed, I head for the elevator sign and find six bays with J. Hunter written above them in bright-yellow lettering. I park beside Jack's red Porsche and collect my purse. I drop a lanyard over my head and make my way to the elevator.

The man standing behind a long desk in the foyer gives me a curious stare as I walk toward him. I push my purse under one arm and smile. "I'm Mrs. Hunter. I believe Tom is waiting for me to arrive?"

"Right away, Mrs. Hunter." He lifts a phone on his desk and presses a button. "Tom, Mrs. Hunter has arrived."

A tall man with sandy hair comes out of a room and walks toward me and then does a double take. I hold out my hand. "You must be Tom. Jack has told me so much about you." I smile. "Have I got food in my teeth?"

"Ah—no." Tom's cheeks pink. "I'm sorry for staring. You remind me of someone I knew in college."

I nod. "Caroline?" I smile and we shake hands. "Yes, I know. I've seen pictures of her. Tragic accident, I believe, like Laura. I hope three's not a charm and that I don't suddenly fall off a building or something."

"I hope not." Tom stares at me. "Jack has had enough sadness in his life. Where would you like to start?"

I glance toward his office door. "Is there someplace in here I can get a coffee?"

"Sure, I have a coffee machine in my office." He smiles and it's a nice smile. "Jack is a great boss. He makes sure we have plenty of coffee so we stay awake on the job."

I shut the door as I walk inside his office and he gives me an inquiring stare. "I'd like a private chat, if you don't mind?"

"Not at all." Tom goes to the coffee machine. "Make yourself at home. Jack is very happy. I've never seen him smile so much, since you married." He hands me coffee in a nice big mug.

I sit opposite his desk and sip the brew he made for me. "That's good to know. I'm happy too. Although I hate the house. I wish we could live anywhere but there. The building is spectacular but it ends at the front door. Inside, the place is a decaying mass of rubble." I sigh. "That's not what I want to speak to you about. Do you mind talking to me about the night Laura died?"

"No, not at all." He smiles. "Jack mentioned you were curious about what happened. I'm glad to help."

I lean forward. "It's difficult stepping into Laura's shoes. I understand she wasn't exactly stable around that time. What do you remember about that night?"

"What exactly do you want to know?" Tom curls large hands around his coffee cup. "I went over it one hundred times with the police."

I stare at him. "So, there was a police investigation? I couldn't find anything about it in any old newspapers. All I found was the coroner's verdict."

"We were all taken away separately and interviewed the day after she fell overboard." Tom shrugs. "I gave my statement about what had happened. Everyone went over it repeatedly but nothing came of it. She was there one moment and the next she'd vanished."

I finish my coffee and place the mug on his desk. "I'd really like to know the timeline. I'm aware of a few things. I know Jack had an argument with Laura and she went on deck and then there was a disagreement between you and Jack that evening just before Laura went missing. It was about you having a relationship with Ruby. I know that Laura told him about it. I also know that she'd just finished an affair with you. Do you believe she told Jack about Ruby to spite you? I know about the non-fraternization rule that he insisted be upheld."

If I ever need an example of the word dumbfounded, I will always think of Tom's expression at that moment. "Ah, I see. Jack doesn't know about you and Laura, does he?"

"I always believed that Laura took that information to the

grave with her." Tom's face drains of color. "How did you find out?"

I lean back in my chair and cross my legs. "Don't worry, I don't intend to tell Jack. He doesn't need to know that information and it would only cause you trouble. I'm sure that over the last seven years you've put all this behind you and have made a better life for yourself."

"I'm married with kids." His hands ball into fists on the table. "It was a stupid thing to do. She was a very beautiful woman and I was just trying to comfort her and things got out of hand. I managed to stop it after a couple of days but she was very clinging and dependent. When she started threatening to tell Jack and told me about missing time and hearing people whispering about her in the walls, I realized how sick she was and ended it. I chased Ruby to show Laura we were over. So yeah, Laura told Jack about me and Ruby out of spite. I was glad to be out of the house. I figured Laura could be dangerous. I know she tried to drown Noah. She hated those kids."

I lap up the new information and nod in all the right places. "And what happened the night she died? I know who the players are, as in who was there at the party. Let's start with the weather."

"The weather was fine when we left but when I went out on deck to speak to Ruby after the argument with Jack, the wind was picking up and it had just started to rain." He sighs. "Jack fired me and I asked Ruby to speak to him. He does what she says most times. Ruby has a way of handling him, as in she just about wipes his ass."

I remain silent and allow him to talk.

"Ruby told me we wouldn't be able to see each other again and that was fine by me." He picks up a pen and taps it annoyingly on the table. "Laura came out on deck and glared at us and then went to the stern. She often went there and stared up at the stars. It was a favorite place for her. That was the last time I saw her." He meets my gaze. "The wind was picking up and a squall was blowing in. I saw Jack heading to speak to the captain. After that we changed course and headed back toward the marina."

So, Jack was on deck at the same time as him and Ruby; that's interesting but it doesn't tell me which one of them murdered her. Or is Tom covering his own back? I lean forward. Is he telling the truth? "Who else was on deck with you?"

"I'm not sure. I didn't really take any notice. Laura, because I watched her walk to the stern. Jack, Ruby and maybe members of the crew, or any of the guests taking the air."

I nod. "So was Laura at the stern when you went inside?"

"I don't know." Tom shrugs. "I didn't look. I didn't care. She'd just ruined my life. That's all I can tell you. Later, everyone was inside apart from Laura and then Jack went to look for her. He figured she'd gone to their cabin but she wasn't there or on deck and all hell broke loose. Jack sent me to wake everyone. Ruby was in her cabin and so were Missy and June. He'd sent the staff to the galley. The men were drinking a special bottle of whisky with Jack."

I ran everything through my mind. "So at this time, you were heading back to the marina?"

"Yeah, the sea was choppy and we were getting thrown all over, but nobody seemed to care. Jack said we were heading out of the storm." Tom gives a shake of his head. "That's all I remember apart from the search. We never found a trace of her." He checks his watch and then pushes to his feet. He looks agitated as if talking about the night Laura died has torn off a Band-Aid. "Are you ready for the tour?"

The friendly man has vanished. Maybe he has something to hide? I stand. "Yeah, sure."

"There's one thing." He frowns. "Why are you rehashing all this now?"

If he suspects I know the truth, could I be in danger? I smile at him, acting nonchalant as I drop the bombshell.

"I found her diary."

THIRTY-SEVEN

My words hit Tom like a sucker punch and, as if too shocked to master the impact of what I just told him, his eyes go blank as he stares into space. His mouth opens slightly—but nothing comes out. I can almost see the gears in his mind spinning, fighting for an explanation to give me. All at once his expression hardens. I stare at him, waiting for the denial, the excuse for sleeping with his boss and once best friend's wife.

"What exactly did she write?" A pulse pounds in his neck as he takes a step closer to me.

I take a step back as he invades my personal space. I choose not to elaborate. "Everything."

"Do you honestly believe that Laura's fantasies mean anything?" Tom shifts from one foot to the other. "She had a very vivid imagination."

I shake my head and meet his gaze. "She writes as if she's leaving the truth for someone to find. I believe she figured something would happen to her."

"You have no idea what she was like toward the end." Tom's lips press into a thin line. "She said so many things that didn't make sense. She saw ghosts and heard voices. I was just trying to help her is all." He barks a humorless laugh. "So much for being Mr. Nice Guy."

I rest one hand on the door handle. I'm not happy with the strange look in his eyes but I raise my chin. What could possibly happen to me in this busy office building? "I know she believed the staff were against her. She mentioned them moving things and spying on her. Do you figure any of them were involved? I understand she might have been a little unstable but I'm certainly not, and some strange things have happened to me since I've been in the house too."

"It's an old house." Tom lifts one shoulder in a half shrug. "It creaks and groans. I believed I'd heard voices at one time but it turned out to be coming through the ventilation grates."

I nod. "Yeah, I've heard them myself but I investigated where the noise was coming from, rather than making myself believe the house was haunted. The diary is mind-blowing. When I arrived here, I was led to believe that Laura was a loving wife and mother and her diary tells me a completely different story."

"So, you figure the diary is going to give you answers, because all it will do is ruin lives? You know that, right?" He raises one eyebrow. "Jack won't be happy if he discovers you've been digging into his past. You're just about accusing him and me of murder. How long do you believe your marriage will last if he figures you don't trust him?"

I can see his point but it doesn't stop me from wanting to know what happened the night Laura died. "I need to know the truth. Someone on that yacht murdered Laura."

"Do you want to know what I believe happened that night? I figure she jumped. It would be the ultimate insult to Jack." He shrugs. "You should destroy the diary before Jack finds out and it comes back to kick you in the butt."

THIRTY-EIGHT

I enjoy the tour of the building. Jack has given his employees every comfort in the massive metal and glass building. As I enter his office suite, I'm impressed with the layout. Julia, his secretary, sits out in front of two closed office doors and an open door to a conference room. Bronze metal plates tell me that one office belongs to Jack and the other to Ruby. I walk right up to the desk. "I'm Mrs. Hunter. Can you please tell Jack that I'm here?"

She doesn't acknowledge my request but picks up the phone, presses a button and avoids my gaze.

"Mrs. Hunter is here." Julia replaces the receiver and moves her attention back to her computer screen.

How rude. A door opens and Ruby smiles at me. "How did you enjoy your tour?" She waves me inside her office. "Come in and take a seat. Can I get you anything? Coffee, water?"

I ignore the seat she is trying to make me sit in and look at her. "No, thanks. I did enjoy the tour. The building is very impressive." I glance over one shoulder. "Jack is expecting me for lunch; maybe I should wait outside?"

"Lunch?" Ruby scans her tablet. "He hasn't made any plans

for lunch today. Maybe you were mistaken? He is very busy with clients all day. Most times he just orders in sandwiches and eats them between appointments. I believe I mentioned on Saturday that taking the weekend off would mean he'd have double work on Monday?"

I recall no such thing. "Well, perhaps I've been mistaken. Can you point the way to the bathroom please?"

She gives me directions and I slip out into the hallway. I use the facilities but while I'm there I send a text to Jack informing him that I'm waiting in Ruby's office to go to lunch. Maybe he made the booking himself and forgot to tell Ruby? He doesn't reply but I guess if he's in a meeting he wouldn't be looking at his phone. I head back to Ruby's office and knock on the door and then enter. "I'll wait here and try to catch Jack between his meetings."

"I'm afraid you may have a long wait." Ruby scrolls through files on her tablet. "We've been flat out all day." She leans back in her chair and stares at me. "It's like this most times."

I feel I need to say something. "Has Jack mentioned searching for a new house? We were thinking something more modern and overlooking the beach. He was going to contact the local Realtors to see what's available. It will be very exciting looking at new homes, don't you agree?"

"Really? How strange." Ruby gives me an incredulous look. "Only just this morning he approved the renovations on the house. Why would he bother if he'd decided to move? Unless he wants to modernize it for you. You enjoy interior design, I believe?" She taps her nails on the desktop and chews on her bottom lip.

I look at her. "Yes, it was an option we discussed."

"I honestly can't imagine Jack wanting to leave Beauford Manor. It's a status symbol around these parts. Moving to a different estate would make people believe his business is failing." She clears her throat. "I'll ask him about it. He usually values my advice."

Her advice about what? I know Ruby is indispensable to Jack. She runs his day so he doesn't have to think about it but it's our decision if we move or not. Is she implying that she would advise him not to move? Or have I got it all wrong? I push my mind back to what Jack said to me. He did mention moving, didn't he, or has my desire to leave Beauford Manor twisted my memory? I give myself a mental shake. Maybe Ruby is gaslighting me. I'm new in her world and she hasn't quite worked me out yet. "Do you really believe that? I'm sure there are other huge estates more suitable to our needs."

"This company is what I guess you'd call from old money. It has generations of Hunters behind it and carries a reputation of trust." Ruby gives me a withering look. "Our clients expect certain standards. Moving is change and they don't like change. Personally, I'd advise him not to move, for the sake of the company." She looks at me, and her eyebrows raise. "Are you sure he mentioned purchasing another estate? Maybe you should ask him to clarify the situation?" She shakes her head slowly and looks at me as if I'm in need of guidance. "I imagine everything is overwhelming for you and it's easy to misinterpret Jack's intentions. He did mention the tour but if there'd been a lunch date, he'd have asked me to make the reservation and I'm afraid he didn't. I'm sure he'll explain when you see him."

I suddenly feel very young, like a kid in the principal's office. I guess she means well but I'm not Laura and forgetful isn't in my vocabulary. I know darn well that Jack asked me to go to lunch with him after I finished my tour. It was *his* suggestion, not mine. Has he really forgotten? I guess I'll find out soon enough. I cross my legs and lean back in my chair. "I'm sorry to interrupt your work. Don't worry about me, I'll just wait until Jack's meeting is over and then I'll have a few words with him before I go home."

She looks away and I glance at my watch. It's almost one. I soon hear voices in the foyer and Jack pokes his head around the door. I'm so glad to see him, I jump to my feet. "There you are. Ruby has been keeping me company."

"We can walk to the bistro from here." Jack flashes me a white smile and holds out his hand. He glances at Ruby. "I'll be back in time for my two-thirty."

"I don't have lunch with Mrs. Hunter on your schedule." Ruby sends him a disapproving glare. "I have already ordered you sandwiches."

"I'm sure you'll enjoy them." Jack grins at her and tugs me toward the door.

In the elevator I turn to him. "She doesn't seem too happy that you're escaping for lunch. Does she schedule your bathroom breaks as well?"

"Just about." He leads the way out of the building and we walk along a busy street until we come to a bistro. "I would have mentioned it to her but she would find a reason for me to stay in the office." He sighs and pulls open the door. "I understand why she needs to be kept informed of my movements; she likes to fit as much into one day as possible."

I can see Ruby is indispensable to him and the running of the office. I push her to the back of my mind and walk through the door. The moment we step inside, a waiter comes forward and takes us to a table. It's obvious that Jack is a regular customer. I inhale and my stomach rumbles in anticipation. The bistro has the wonderful aroma of fresh coffee laced with the mingled sensory delights of foreign spices and baking. I glance around at the cozy tables, each with a pristine white tablecloth. A low mumble of conversation winds its way around us along with the clink of polished silver tableware. I glance at the menu and my heart misses a beat at the prices. I could feed myself for a week for the price of lunch here.

"Is there a problem?" Jack's eyes narrow. "If there's nothing you like, I can ask the chef to prepare something else."

I smile at him. "It all looks wonderful. What do you recommend?"

"A favorite for me is the lobster salad roll with coleslaw and hand-cut fries. It goes well with a glass of Sauvignon Blanc." Jack's gaze moves over my face. "You look so beautiful. I can't believe you wanted someone like me."

I laugh. "You say the nicest things. I'll have the lobster as well."

"Did you enjoy the tour?" Jack orders and then swings his gaze back to me. "Did Tom answer all your questions?"

I lean back in my chair, wishing I could tell him everything I've discovered but I hold my tongue. "He was very informative." It wasn't a lie. "There's so much about you I don't know. You've all been together since college. It was inevitable that the conversation ended up with Laura's accident."

"Really?" Jack raises one eyebrow, breadstick in one hand. "What did he say?"

I lean forward and rest my hands on the silky clean tablecloth. "He didn't actually say much, I asked him questions. Do you recall where he was that night?"

"The accident again?" Jack lets out a long sigh. "You need to drop this madness now, Willow. This obsessive behavior isn't healthy."

I cover his hand and look deep into his eyes. "I'm not Laura and I'm not crazy. Indulge me. *Please*, Jack. Put my mind at rest. Try and remember."

"It's been a long time, Willow, but when the weather changed, I went to speak to the captain; it was too noisy to use the phone. As I went into the wheelhouse, I saw Laura looking at the stars. Ruby and Tom were on deck." He drops the breadstick onto a side plate and narrows his gaze. "Two of the crew were preparing for rough seas when I went back inside. I told all this to the police when they questioned us. Later, Ruby and the other women went to their cabins, everyone had been drinking. The men, including Tom, sat around drinking whisky and talking about old times." He frowns at me. "You're not suggesting Tom had something to do with her death, are you?"

I meet his gaze. "I'm not sure. I've been thinking about it and he had a motive as she'd told you about his affair with Ruby."

"If Tom had tried to toss Laura overboard, he'd have gotten hurt. She could fight like a wild cat and he didn't have a mark on him." He sighs. "Can we drop this and enjoy our time together?"

I squeeze his hand. "Sure, I'm sorry."

My conversation with Ruby springs to mind. "Ruby mentioned you plan to go ahead with the renovations. Is there any point to that if we plan to move?"

"That was last Friday." Jack frowns. "I haven't signed anything yet. I'll call the supervisor when I get back to the office and cancel them. It slipped my mind this morning."

Last Friday? Didn't Ruby tell me he'd given the go-ahead this morning or had I misheard? Perhaps I need to stop obsessing over Laura's death and get my head on straight. I glance at my phone. As I'm suddenly becoming so forgetful, I'll make notes on my calendar and then I'll know for sure if I'm falling down a rabbit hole—or being pushed.

Our meal arrives and we eat slowly. I enjoy every morsel and when Jack recommends the raspberry sorbet for dessert, I accept. I look at him across the table. "Now you have me to make sure your suits are dry-cleaned and you're dressed for every occasion, why does Ruby need to live with us? Surely as she doesn't need to be on hand twenty-four/seven, she'd enjoy a place of her own. Maybe now she's not working weekends, she might be able to find herself a husband. It's like slave labor expecting her to work the hours she does. You only really need her to organize your work day and make reservations for you, don't you?"

"You're not jealous of her, are you? Because there's absolutely no need for you to be jealous of Ruby. I have never had any feelings for her whatsoever. Laura always believed there was something more between us and I'm not sure if I could cope with that again." He runs a hand down his face. "I met Ruby when we were helping in an office of a candidate during an election. You know the way most students do. She impressed me how well organized she was, so when I started working in the company, I asked her if she would be interested in becoming my personal assistant. She's been with me ever since, and I've never had a problem with her."

I laugh and squeeze his hand. "Jealous of Ruby? Heavens, no. I'm sure if there was anything between you, it would have developed by now or if you'd had a relationship, I doubt you'd still be working together. I just find her a little defensive is all. I mean, before we left for lunch, the look she gave you for not informing her you'd be out almost turned me to stone."

"Yeah, she can be a little intense sometimes." Jack sips his wine and sighs. "I usually just go with the flow to keep her in a good mood. You're right, she does need a man in her life. As far as I'm aware there hasn't been anyone since her breakup with Tom." He stares into space and then smiles. "I have apartment buildings. I could offer her one rent free as part of her employment contract. Her contract comes up for renewal the end of this month."

I blink. "So, her living with us is in her contract? Whose idea was that?"

"She practically writes her own contract. I approve it and then it goes to the lawyers." Jack's blue eyes scan my face as if trying to read my motive. "Why?"

I shrug. "We need our time together, the kids need their dad and Ruby needs a life. I figure it's time to cut the cord, Jack."

"What exactly do you mean?" Jack turns his glass around in his long, manicured fingers.

I smile. "Bring in an assistant PA, to ease her workload. I know Ruby is very protective of you." I laugh to make light of the uncomfortable situation. "She wanted to send me home today and insisted I'd made a mistake about our lunch date. I'm your wife. If I decide to wait to speak to you between meetings, that's my business not hers. Same with your secretary. She guards you like a pit bull."

"That's so funny." Jack laughs so loud diners on other tables glare at him. "I guess it's because you look so young. They can't believe I'm married to you. I'll have a word with them." He shakes his head. "In corporate business, sometimes it's good to have a couple of pit bulls guarding the CEO's office. I often have people trying to speak to me but, you, my love, I'll always have time for. However, please, if I'm in with a client, unless the house is on fire or the kids are in danger, wait until after the meeting."

I grin. "I understand, but you will consider giving Ruby some slack? I figure she's earned it after all these years."

"I will but getting her to accept is another matter." He chuckles. "I guess if she refuses, I can fire her? The problem with that is I might come to work the next day and find my building razed to the ground."

I look at him as he waves for the check and I'm not sure if he's joking.

THIRTY-NINE

I've often wondered why the wives of the wealthy work for charities and other useful distractions; it's because they are bored silly. The moment I arrived home this afternoon, my options were to walk around the garden, watch TV or go and sit in my room. The children won't be home for hours. I need something to pass the time. I'd enjoy watching Pierre prepare for the evening meal but the upstairs–downstairs mentality that I'd assumed had vanished in Victorian England is well and truly alive in Rhode Island. I'd like to spend time in the kitchen, as it's always the hub of a house, but the moment I step one foot inside I feel like a foreigner. The longer I'm here, the worse it gets but I have heard Ruby telling the staff to remember that I'm not one of them. The thing is, when I arrive, any conversation ceases immediately and starts up again as I leave. I've made a habit of pausing to listen and it's usually about me. I nod to the staff working in the kitchen, fill a mug with coffee, add the fixings and walk out the door. I pause in the hallway.

"What's wrong with her today?" Sue's voice drifts toward me. "I figure Mr. Hunter has had a few words with her about taking our keys. I mean, who does she think she is? She arrives here and then tries to change everything. I knew he wouldn't agree to it."

"I wonder how long this one will last." Amy stifles a chuckle.

"If she keeps going up to the third floor, anything might happen." Sue lowers her voice and I can almost see her leaning closer to Amy. "Strange things happen up there and I heard that more than two of the women that lived here in the past had been dragged away screaming after wandering around up there. A hundred years ago if a person ended up in a sanatorium, they never left."

"What did you hear about the third floor?" Amy's voice rises. "Do people say it's haunted? I've always figured it was just rats that lived up there."

"Nah, they don't say it's haunted." Pierre chuckles. "Think about it. The rooms are so tiny and claustrophobic and you can hear conversations, like whispering through the heating ducts. Those women figured they'd gone mad."

So, they hoped I'd go mad and be locked away in a psychiatric ward? How nice. I climb the stairs and this time I stare into the eyes of Laura. Secrets and lies surround her and I have no solution to the mystery of her death. Strangely, I feel sorry for her, even though the woman is a thorn in my side and dominates my marriage. For my own peace of mind, I need to get to the end of her story. Inside my bedroom I set my coffee on the desk in front of the window and stare at the rose bushes swaying in the breeze. Diving back into Laura's diary is placing my own peace of mind at risk. I believe reading the thoughts of someone who is obviously mentally disturbed is upsetting me more than I realize.

Reluctantly I take the laptop out of the drawer, place it on the table and plug it into the power. It's as if something is compelling me to do it rather than my own free will. I can't fight against it. I need to know what happened. Trepidation creeps over me as I open the files and scan the last few entries before Laura's death. Two people mentioned she may have taken her own life and now Sue is implying the same thing. Not many people got close to her but Jack and Tom had intimate relationships with her so may have seen something in her behavior I've missed.

August 26

I took photos of Ava today and transferred them to my laptop. When I took the photographs, Ava refused to smile at me; she pulled a sad face and tugged at her hair. She always liked me to brush her hair in front of the mirror and now all she does is call for Jenny. It's as if I'm not her mother and never had children. Maybe it's a good thing because now they'll be just the way Jack wants them to be.

I make a note of the date and go through the image files until I find the photographs mentioned. I'm shocked and check the dates and go back and forth many times but what Laura describes is chilling me to the bone because I see a toddler with long dark hair. She has inquisitive dark eyes and a smile that would melt anyone's heart. Why did Laura see her as sad? What type of mental disorder did she have that caused her to see things differently to other people? Laura had been under supervision by a psychiatrist. If there had been any problems, wouldn't Jack be dealing with them by now? Unless her condition had deteriorated because she wasn't taking her medication. I imagine Jack being at his wits' end with her. It must have been a terrible time for him. I'm disturbed and weird thoughts are flying through my mind but I must read on.

August 27

I lost time again this week. I have gaps in my memory. Earlier, I passed Ruby in the hallway and noticed she was wearing my scarf. I asked her about it because it was a silk one I'd purchased in Paris. She laughed at me and told me I'd given it to her for her birthday two days previously. I know the date of her birthday—Jack always makes sure she has a special dinner with us—and it's not for a day or so. I checked the date on my laptop and I've lost two days. I have no recollection of what happened over that time. Someone is doing this to me and now I'm sure Jack is involved. I mentioned Ava's reluctance to be with me and he wanted me to spend more time with the children—not alone—never alone. He had Jenny bring them to us and I stared at Noah. He wasn't my son. I didn't recognize him and yet Jack acted as if nothing was wrong. They've switched out my son for another baby. Where is Noah?

What?! I stand so fast the chair tips over and clatters to the floor. Shock trembles through me and I take a few steps away from the laptop as if demons are going to pour from it. Missing time was bad enough but I know enough to know not being able to recognize her own child or misreading their expression is paranoia. The entire entry is laced with confusion and the unsettling idea that someone was manipulating her reality—but who—and why? By this time Tom wasn't living at the house, so that left Jack. If Laura's condition wasn't induced by drugs maybe she did take her own life. She'd been living in a confused state of hell for months.

I can't read on and close the laptop and hide it back in the drawer. I need to get out of this horrible house. I grab one of Jack's ball caps and head out the back door and walk to the beach.

The sound of the waves crashing on the wet sand and the

sun sparkling on the ocean lift my spirits. I've only known Jack for a short time. It hasn't even been six months yet but I believe deep down in my heart he's a good man. I admit I had my suspicions but I really don't believe that he murdered Laura. I will speak to him when he returns home about her health the few weeks before her death. One thing I can't get my head around is the fact that she was well enough to go to a celebration on the yacht the night she died. From what the staff told me previously, and the diary entries, she sounded too far gone to be able to be taken out in public.

I walk, leaving my footprints in the pristine sand. The shore break wets the beach and, as the wave is pulled back into the ocean, it leaves a golden sparkle and the sound of rolling pebbles. I allow the sound to filter through my brain, calming me and helping me to think clearly. Laura mentioned the fear of being drugged and took every precaution. Why did she believe she was being drugged? It doesn't make sense that the medication given to her by the psychiatrist would cause paranoia and delusions. I need to discover what medication she was taking and then search for it on the internet to find out what it's for and how it affects people. I'm wondering now if it's time to tell Jack about the diary. My only concern is that if Tom isn't involved, what will happen to him when Jack discovers he had an affair with Laura?

My head fills with images of Jack and my stomach drops. Just being with him makes me believe my life has changed for the better. My time with him is wonderful. I honestly couldn't ask for a more considerate or gentle husband. I don't believe he intentionally deceived me about his tragic past but I didn't expect to be thrown into a web of lies and deception. It's over seven years since Laura died and yet it's as if she's still here, waiting for the truth to come out about her death. I don't know if she jumped or was pushed. In her state of mind, anything is possible. When I read her diary, I felt sorry for her and now, knowing her inner thoughts, I feel as if I've lived through the breakdown with her. I turn and stare at the house. I can make out Laura's bedroom window—*Laura's bedroom*—Laura's home. Laura, Laura, Laura...

Will she ever be gone from the house and my life?

FORTY

I really enjoy spending time with the children. From when they come home from school until I read them a story at night is a happy, fulfilling time for me. They greet me with hugs and I know deep down in my heart that I will make them a good mother, and hope that someday I will have a child of my own. I haven't discussed children with Jack. I'm not sure why the topic hasn't come up but I now believe it's because of what he went through with Laura. Things seemed to be okay with her before she had Ava and, from that point onward, she deteriorated rapidly—unless someone in this house caused her to become unstable. It's this issue that weighs heavily on me now. Each evening, we sit with the children while they eat their dinner but we prefer to have ours after they've gone to bed. It's a nice relaxing and private time for us together.

After my tour of the office, Jack enthusiastically asks me questions about my impressions. I discover he designed and built the building after his grandfather's death. The previous building had been old and didn't have the modern edge necessary to bolster his image in the building industry. I listen and nod in all the right places but questions about Laura's last days are burning on my tongue. As the dessert dishes are cleared away, and a fruit, cheese and cracker board appears on the table along with our coffee, I turn to look at him. "I know you really don't want to discuss this but there are some things I need to know about your past."

"It's difficult putting Laura behind me when you're constantly bringing her up again. No good will come of talking about her and rehashing her life. Let it drop and leave the past undisturbed."

I need to know and push him. Seeing him tense, I know I've hit a nerve. "Please, Jack. You said no secrets, so let's be honest with each other, no matter the cost."

"You just won't let it lie, will you? She's dead—end of story." Jack gives me a withering look. "Okay, if you've got something on your mind, we need to get it out into the open and then move on with our lives. We won't be taking Laura with us to the new house."

Relieved, I smile at him. "That's good to know." I add sugar and cream to my cup of coffee and stir slowly, gathering my thoughts. "You mentioned one time that you believe Laura took her own life just to spite you. Why would you think that?"

"When I discovered she'd left Noah in the bathtub and walked away, I gave Jenny instructions not to ever leave the children alone with her." Jack runs his finger through a drip of coffee running down the side of his cup and then raises his gaze to me. "In truth I wanted to have her placed into psychiatric care. When I told her she wasn't to go near the children unless someone was with her, she went ballistic. Things went downhill from there."

I sip my coffee. "What kind of things?"

"She frequently told me how much she hated me." He sighs and stares into space. "She became paranoid and believed everyone was out to get her. She got it into her head that someone was drugging her but I gave her the medication each night."

I lean forward on the table, cupping my chin in the palm of my hand. "Oh, I was under the impression that Sue gave her medication three times a day? What medication was she taking?"

"It was a mild antidepressant." Jack blows out a long sigh. "I spoke to the psychiatrist about her sudden change in personality and they insisted it wasn't the medication. They changed it just in case to something else but it made no difference. Laura was losing weight; Sue made sure she took vitamin supplements three times a day with her meals. Not drugs just vitamins."

I frown. "If she was so paranoid, why take her on the yacht?"

"It was really strange." Jack rubs the back of his neck. "She went through a few days of euphoria. She was laughing and happy and back to her old self. Then she locked herself in her room and I could hear her crying but she refused to open the door. I called the psychiatrist and they just told me to watch her. When she finally opened the door, she was acting normally again. I made sure Sue watched her closely over the next week or so. It was as if someone had waved a magic wand and she was back to normal. I wanted to give her some encouragement so I arranged the celebration for our wedding anniversary." His gaze met mine. "I would never have taken her out on the yacht if I'd believed she was a danger to herself. Nothing happened during the evening that pointed toward her taking her own life."

Everything he said followed the diary entries exactly. She had stopped eating the food and was having an affair with Tom. She wasn't taking the drugs causing her hallucinations and unstable personality. When she broke up with him, she cried and then pulled herself together. I look at him. "Do you believe she considered that your marriage was over or did you make it clear to her that there was a future for the both of you?"

"I was positive with her all the time." Jack shakes his head. "She, on the other hand, spent most of her time accusing me of having affairs. I don't think she ever truly loved me and yet she was jealous of my time with other people. The psychiatrist mentioned that she had narcissistic tendencies so perhaps that was just part of her personality. She needed to be the center of attention all the time."

I gather my courage and clear my throat. "Did you ever suspect that Laura had an affair and that was why she had a sudden change in personality? She was getting the attention she craved and when it ended, she cried for a day and then pulled herself together and decided to keep going?"

"How the hell did you know about her affair?" Jack stares at me with an incredulous expression on his face. "I've never spoken about that aloud. Of course I knew about the affair; I was sleeping right next door. I'd need to be some kind of fool if I believed it took Tom an hour to deliver takeout." He barks a sarcastic laugh. "She was just using him like she used everybody but he was smart enough to walk away after a day or so." His eyes flash with anger as he looks at me. "Did Tom tell you? I'm surprised, because he values his position in the firm and would know you'd tell me."

I shake my head. "No, Tom didn't tell me. Laura did. She wrote everything in her diary. I found it in the attic. The thing is, Jack, I believe either someone was drugging her with a hallucinogenic—" I squeeze his hand "—or it came from something she was using, maybe a hand lotion, or cosmetic. It must be something you don't use. Did she buy things from overseas, maybe?"

"A diary? She never mentioned a diary. What diary and what does it say?"

I touch his arm. "I found it in the attic; it covers the months before she died. She believed someone was drugging her. It's all in there. It's a tragic story of her losing her grip on reality." I meet his gaze. "Do you want to read it?"

"No." Jack wiped his mouth with his hand as if removing a taste from his lips. "I lived it."

I nod. "Now about the cosmetics?"

"Yes, she purchased tons of lotions and cosmetics from wherever we traveled." He frowns. "It must be something she used because no one here would poison her. Why would they? What did they have to gain?" He shakes his head. "Laura died and nothing has happened in this house to anyone else, nothing has changed. I haven't been seduced by any of the staff, or poisoned. Maybe you're clutching at straws." He closes his fingers over my hand and rubs his thumb over the back. "Have you considered that maybe she was just crazy?"

I nod. He makes sense but I need to collect Laura's cosmetics, creams and lotions. I want to get them tested for possible drugs or side effects. I look at him. "To put my mind at rest, would you mind if I had her used cosmetics tested for possible drug contamination?"

"If it makes you happy, go for it." Jack smiles at me. "As far as I'm aware, nothing's been touched in her dressing room since she died. I don't have a clue where to send them for testing. I'll ask Ruby to search for a laboratory." He sighs. "If Laura was using contaminated cosmetics, it would solve many unanswered questions."

I need more information. "Just one thing, the argument you had with Tom the night Laura died... was that fueled by his affair with Laura?"

"Yes and no." A muscle twitches in Jack's cheek. "I knew about him and Laura, and I didn't really care. It was an insult to my ego but I'd deal with it. She was sick and he made her better. No, it was seeing him lip-locked with Ruby on the yacht. It just made me mad a guy can use women like that, and I exploded. I used the non-fraternization rule to get him out of my house but

I needed to keep an eye on him, so I kept him in my employ. It was Ruby's idea. She figured he might cause problems being fired after I argued with him, publicly. Keeping him on full salary and giving him an apartment to live in rent free squashed all that."

I nodded. I feel he is being honest with me. "That was a good idea. Thank goodness you have Ruby."

"Now can we stop talking about Laura?" Jack raises both eyebrows. "I want to show you some of the houses in this area listed for sale." He pulls a thumb drive from his pocket. "Why don't we take our coffee into the sitting room and I'll slip this into the TV."

I meet his gaze. "You've found houses for sale? So soon? I can't wait to see them."

"If we see something we like, I'll make an appointment to view them next weekend." Jack stands slowly. "It's not something I want to rush into, Willow. We must be sure it's the one for us."

I refill our coffee cups and hand one to him. "I want to be sure too." I give him a long look. "I don't want to end up writing a diary because the house drove me insane."

My intention to spend the entire weekend with the children ended abruptly when I discover Jenny is taking them to the circus. My acute fear of clowns means that I can't walk past a flyer for a circus with a clown face on it, let alone go inside the big top. I take Jenny to one side and make sure she doesn't purchase anything with a clown face on it and bring it back to the house. With Jack ready to head out the door to play golf, I kiss him goodbye and watch him and then the children drive away. I walk into the kitchen and find Amy and the other house-maid I rarely see, Lucy, unpacking the dishwasher and stacking the shelves. They both look at me as if I'm a Little Green Man just landed from space. "I need a pair of disposable gloves and a plastic storage container of some kind. Maybe twelve by twelve?"

"The storeroom is through here." Amy leads me to the back of the kitchen. She slides open a door to reveal a wide room with shelves all around

Inside is like an Aladdin's cave, with everything imaginable packed on the shelves. It's brightly lit and I follow her to an area housing boxes of disposable gloves. We move on to another shelf where there is a variety of plastic storage containers. I select a box of gloves and two containers. Back outside in the kitchen, I turn to Amy. "Come with me. I'm going to collect a few things from Laura's dressing room and will need your assistance."

As we climb the stairs, I notice Amy's reluctance and turn my head to look at her. "Did you work here when Laura became unwell?"

"Yeah, I was here." Amy flashes me a dark look. "I started working here when I was seventeen. She became very difficult just before the accident."

I can almost feel her hesitation to enter Laura's dressing room. She hangs back, looking all around as if her old mistress is going to jump out of one of the closets. "I know it's spooky in here but I want you to put on a pair of gloves and help me collect any of the makeup and other things that Laura used. Don't bother with the unopened bottles of lotions or face cream; place them inside the plastic containers. Don't open them or smell them. Some of these were purchased overseas and I believe they might be contaminated. I'm going to have them examined by a laboratory to find out if there was anything in them that might have caused her erratic behavior."

"It smells like her in here even after all these years. She just about bathed in perfume. I could smell her coming." Amy sighs as she collects the cosmetics on the dressing table. "I doubt you will find anything." She carefully loads the creams and lotions into the box.

I take the jars of face cream and place them in my container. "What makes you say that?"

"She had postnatal depression after Noah was born. I believe that was the cause of her decline. She really didn't want to have another baby. She told me one time that she had no maternal feelings whatsoever. So, it was just as well Jenny was here, especially after Laura tried to kill Noah." She must have caught my expression of shock. "We all know about it, it's not a secret. Mr. Hunter and Laura could be heard arguing all over the house. Jenny was in tears and took the children down to the kitchen and we all cared for them. Ava and Noah were screaming. It was dreadful."

I take Laura's perfume and then go to her bedside table and open the drawers to search for anything else she might have been using. I turn on the lamp and spot a paperback novel, with writing all over the cover. I flick through the pages. There must be over three hundred of them and the bold writing covers them all. It is the same three sentences, repeated over and over again: *Don't drink the water. Don't drink the water. Don't drink the water.*

Is this a warning or was she so disturbed she needed to remind herself? Trembling, I stare at the writing. It becomes more and more illegible as I turn the pages and the last few lines are squiggles. Three hundred pages of the same words goes way past paranoia and steps into the realm of insanity. I'm suddenly afraid of what I've stumbled into. My hands shake and the book slips from my hands. I watch it fall as if in slow motion and it lands on the floor in a puff of dust. Did Laura work out who was drugging her by a process of elimination? The need to run as far away from the room as possible grips me but, if she was right, I need proof. I turn three-sixty degrees and slowly scan the room, searching for bottled water, and find nothing. I go back into the dressing room, and the smell of Laura's perfume accosts my nostrils again, suffocating me. I pull out a garbage bin from the dressing table and under the tissues are two half-full bottles of water. I collect them and add them to my box. Beside me, Amy is sealing her container and I turn to her. "I'm done here. Let's go."

Sweat trickles down my spine as we head down the stairs and I can feel Laura's eyes boring into my back. I send Amy back to the kitchen and go to Jack's office. I seal the boxes with tape and then, using a Sharpie, write my name and address on both containers and the tests I require. I'm trembling and breathing heavily and try to calm myself. Laura believed someone in this house was drugging her and she left a warning. Who can I tell about the book? Who can I trust? *No one.*

I run through names in my head. Three people—Jack, Tom and Ruby—were in the house when Laura started to decline, all were in the photographs I found taken on the day Caroline fell from the mountain trail and all three were on the yacht. If I discover Laura was being drugged, it could only be one of them —or could it? None of the staff liked her, did they? In fact, they were all scared of her. That gave all the staff a motive to drug her. If she'd died or been sent away to a psych ward, their lives would have changed for the better. This would mean Laura's death was an accident after all. I run the reasons why the other three might want Laura dead and my mind goes to Jack. He had a motive and so did Tom but if Ruby had a motive, I'm not seeing it. Was there something between Jack and her at that time, which he refuses to admit? I doubt it or Laura would have mentioned it in her diary. In any case, I know Ruby was involved with Tom at the time—that's how he lost his job. I need to look closer at the staff. From what I hear, life has been better for everyone involved since Laura disappeared, and now I've arrived to upset the apple cart. Am I next in the line of fire?

My things went missing, I heard noises, saw a face in the mirror and in a window. Perhaps they're trying to get rid of me too? But who is doing it? Tom doesn't live here anymore but he is involved with the firm. If he murdered Laura, who knows what hold the others have over him? Maybe I'm not looking outside the box. What if I'm correct and it's the entire staff? Each doing their bit, like moving the flowers and my phone, and then shutting me inside rooms in the hope I'll go crazy like Laura? I look over my shoulder at the open doorway and run to close and lock it. I run a hand down my face. I can't think straight. The idea of becoming like Laura frightens me.

I stare at the boxes. I can't tell anyone about finding the book—not yet. First, I need to know if they drove her to madness or drugged her. I know if I mention it, Jack would ask Ruby to help me and, until I'm sure, I must do everything myself. I grab my phone and ask it for the address of a drug-testing laboratory and it gives me the details. I go to the website and download a form to submit samples for testing. Using a large post bag from Jack's office supplies, everything is ready to be mailed on Monday. I lean back in Jack's chair and take a deep breath. "And now we wait."

FORTY-TWO

MONDAY

We spent a nice Sunday with the children. We walked to the beach, built sandcastles and later went for pizza. It was a typical family day and I loved every second of it. Nothing bad happened and everything was perfectly normal. Being with Jack and the children is like breathing fresh air, and all my concerns vanished over the time I was with them. More determined than ever, this morning, I drove to the post office to mail the package. I want to be sure it arrives without a problem and send it by Priority Mail Express. As I drive into the garage, Ruby comes out of the house and stares at me. I wonder why she's at home and not at work with Jack. I climb from the SUV and walk toward the front door. "Morning, did you want to speak to me?"

"Is there anything I can help you with today?" Ruby walks beside me. "Did you persuade Jack to send Laura's things to Goodwill? I'd be happy to help you pack everything."

I laugh. "No such luck." I give her a side eye. *Can I trust her about the drug testing? Maybe, but I'm not risking it.* "I'm just shopping online today. I can't think of anything I need help with right now, but thanks for the offer."

"I'm working from home today if you change your mind." Ruby walks into the foyer and pauses. "Jack is taking a client to lunch and then he'll be home early. We'll catch up with a few things and then he's all yours." She turns back to me. "I know you've been digging into Laura's death but it was an accident. This house does weird things to people. As a friend, I wish you'd drop it. Laura went a little crazy toward the end and I'd hate to see that happen to you too. Jack loves you very much and I've never seen him so happy."

Was that friendly advice or a warning? I can't tell the difference any longer. I search for an answer and smile. "That's good to know." I head for the kitchen. "Thanks, Ruby."

After grabbing sandwiches and a mug of coffee from the kitchen, I head up to my room. I recall seeing more diary entries listed in the file on Laura's laptop. I need to know what her frame of mind was on the night of the anniversary celebration. Jack mentioned she'd recovered. I need to see the truth in her own words. I open the laptop and scroll through the pages as I nibble on my ham and rye sandwich. I find the final entry.

September 15

I'm feeling better and today, I woke with more clarity than ever before. Jack is pleased with my progress and has organized a celebration for our anniversary. I've known for a while now and, each day, I climb further out of the abyss. Now, I must try and focus on the small ray of sunlight that is my future. The party is just two weeks away and I must ensure it goes ahead. I'll ask my hair stylist to call in a makeup artist today. Convincing Jack I'm well and ready to start entertaining again is paramount. When Jack comes home, I'll be the socialite he married. I'm looking forward to being on the Laura again. I know it's too late for us now but at least in front of our friends, if only for one night, Jack will act as if he loves me. I guess then,

I'll be in the hands of fate. Nothing will ever be the same between us but I'll be able to go out on deck, feel the wind in my hair and be free under the stars.

A cold ball forms in my stomach and crawls up into my lungs, making me catch my breath. I lean back in my chair as the wheels in my brain turn slowly, digesting the underlying menace in Laura's last words. On the surface, the entry looks like a normal, perhaps wistful person, but it covers an awful truth. I can imagine plans being made. With the drugs removed, slowly Laura would return to normal, and this entry proves that; it also proves that someone was controlling her. Jack knew about Laura's affair with Tom; perhaps after she tried to murder his son, it was the straw that broke the camel's back. After removing the drugs, he'd plan a nice public party, take her out to sea and then make sure she never returned. Everyone knew that Laura was unstable, and if the cops didn't believe she'd fallen overboard by accident, Jack could use the same excuse he'd given me that she'd taken her own life.

Perhaps his argument with Tom was an excuse to take the attention away from Laura when she went out on deck. All eyes would be on the men arguing. It was a perfect ploy. The weather had worked to his advantage too. He needed an excuse to go on deck to speak to the captain. An excuse and an alibi. I stare at the laptop. It's all here. The defaced book is the final nail in the coffin. Laura knew someone was drugging her and the only person she mentions is Jack. The pain of betrayal grips my heart. I love Jack so much. Am I prepared to lose him? What can I do?

I close the laptop. Maybe Jack has changed? It's been over seven years and he is such a kind, loving husband. If I go to the cops and they can't prove he did anything, he'll divorce me in a second. If I do nothing, I won't be able to live with myself. It's not something I can talk to him about. Can you imagine the conversation? "Hey, Jack, did you throw Laura off the yacht because she tried to murder your son?"

I can almost see his face. He'd smile and stare into my eyes. "Yeah, wouldn't you?"

My hands tremble and my pulse races. Would I? As a parent, would I kill a threat to my kids? Should I blame Jack for protecting them from someone who considered them a burden? My mind is twisting this way and that, unable to make a decision.

Outside, I hear voices, and go to my door to peer out. I scan the hallway in both directions but there's no one there. Suddenly I can't think straight. Am I hearing voices now too? I go and stare at myself in the mirror. I've changed in the last few weeks since we arrived in this house.

This isn't the first time strange things have happened to me. It's as if I'm running a parallel path with Laura. Could Jack really be involved? No, that's not possible—is it? Realization crashes down on me. I face-palm and shake my head. If he killed Laura, I've put myself in danger by digging into his past to discover what happened to Caroline and Laura—Oh—My—God! If I'm married to a killer, I'm now his biggest threat.

FORTY-THREE

Leaving the laptop on the table in front of the window, I run downstairs and almost collide with Tom. I stare at him. "What are you doing here?"

"Jack has a few things for me to do. If you'll excuse me?" Tom nods and heads along the hallway.

I don't trust him but I'm not alone. I head to the kitchen, glad to be with people. I'm thirsty and, if I'm going to drink the bottled water, I'll be taking it from the fridge myself. I'm guessing it's only a matter of time before someone tries to drug me. My mind is in turmoil and I suspect everyone. As I take a bottle of water from the fridge, Ruby walks through the door. I crack the bottle open and take a long drink.

"Oh, there you are." She waves a piece of paper at me. "I have the list and times of the viewings for next weekend but Jack called just before to tell me that an estate only two years old has just come onto the market. He was able to get a viewing for later this afternoon."

I smile at her, wondering why Jack would go through this charade if he planned to kill me—would he? It would make a good alibi. "That's wonderful, I can't wait to see it."

"Well, you can take a peek of it from the roof if you'd like?" Ruby grins at me. "Jack said you can see it clearly from up there. It overlooks the beach. It's a large white building surrounded by manicured grounds. There's a tennis court and a go-cart track the kids will love." She glances at Sue and Amy. "Staff quarters and it has all very modern conveniences. He figures you'll love it. The owners purchased it and only lived there for three months before they moved to Florida."

What if Jack sent Tom to do the deed? Tom will never find me on the roof with Ruby. I nod, wanting to be anywhere else but here with him right now. The house sounds like my dream home but what if I never get to live there? I force my face into a smile. I need to get out of here. "It sounds wonderful. How do we get to the roof?"

"Via the staff quarters." Ruby walks away, swinging a bottle of water. "It's quite a climb but it's worth it. The view is spectacular."

I picture the roof in my mind. It's all peaks and slate tiles. "I'm not planning on climbing up the side of a roof. It's too dangerous."

"There's a flat bit between the peaks, where the AC units are." Ruby looks over one shoulder at me. "It's a tar and gravel area and perfectly safe. You're not scared of heights, are you?"

Taking a glance behind me to make sure Tom isn't coming, I follow her through the staff quarters. "I don't like heights but I'll manage."

The staircase leading to the roof is behind a plain door. The creaky wooden steps seem to go up forever and I'm out of breath by the time we reach the top. The moment I step onto the roof, the wind catches my hair and blows it around my face. I stand to one side as Ruby places her bottle of water on an AC unit and pins back the door on a hook. The scenery is spectacular and I take a deep breath of the salty sea air and scan the area. Seagulls glide and dive, their familiar noise like people calling comes above the crash of waves on the beach. It's a beautiful day, sunlight dances on the ocean and in the distance, yachts' sails billow as they tack the waves. As the wind swirls me, pushing me toward the edge, my stomach knots. The area wasn't built as a lookout; I see the edge of the metal gutters and it's a sheer drop to the ground. Anxiety grips me but I push it down. I so want to see the house. "Which way is it?"

"To the right." Ruby moves up behind me. "The huge white one tight against the coastline."

I move around chimney pots to get a better view and, after taking another drink, place my water on the top of an AC unit. I take a firm grip around a pipe and then shield my eyes from the sun and peer at the dazzling white structure that spreads out in all directions. I hear a crunch of shoes on the gravel behind me but I don't move. In my peripheral vision, I see Ruby swap the bottles of water. A shiver of apprehension grips me. The threat isn't Tom after all, and the answers were right under my nose—Ruby drugged Laura. *Ruby*—I can't believe it and now she's trying to do the same to me, but why? My pulse quickens but I try not to react as the puzzle pieces drop into place. Ruby who's always been there, doing Jack's bidding, but is she an accomplice to murder—or is she acting alone? I take a breath and will my mind to work faster. I feign interest on the view but keep one eye on her. The knowledge it's her is rocking me to the core. If I hadn't seen her, I'd never have believed it.

Clarity of mind breaks through the panic and suddenly it makes sense that whoever suggested the party on the yacht must be the killer. It was the perfect opportunity to dispose of Laura. I turn around, putting my back to the ocean. The wind whips my hair all around like Medusa.

"I was talking to Jack about the party on the yacht. It's nice to know that Laura had one wonderful evening before she died. I know she'd been unwell for a time. Whose idea was it to hold it on board the *Laura*?"

"That would be me." Ruby smiles. "I do everything for Jack. He couldn't manage without me."

I nod, keeping my expression neutral. "I understand that Laura had a few problems over the last few months before she died?"

"She did and that reminds me." Ruby's lips curl into a smile. "Did you find your phone? It's strange your phone went missing. Laura's did too and then she kind of unraveled mentally. You know Jack was worried about you. He said you were searching your pockets all the time and not sleeping."

I see triumph in her eyes. She believes she's pushing me off balance but right now I hold all the cards. "I found it, so no big deal."

"Is it true you believe people are watching you and talking about you?" Ruby shook her head. "I told Jack he should take you to see a psychiatrist. He left it way too late for Laura."

Knowing that Jack had been talking to Ruby about things that I told him in private upsets me but I stand my ground. "Did you know that Laura left a diary? It details everything about the last six months of her life. She believed someone was trying to kill her and it was the same person who killed Caroline." I stare right into her evil eyes and see a flicker of doubt. "Are you going to try and kill me now too?"

"You think you're so damn clever to have figured it all out, don't you?" Ruby looks away and then back at me. "You know nothing."

I swallow my rising fear. "Obviously I figured it was Tom."

"Tom? He wouldn't hurt a fly." Ruby snorts with laughter and then her eyes turn to black beads. "Have you any idea what it took to get where I am today? I'm the only one Jack needs, but first he flaunts that spoiled brat, Caroline, in front of me, then Laura, and now you. He never loved you. You're just a toy—a distraction."

Relief floods over me. My kind and gentle Jack is innocent.

A great weight lifts from my shoulders but I can't let my guard down—not for a second. It's suddenly clear that Ruby's been manipulating him for years and, from her expression, she plans to take me out of the equation. I won't let her win. I must fight. I scan the roof for an escape route but there's one way on and two ways off—and one is falling over the edge. I swallow hard and my dry tongue rasps over my lips.

There's no one to help me and no one will hear my screams until I fall to my death. I must out-think her. My heart pounds so loud I can hear it in my ears. If I can just reason with her, she might change her mind. I take short steps backward as she moves closer. "No, you're wrong. I know Jack loves me. Think about it, Ruby. You've had years with him. Don't you figure he'd have married you by now if he cared for you?"

The words have fallen from my mouth before I realize.

"That's a lie!" Eyes wild with rage, Ruby leans closer and drops her voice to a menacing whisper, her lips curl slightly. "You ignorant fool. He needs me to protect him. Caroline was a selfish manipulative little princess and when Laura came along —" she barks a laugh "—I mean, surely you'd know what she was like if you've read her diaries—treated him like dirt. I needed to drug her to keep her out of my way." She laughs maniacally. "She was so out of it, she didn't remember it was me who put Noah in the bathtub. I did it right in front of her and then told her to leave and she did. She was my puppet."

I stare at her horrified. "You tried to kill Noah?"

"No, there was no need to kill him. I told Jack Laura left him crying in the bathtub." She moves closer, invading my personal space. Her eye twitches. "Now you come along playing the detective." She pokes me in my chest. "You don't get to take him from me. Not you. Not any of them."

I can see her unraveling before me and know she'll push me over the edge but I'm ready for her. I must keep her talking and edge away from her. "So, you pushed Caroline into the waterfall, pushed Laura off the boat and now you're planning on tossing me off the roof? Why? I'm no threat to you."

"Jack has me, so you need to die. I'll tell him you jumped. Everyone knows you're crazy." Ruby moves closer and laughs. "Laura was pathetic and it took nothing to shove her on the wet deck. I chose just the right second as the wave hit. It was so easy. She just slid right under the railing and vanished in the breakers. I figured it was over but then I heard her screaming. I threw a life buoy at her head to shut her up. It hit her right in the temple and it was bye-bye, Laura."

I step back and wind rushes around me. I'm dangerously close to the edge. Movement over Ruby's shoulder catches my attention. Jack is standing in the doorway and emotion fills his expression. I move my attention back to Ruby. She expects me to argue but I won't give her the satisfaction. "I think you've been working too hard and you're stressed. Why don't we go back to the kitchen and we'll talk this through? I'm sure there's a good reason why you killed Caroline and Laura."

"Yeah, come away from the edge, Ruby." Jack's voice is low and in control. "We need to talk."

"Jack, she's lying." Ruby spins around, grabbing my arm. "She's trying to turn you against me." She pulls me closer to the edge. "Everything I've done was for us, Jack—for *you*. I killed them for *you*."

"You're very loyal." Jack moves slowly toward me. "You know I value the work you do for me, and I always have, but I could never love you." He curls one hand around my other arm and plants his feet. "Let Willow go and we'll talk. Just you and me."

"I won't let her take you from me." Ruby's fingers dig painfully into my arm as she pushes me toward the edge.

I bend my knees and dive toward Jack and he drags me from her grasp. We both tumble to the hard ground. I glance behind me and cry out as Ruby's arms windmill. Balancing on the edge of the roof, she tries to straighten but one foot slides into the gutter. Wide-eyed, her mouth open in shock, she frantically grasps at air. She seems to hang for a second, her hair flying in the wind and then, with a feral scream, she falls out of sight. The next second Jack's hand covers my ear and presses my head against his chest. I'm thankful I don't hear her hit the ground. I know she's dead, no one could survive that fall and I'm not getting up to look. I examine Jack's ashen face. "Did you hear everything?"

"Just about." He sits up and rocks me in his arms. "All this time, I figured she was helping me but she was controlling my life. I've been such a fool." He pushes hair from my face. "I almost lost you too."

I shake my head. "But you didn't." I'm trembling and so is Jack. "Just hold me."

Below, people are shouting.

"Call nine-one-one, call nine-one-one."

"Are you okay?" Tom rushes onto the roof and drops to his knees beside us.

"Yeah." Jack's arms tighten around me.

Exhausted, I bury my face in his neck. The nightmare is over.

EPILOGUE
THREE MONTHS LATER

I've never been involved with the police before. The last few weeks have been quite harrowing. Forensic teams searched all over the house and, even though it's been seven years since Laura died, they still managed to find evidence in her bedroom. The items I'd packed and sent to the laboratory for drug testing have been collected by the police and taken to be forensically examined. The water in the bottles I'd discovered in her dressing room had been laced with a hallucinogenic drug and had Ruby's fingerprints all over them. We endured weeks of questioning. They'd taken the information I'd collected about Laura, her laptop and the various newspaper cuttings, along with the book. For a time, I was concerned that Jack or I would be blamed for Ruby's death. Luckily, the staff had told Jack I'd gone to the roof with Ruby and he'd followed. Hearing Ruby screaming at me, George, Sue and Amy had eavesdropped on what was happening. The moment the police arrived, we were all separated to tell our stories. This time all the stories were the same.

The staff remained in the house, apart from Jenny. She came with us to stay at a hotel. I couldn't live in that terrible place a moment longer. Once Ruby's death was ruled accidental, Jack sent in a team of professional cleaners. They removed everything belonging to Laura and took it to Goodwill. Her portrait was sent to her family in France. The yacht was sold as Jack has lost his desire to go sailing alone and intends to spend more time at home.

His new PA is a man named Dudley and he's very efficient and will join the household when we move. Talking of moving, we've been viewing houses and found one further down the coast that is perfect. It's the size Jack needs to fit with his lifestyle, it's modern and has everything we need for a growing family. Yes, I find I'm carrying his child and he is ecstatic and so are Ava and Noah. I'm waiting in the hotel foyer for the children to arrive. We plan to have a final walk through, although I made it clear to Jack that the house is my dream home.

The glass doors to the hotel swish open and a blast of cool ocean breeze rushes in along with the children followed by Jenny. They run to me as usual for hugs. "Are you ready to see the house we like?"

"That would be neat." Ava slips her hand in mine. "Are the bedrooms huge?"

"Yeah, they're all really nice." Jack nods to Jenny and takes Noah's hand. "There are stables there as well. Maybe you can have ponies?"

I turn to look at him in surprise. It's not something we've discussed. "Really? Do you plan on mucking them out each day or will you hire someone? The children will need someone to teach them to ride as well."

"All doable." He leads the way out to the sidewalk. "Ah, here's our car."

I smile as he slides behind the wheel of my SUV. I don't mind that he likes to drive. With the children safe in their car seats, we head along the coast road and, a few minutes later, pull into the driveway of a huge estate. The gates are open but entry is by a keypad and Jack assures me the security is second to none. It's strange, the house is so welcoming, I feel like I'm coming home. The landscaped gardens spread out and we drive past colorful garden beds and manicured lawns. The outside is spectacular and, on the inside, everything is pristine and modern. As we stop outside the grand entrance, the sea breeze brushes my cheeks and, above, seagulls drift in the thermal currents.

We are so close to the beach, small patches of sand pile up along the footpath and grind under my shoes. The Realtor is waiting for us at the front of the house and we smile and head inside. There's no need for her to give her spiel about the attributes of the property because this is the fourth time we've been here. In fact, this time, Jack gives her a nod and she goes outside and closes the door behind her. We leave the children to explore. I listen and smile at Jack at the whoops they make as they go from room to room. We head for my favorite room. The kitchen is everything I've ever wanted, all white marble and stainless-steel appliances, although I doubt I'll be spending much time here as Jack has already mentioned hiring a new chef and, in fact, an entire staff, except for Bill the gardener. The rest of the staff from the old house will be staying at Beauford Manor as the new owner has made it part of the sale.

I pull up a chair and sit at the island. "I'll be making my own rules if we buy this house. Thank goodness I won't have Ruby telling me what I can and can't do."

"Let's not talk about her and ruin our day. In fact, let's never mention her name again." Jack runs his fingers over the counter top. "Deal?"

I laugh. "Sure."

"This place has a good feel to it, doesn't it?" Jack comes behind me and rubs my shoulders with his large warm hands. "The kids love it too by the noise they're making."

I nod, lean back into his massage and sigh. "I don't want to change a thing. Everything in here looks new. Can we look through again?" I stand and we walk into the family room and stare at the ocean. "It's so beautiful. The views from every window are spectacular."

The house is quiet apart from the running footsteps and exclamations of the children as they claim their rooms. The slightest hint of fresh paint lingers but the house is filled with ocean air. Sunlight pours through the windows, casting long shadows across the highly polished floors. I lean into Jack and his arm comes around my shoulders, solid, dependable and all mine. I make a wish and look up at him. I so want to live here. "Could this be your dream home too?"

"Anywhere you are is home, Willow." He cups my cheek. "And all I want is to make you happy."

Excitement rushes through me and I turn and wrap my arms around him. "Can we buy it?"

"I figured you'd say that." He grins and holds up a set of keys. "It's ours."

And just like that we leave the past behind.

A LETTER FROM D.K. HOOD

Dear Reader,

Thank you so much for choosing my novel: *His Next Wife*.

I really enjoyed writing another psychological thriller. Delving into the minds of the characters and adding a little mystery along the way was a wonderful experience.

If you'd like to keep up to date with all my latest releases, just sign up at the website link below. Your details will never be shared and you can unsubscribe at any time.

www.bookouture.com/dk-hood

If you enjoyed *His Next Wife*, I would be very grateful if you could leave a review and recommend my book to your friends and family. I really enjoy hearing from readers so feel free to ask me questions at any time. You can get in touch on my Facebook page, X, through my web page, or D.K. Hood's Readers' Group on Facebook. Here we chat about books, have giveaways, and, from time to time, I offer members the chance to volunteer to be an extra in one of my upcoming stories. Anyone who appears as an extra receives a special gold seal and an autographed bookplate for their paperback.

Thank you so much for your support. Until next time,

D.K. Hood

KEEP IN TOUCH WITH D.K. HOOD

www.dkhood.com

facebook.com/dkhoodauthor
x.com/DKHood_Author

ACKNOWLEDGMENTS

To my editor, Helen Jenner, for her constant help and support. Her guidance is gold.

Also, to #TeamBookouture, the amazing professionals who work tirelessly to make sure each of my books is as good as it can possibly be.

PUBLISHING TEAM

Turning a manuscript into a book requires the efforts of many people. The publishing team at Bookouture would like to acknowledge everyone who contributed to this publication.

Audio
Alba Proko
Sinead O'Connor
Melissa Tran

Commercial
Lauren Morrissette
Hannah Richmond
Imogen Allport

Cover design
Emma Graves

Data and analysis
Mark Alder
Mohamed Bussuri

Editorial
Helen Jenner
Ria Clare

Copyeditor
Donna Hillyer

Proofreader
Claire Rushbrook

Marketing
Alex Crow
Melanie Price
Occy Carr
Cíara Rosney
Martyna Młynarska

Operations and distribution
Marina Valles
Stephanie Straub
Joe Morris

Production
Hannah Snetsinger
Mandy Kullar
Nadia Michael
Charlotte Hegley

Publicity
Kim Nash
Noelle Holten
Jess Readett
Sarah Hardy

Rights and contracts
Peta Nightingale
Richard King
Saidah Graham